JUST DESSERTS

THE AMERICAN WHO WATCHED BRITISH MYSTERIES

BOOK THREE

JUST DESSERTS

ARTHUR JOHN

AN AMERICAN WHO WATCHED BRITISH MYSTERIES NOVEL

Ainsley Publishing

ISBN: 979-8-9926415-4-7

Library of Congress Control Number: 9798992641547

FOR NATALIE AND AINSLEY

1

Detective Marlowe's night had been going as smoothly as the top of his bald head. The day at the expansive downtown brick-walled City Police Station hadn't been crimeless for every officer, but for him and his team, it was solely filled with paperwork, end of the month catch-up aligning blissfully with a moment when they'd just wrapped up a case and were waiting for the next. He'd even had his two junior detectives—reliable, steady Tessa Morven and energetic young detective Jamie Nelson—knock off early. When he left the station soon after, the dusky fall Friday evening's start was cloudless. Instead of braving crowds for a drink at his favorite bar, Gary's, Marlowe decided to head home, looking forward to ordering a double-sized hummus, extra pita bread, and dolmas from Shaw's Schwarma, and hours of relaxing watching *Gunsmoke.*

The first drop of rain from the nearly cloudless sky hit him around 5:30 p.m. as he parked his wet-sand colored 1987 AMC Matador on the street in front of his apartment building. His delivery driver showed up on a bike at six, dripping wet. The sky, as it often did in the City, turned from clear to dark clouds to rain as quickly as if changing coats from light-weight jean jacket to thick peacoat. *Well,* he thought, adding an extra few dollars tip for the tattooed delivery person, *nothing new about that. The City's a cantankerous horse.*

The moment he went to press play on his second *Gunsmoke* episode, one entitled "Daddy Went Away," the phone rang. He'd gone back for a second round of hummus and had a pita triangle poised for dipping. In that brief time between ring and answer, he hoped for a wrong number, knowing it wasn't. It was an operator from the station, relaying a message that he needed to head out. A death had been reported. He asked them to call Morven and Nelson, was told that was in process, and was given an address to report to: 2000 4th Avenue.

Shucking on a sports coat the color of his car over a now-wrinkled, white button-down shirt with one tan speck of escaped hummus splotched under the third button. He hooked on green suspenders with golden highball glasses on them, and settled on his head a sky-blue baseball cap with a stylized golden S on it, representing the local baseball team, the Seafarers. Making it halfway into the hall, he remembered the rain and went back to grab a windbreaker matching the hat's color.

He first headed toward his car but paused. The rain was coming down steady and thick, harder than the City usually received. Heavy enough to match what television shows set in the City depicted, those shows usually written by people who'd never been, only knowing its rainy reputation. The address he'd been given fell in the center of the Tolltown neighborhood, the northern part of the City's downtown. Tolltown was thick with bars, restaurants, cafes, bubble tea shops, higher-end clothing boutiques with names like Morses Glamourous Garb, delis, a scattering of mom-and-pop groceries, one of the City's few remaining records stores, Pete's Platters, and lofty apartment buildings stretching up into the sky. In short, a place where parking on a Friday night is difficult, if not perilous.

Gazing up the street, rain pooling on his cap's brim, Marlowe saw a sight that invariable made him smile inside, but tonight brought the grin forward. A marked police car was parked at the curb, which wasn't as remarkable as it might appear. Joe D's Jellies, the City's top spot for jelly-filled doughnuts, was steps around the corner. The small shop's offerings were so tasty, it got away with serving nearly nothing but doughnuts filled with an array of jams and jellies, from standbys like strawberry to more adventuresome fair like cider, hops, and sage, a Marlowe favorite. It stayed open later than most baked goods shops too. Cops and doughnuts may be a cliché, but clichés are often that for a reason. While it wasn't completely approved, he knew as a senior detective he could bum a lift from the officers and get to the scene much quicker than driving and having to find parking.

Which is why he was soon seated comfortably in the back of a police car, the location usually reserved for those suspected of a crime. The two officers hadn't been as put off about driving him as he'd expected once he'd flashed his badge and explained. They were officers he'd not met before, so once settled in the back, he introduced himself properly.

"I'm William Thackeray," the driver said as he pulled out into traffic, "and this is Simon Edwards, sir." The hair peeking out from under his hat was luxuriously curly, bouncing as he enunciated each word distinctly. His partner didn't have a beard, but boasted flaxen sideburns. Add in Marlowe's thick mustache, and the trio could have been a 1920s barbershop singing trio.

"Thanks again for the lift. Figured parking would be a bear down in Tolltown."

"Not a problem, sir," Thackeray replied. "This little chapter in our evening may affect history, who knows."

Marlowe wasn't exactly sure what the officer meant, but they were kind enough to provide a ride. "I do appreciate it, especially with the rain."

"I don't mind the rain. I think of it like a mirror. If you frown at it, it frowns. If you smile at it, it smiles."

"That's a positive take."

"I like to be positive, sir."

"Detective Marlowe is fine. Sir makes me feel too formal."

The car quieted, stopped at a light. Officer Edwards finished the last bite of a doughnut and started singing. While Thackeray's voice was oddly reedy and high-pitched for what appeared even sitting to be a large man, Edwards's was as sonorous as an opera singer, filling the car. "Rain, rain, midnight rain, nothing but the wild rain in this police car, and us three, nothing but the rain and me."

Marlowe wasn't sure how to reply, and the car went silent again before Thackeray spoke as he turned right onto 4th Avenue. "Edwards does love a tune, sir. I mean Detective. Not much of a talker, but a grand singer."

"How long have you two been partners?"

"Thirteen years to the month, Detective." Thackeray smiled. "Not every minute perfect, but most. It's hard, as you know, dealing with criminals, and harder dealing with those not so much criminals, if you get my drift. The wicked are wicked, I've found, and will go the way they'll go. We book them, and they get what's coming. It's when the virtuous do mischief, not so much with intent but almost by accident, heat of the moment stuff, that can wear one down. But we do keep going, Detective."

Looking out of the front window, wipers scraping across the windshield, Marlowe saw two blocks away the blue lights of police cars and red and white ambulance lights. They twinkled almost festively in the downpour. Traffic slid from slow to completely stopped.

"Probably best for us all if I dismount here and walk the last two. Feels this street's going to be stuck for a bit. If you drop me here, you can cut this corner."

"Very sound judgement, Detective." Thackeray nodded, pulling the car into a loading zone.

Opening the door, Marlowe said, "Can't thank you both enough. Saved me lots of time, and I enjoyed the ride."

"Thank you, Detective," Thackeray replied, Edwards giving a short nod and smile. "I see you share another sentiment of mine, always leaving with a kind word. I'll return the favor by saying we've yet to have a senior detective in the car as nice as you, or with such a mustache." He chuckled as Marlowe left the car. "Of course, you are the only senior detective we've ever had in the car."

Marlowe gave a short salute, shut the car door, and pulled his slicker tight. The rain remained in bucketing mode as he walked nearer the action. Even with wet weather, crowds milled in front of the varied array of bars and restaurants he passed: Hillwood Hops Brewpub, Inspector Slices, Hobson's Choices, Jaime's. The latter was a friendly dive bar Marlowe had visited before that had flyers for old rock shows as wallpaper. Some people tucked under awnings, some under umbrellas, some just got wet. The rain did make maneuvering around them easier, as he hugged the streetside of the sidewalk farther from the crowds.

Police tape, police cars, and numerous uniformed officers were present, shooing off gawkers and directing traffic. The tape and the bustle blocked the corner of 4th and Arlington, as well as half of both streets. An occasional siren burst forth, breaking up tentative honking from the city's normally amiable drivers. Before crossing Arlington, Marlowe took a long look up at the building occupying a quarter of the whole block in front of him. Built from caramel-colored brick and forty-stories high, it wasn't majestic but had an austere quality that made it stand out amidst Tolltown's other buildings. Hotel Herre occupied much of the building, but the ground floor was a restaurant he'd never visited, Il Signore Piccolo. Italian, unless the name translated into a cryptic play on words or culinary traditions.

For a few steps, Marlowe circumvented the tape and officers, hat pulled down, to get a view of the front of the building. *Soak it in*, he thought, instantly regretting his choice of words. He ducked under a solitary large oak tree breaking the sidewalk flow after crossing Arlington, its few branches dipping forlornly, either from the rain or from a distant deciduous memory of when the area was a massive forest. The building's fifteen-foot-tall, shining steel and glass front doors were mostly hidden by the swarm of police, emergency crews, and a few non-uniformed people. It was the only entrance, so must go to both hotel and restaurant, he decided. Victorian-sized windows fit into the building's sides regularly for the first two floors before shrinking to normal height as the eye traveled higher.

Was it the setting for a crime? Or just an accident; a misstep causing a sudden shift in someone's life as a result of chance, fate, or a bone stuck in the throat? Probably not given the volume of police and activity, unless it was the mayor, a local sports or music star, or other luminary. Removing his hat, he knocked it against the tree trunk in hopes of drying it, even as drops splashed his head like tiny wet insects. *Better join the party.* Cap snugly back on, he walked up to the nearest officer behind the tape, removing his badge.

Marlowe had nearly made it to the door, giving short head nods to officers he knew while walking, when the door opened. A woman slightly taller than Marlowe walked out. She wore a knee-length, olive-green rain slicker with high collar and no visible buttons, under which she had on sea-green slacks, their press lines holding up even with the weather. An umbrella matching the coat in color was hooked casually over one arm. Dark-brown hair encircled her head in a crown braid, under which intelligent eyes peered out. Seeing Marlowe, she smiled wide.

"Detective Marlowe. Cozy night."

"Detective Morven. Not the finest weather for it. Glad you're here, sorry your evening was interrupted."

Marlowe's reply may have been laconic, but he was incredibly happy to see Detective Morven had already made her way to the scene. They'd been working together for a few years, and he relied a lot on her. More than anyone else he'd ever worked with. She was steady, insightful, and concise, bringing a sharp, intelligent energy that balanced out his tendency to mosey. He knew she wouldn't be on his team forever, that she'd one day have her own team, but tried not dwell on it.

"No worries. Wasn't doing much more than couch surfing. It's wild down here." She gestured toward the controlled chaos around them, at the same time stepping away from the door and out of the way of people entering and exciting. An overhanging decorative brick shelf a few floors above blocked a chunk of the rain while they talked.

Marlowe leaned against the wall. "Seems it. What do we know? We needed?"

"From what I've gathered, yes. I talked to one officer on the way in, and one when I briefly went inside. The latter and a few others are keeping restaurant patrons as calm as possible and ensuring they don't leave. I asked him to grab more officers and to have them start taking names and details. But the action for us is upstairs, above the restaurant. One dead body. It seems suspicious."

"How so?"

"From what I was told, the body was found in a locked room."

"Hotel room?"

"No, there's a culinary and cooking school space above the restaurant, with offices. The body was found in an office. Not sure under what circumstances. That's what I've picked up at this point."

"Cooking school upstairs. Odd."

"Owned by Douglas Small. Local restaurant king, famous chef, author. Put the City culinary scene on the national map, in a way. That's what the newspaper articles say. You know him?"

"Of him." Marlowe leaned back farther, resting his head on the wall.

Morven paused a moment. "Odd might be just the word, because Douglas Small is the dead body."

Rain splattered around them on the ground. A siren cut into the night. Voices from the surrounding area jumbled into a quilt of muted syllables highlighted by an occasional brighter, louder word.

Marlowe spoke, a little louder after the siren. "That's a wrinkle. Big name. Better get inside, take a deeper view of the landscape."

Morven was pulling the door open when a voice broke out above the rest from beyond the police tape.

"Detective Marlowe."

They turned, looking up the block. The voice called again, loudly:

"Detective Marlowe."

A uniformed officer moved in the direction of the person speaking. An open, full-sized white umbrella with croissants on it was held low enough the speaker's face wasn't visible. Both recognized the voice, however.

"Morven, I believe that's—"

"John Arthur," she said simultaneously.

"Yep. Again. I should go make sure he's not arrested. You head inside. I'll be not two shakes behind."

She grinned. "Check. Don't let him ramble. I'll see you upstairs. Nelson's there. He came in on a bike as I arrived, and I sent him up."

"Good to hear. Was wondering."

She slipped gracefully through the door as Marlowe headed toward where John Arthur was now talking animatedly with the officer.

As Marlowe took a few splashy steps to the police tape boundary, he caught the trailing end of what John was saying.

". . . probably a gin, no ice, no slice. Am I right?"

Marlowe cut in, holding up his badge for the officer. "Excuse me. Detective Marlowe. I know this man."

"Officer Crabbe, sir." The officer, a thin-faced man with a long upper lip and whisps of reddish brown hair curling out from under his police rain hat, ducked the edge of John's umbrella, dangerously close to his head. "A moment?"

"Sure. John, hold on here at the tape."

Marlowe and Officer Crabbe turned slightly. The latter leaned in, whispering, "You sure he's okay, sir? I heard him calling and went to calm him down. When I told him my name, he said it was amazing and asked me if it was spelled with two B's and an E, which it is. Then he asked me if I liked savory pies and started in about drinks and if mine was a G and T. I couldn't get a word in."

Marlowe couldn't help laughing lightly. "He's all right, just can go on a bit. Has some peculiar interests. Guessing your name aligns with one. Tends to forget not everyone knows what he knows. But harmless. Nice guy. I can handle him."

"Thank you, sir. I'll move on then."

Marlowe gave him a quick shoulder pat as the officer walked off, then stepped nearer to John, who leaned in over the police tape. A few years older than Marlowe, John wore a gray puffy jacket with two pins on the chest. One black with "Be Nice to Dogs" in red lettering, one black with the white outline of a thick-chested dog. It had the word "Staffy" on it, also in white. He had on russet-colored trousers, shoes matching the jacket, and nearly clear eyeglasses, a few specks of gold in them reflecting the flashing lights. Almost as bald as Marlowe, John's graying hair tufted around his ears, a few brown strands surfacing within the gray.

"Detective Marlowe, can you believe it?"

"What's that, John?"

"Officer Crabbe. Like *Pie In the Sky*. You remember we talked about the British show featuring the police detective turned chef. Richard Griffiths played Inspector Crabbe beautifully. I felt with sharing that name, the officer had to be of English descent, and had to enjoy a good, savory pie."

Marlowe first met the curious older man on a previous case, one John ever since insisted on calling The Case of the Nine Neighbors. At first, John had been a suspect, as he'd found the murder victim–the first victim of that specific case–in a neighborhood park near his house. Marlowe and team had had a hard time agreeing whether that discovery equaled cover-up or happenstance.

John hadn't made it easier, either. The elderly widower, who lived alone with his brindled bundle of doggy energy, Ainsley, was mildly obsessed with British television mysteries past and present. Maybe more than mildly. He dropped quotes, facts, and lessons from them into conversation without warning. Believing his mystery watching gave him insights into solving crimes, John would show up at the station or crime scenes, talking to Marlowe, Morven, and Nelson about Sherlock, Poirot, Father Brown, Miss Marple, and many more.

Turned out John was partially right about the insights, as his television mystery inspired learning helped them solve that case. Then, a few months later, John was again coincidentally at a murder scene, a kids' baseball game. During that case, he'd unveiled more television mystery driven theories. Marlowe admitted to himself that he liked the man and that John could be helpful. But he could also go on and on. You had to put down some boundaries.

"John," Marlowe gently interrupted, slowing the man's flow of words.

"Too much British mystery TV talk for a rainy night?"

"I'd say. Hold up that umbrella and tell me what you're doing here."

John's umbrella had slipped, scratching Marlowe's hat. The older man raised it higher, leaning farther over the police tape so it covered both of them partially.

"I was next door at Julie McK's, the wine and antipasti place. Cozy spot, like a series of connected English drawing rooms. Deep comfy chairs, small wood-carved tables, knickknacks, oldish books on shelves. Solid wine list. They had Sagrantino, my favorite red wine, from Montefalco."

Marlowe gave a negative shake.

"Only in bottle, too expensive, so I had a glass of a Sangiovese blend. Not bad. I was there with Neville and Florence Cassell, you remember them."

The Cassells had been suspects in the first case, the one where John found the body. Marlowe nodded but said nothing. He knew sometimes it was best to just give John his lead, let him get his narrative out.

"I hadn't caught up with them in a while. Too long. They're still somewhat shocked by the outcome of The Case of the Nine Neighbors. I am somewhat myself, honestly. They weighed moving from the neighborhood, but decided to stick it out. Florence couldn't leave her trees. Maybe Neville had one to many glasses of Chardonnay, as he was getting maudlin. We'd gotten up to leave when I saw the police activity swarming.

Buckled them into a taxi, sent them home, and came over. Then I saw you and knew it must be a murder."

"Don't jump the gully before you've seen the other side, John."

"I'll bet that's a grandfather saying."

Marlowe's grandfather, who had been in policing his entire adult life, was known for a deep vault of country sayings, which Marlowe trotted out as fit the occasion. His grandfather had raised him, and the influence ran deep.

John didn't give chance for a reply, however, going on rapidly. "The confluence of patrol cars, an ambulance, officers buzzing around like bees around a rhododendron, points to more than, say, a heart attack after an extra-large portion of tiramisu or an accidental hotel room overdose. Then you show up, head of the murder squad. Ergo, murder." He gave Marlowe a ta-da gesture, causing the umbrella to shake.

Taking a deep breath, Marlowe said, "John, I just got here. I haven't even been inside. And I'm not the head of a murder squad, just a detective. One who should get to work."

"I know, crime waits for no man. But Marlowe." He put a hand gently on the detective's arm. "If the crime has to do with Douglas Small—"

Marlowe raised a hand, palm out, causing John to pause and reroute his thought mid-sentence.

"A palm stop. The time-honored police gesture."

Marlowe ignored the palm talk; he'd heard it before. "Why did you bring up Douglas Small?"

"I'd like to say it was completely intuition after years of British mystery watching, but I'll come clean. I walked around some before I saw you and overheard an officer mention his name. I wasn't eavesdropping, just happened to hear it. If someone murdered him, that'd be big news and demand a response this busy. So I bet that was it."

"Loose lips," Marlowe said to himself. Then to John, "Just because you heard his name, why would you think he'd be the victim?" Marlowe knew he needed to be getting on, but John's insights were sometimes uncanny.

"I knew him a tiny bit. Interviewed him for a couple of articles years back when I was freelancing with restaurant and bar writing. The first one, he was launching a line of branded cook- and bakeware, Small Supplies. The second was when his bar book, *The Small Bartending Book*, came out."

"You wrote a few cocktail and bartending books. Competitor?"

"I suppose. Does that make me a suspect? Or just a person—"

"Of interest." Marlowe knew John well enough now to know where his TV police talk would lead. "No."

"Shame in a way. I had such a reliable alibi. Anyway, I talked to him here and there as you do in culinary circles, when I ran more in culinary circles. Took a couple classes at Small's Cooking Classroom, the one here—a cocktail one for the story when the book came out, and then an intro to baking when I decided to learn to bake. Mostly a failed experiment, my baking. He is, or was, a brilliant chef *and* decent baker, a combo that doesn't happen often. Like many chefs, brilliant or not, he was a hard-driving, edgy at times, charming at times, prickly when challenged, his-way-or-the-highway type. An *enfant terrible* when starting out, doing things not so regular here in the City. Quite a name for a time in the celeb chef explosion, though faded a little lately. Still the biggest in restauranteurs here by a fair stretch, which equals a host of bobbies and SOCOs out on a rainy Friday if I'm right and he's involved."

John's rambling might be a bit unstructured, but it was providing some solid background so Marlowe stayed silent, letting the man continue.

"To get you down here, and Detective Morven, who I saw, my thought is it's either him murdered, or it could be that he's murdered someone in the restaurant or class, though that feels flimsier, less logical. As Humphrey said in *Beyond Paradise*, 'Surely poisoning your customers is bad for business.' I doubt a business-focused type like Small is going to be a killer. But be killed? I could see it. Interestingly, Detective Inspector Humphrey Goodman, played by the hilariously charming Kris Marshall, started in *Death in Paradise*, the long-running, island-set, murder-of-the-week show with a fish-out-of-British waters detective inspector, or inspectors, as now there have been many different lead actors. In the fiction of the show, Humphrey fell in love with a visiting tourist, which caused him to move back to London, get married to said love interest, and move to a seaside town in Devon, where he—"

"John." Marlowe's interruption this time wasn't as gentle. John tended to go even more pedal down than usual once he wandered onto the trail of a specific British show. Marlowe knew he'd better cut it off and head inside. The man was incredible accurate often, at times too much for Marlowe's liking, but tangential British television talk tended to go on too long. "Interesting theorizing, John. Maybe we'll talk more. I've gotta get inside. Stay dry as possible. Pet Ainsley for me."

"I wish she was here, even in the rain. Every moment is better with a dog. Sadly, not a dog-friendly restaurant."

Even though he felt a smidge rude to the man he'd become friends with, Marlowe turned to leave as he talked, thinking it the best way to keep John from continuing conversing. He wasn't completely right, as John's voice rang out to Marlowe's retreating bulk.

"Marlowe, I have more information as you need it. Stop by the house, or I'll come to the station. I've got great background on the culinary scene in the City."

Marlowe raised one hand to over his shoulder to wave. John could talk morning to night, but you couldn't fault the man's enthusiasm. He knew a chunk of it grew out of the loneliness John felt since his wife, Marlene, died in a car accident, that her absence propelled the relentless conversing. Filling the silence, John told him. Heading in the door, a thought entered his mind unexpectedly. *Maybe I should hire John as a consultant.*

He laughed at himself, slightly confusing the officer inside taking a quick view at his badge. John would certainly love that. Consultant to the police. His dream. And was it such a silly idea? John had helped them with two confusing cases. Heck, John had put the final nails in *solving* those cases. John's insights were usually very incisive. Why not bring him in in a more official way.

The department had consultants for forensics, computer issues, accounting. Even the cooks in the canteen were civilian consultants if you expanded the view. John's knowledge of the world Douglas Small lived and operated within–if he was truly a murder victim–might be crucial. He'd have to run it by the team, make sure Morven and Nelson were okay with the idea. Both were friendly with John after the past interactions. Nelson arguably idolized the man. The young detective had taken a list of British television shows from John and was working his way through the ones about the small village spinster detective. The hard sell would be Marlowe's boss, Captain Innocent.

He almost bumped into another officer walking across the lobby. *Better watch my musing*, Marlowe chastised himself. Refocusing on current surroundings, he found himself at the bottom of a wide wooden staircase leading to an open, thirty-foot landing with yellow couches along its cable railing. A sparkling chandelier that looked like the bulbous whisk of a hand mixer hung above the stairs. To his right was the hotel check-in area, a series of walnut wood desks painted black topped by computers, with a hallway beyond leading to an elevator bay.

To his left, bifold glass and metal doors were open. Lush cream curtains with willowy crimson stripes were pulled back from sides, revealing the beginnings of a restaurant: maître d podium, round tables (mostly full) topped with red-and-white checked cloths, the corner of an open kitchen. On either side of the stairs were wooden doors set into walls. Officers and a few gathering forensic personnel in white body suits filled the spaces between furniture like an invading army, with only a few civilians remaining. Another pair of officers perched at the top of the stairs, as if castle sentries on a rampart. Marlowe headed up, badge in hand.

2

At the top of the stairs, Marlowe noticed two things. Against the landing's back wall on the right side, a group of people gathered, either sitting on yellow couches or standing nearby. They appeared herded, twelve in total, with two uniformed officers playing the role of Border Collies. Each wore some manner of white chef coat and black pants. The white clothing stood out brightly against cherry-colored walls that wouldn't have been out of place in a Vegas speakeasy. A glance caught a range of emotions on the group's faces: crying, annoyance, anger, shock.

A sizeable African American man stood beside a doorway on the landing's far left, a door that officers and forensic personal walked back-and-forth through or clustered close to. Over six feet tall, carrying a sculpted 220 pounds like a profession linebacker, broad shoulders, thick biceps, a bushy mustache, and intense brown eyes, the man would have been intimidating except for his abundant smile.

"Detective Marlowe." He reached out a hand to shake. "I've been wondering when you'd arrive."

"Sergeant Troy, didn't know you were here. And all gussied up." Sergeant Troy wore an immaculate charcoal dress shirt with a tiny, white octagon pattern, mitered cuffs, and a single patch pocket, steel-gray pants, and hazelnut leather stitched shoes. Marlowe knew the officer well, as they'd both been years in the service and had spent time hanging out at various cop bars after hours.

"I happened to be having dinner downstairs with Doc Jones Peterson, currently inside with the body, when it, well, kicked off is an accurate phrase."

"That was lucky. Or unlucky. Makes for a short trip."

"Detectives Morven and Nelson are inside too."

"Good. Feel up to giving me a version of what happened from your point of view? I'd enjoy hearing it firsthand."

"Happy to. We'd ordered dessert, a panna cotta frutti di bosco for me, when I thought I heard a scream. The music wasn't overly loud, but loud enough to make me doubt. I definitely heard a second scream, nearer. The doc and I got up and left the room, flashing my badge along the way, asking people to stay in their seats. Ran into a man in a chef outfit coming down the stairs, yelling, 'Help, help, I think he's dead. Murdered.' Jim Sean. He's over with that group, class attendees from tonight. Left him on the top step with the doc, instructing the latter to not let anyone else up. I gave him my badge to add authority. He was very excited, but managed to keep the crowds down."

"Moving into the classroom area, I identified myself as police, asked where the trouble happened. One attendee, Kevin Holman, led me down the hall off the front of the room to an office, outside of which were two more people, Chester Rowan and Louisa Sweeney. I discovered the body of Douglas Small inside the office. Checked his pulse, though I knew. I called it in to the station. All cars."

Troy made a circling sign with one finger, imitating a spinning siren. "Most of this group in white was huddled around the student tables. You'll see the setup. Some were on phones, calling 911. I hope. Then I marshalled everyone in that area out to these couches and have been helping since."

"Thanks, Troy, bunches. Very helpful. Both the overview and getting things rolling. Two quick questions."

"Sure, Marlowe."

"You said you knew once in the office he was dead."

Troy leaned closer to Marlowe. "There is, you'll notice, a large knife in his back."

"Understood. Second, not as important. You and Doctor Peterson having dinner—work or fun?"

Sergeant Troy smiled. "You know the doc, he's expansively into what he calls the am-drams. Amateur theater productions. We were talking at a scene once, as you do, and it came up that I'd done a play or two back in high school. He's been trying to get me on stage ever since, and tonight gave it a shot once more. 'All the world's a stage,' he quoted, as he does. Standing up here on this landing looking down over the controlled chaos, I believe he might be right."

"He might at that. Thanks." They shook hands once more, and Marlowe went into the next room, noticing a polished brass sign on the wall behind Troy. It said in black lettering: "Small's Cooking Classroom. Work harder. Cook better."

The room was vast in relation to what Marlowe expected following the fairly slight landing. Walls stark white, wood floor painted black and buffed to a fine sheen under a lofty, twenty-foot ceiling with visible metal ductwork and lots of venting, matched by wall ventilation ducts. A six-by-four-foot slightly raised rectangular kitchen-island style table stood six feet in front of eight other four-by-three-foot tables, each approximately four feet from the one nearest. With the room empty, it appeared as though the larger table was lecturing the smaller.

The tables were kitted out for a kitchen classroom: gas burners on right side tops, double ovens on left, proofing drawers and utensil drawers, multiple outlets and side shelves holding mixing bowls, books, more tools. Currently, unclean pots and pans, flour flowers, and what appeared to be half-made cakes, kitchen utensils in need of a wash, and more culinary detritus was scattered over the tables. Everything was brightly detailed by powerful hanging lights.

The back wall's full line of high and hearty industrial-chic metal shelves broke in the middle thanks to a single open door, above which two crossed chef's knives were mounted like heraldry. One set of shelves held almost every imaginable type of kitchen and baking gadget: stand mixers and hand mixers, skillets and saucepans, food processors, stockpots, cake, muffin, sheet, and loaf pans, juicers, ice cream makers, blenders and immersion blenders, ceramic jars blooming with spoons, whisks of various colors and types, ladles, offset spatulas, and pastry brushes. A whole shelf section seemed a breeding ground for rolling pins.

Another shelving unit held dry ingredients in tightly-sealed containers: different types of flours, confectioner's, brown, and white sugars, nuts (crushed and whole), seeds, and dried spices adding muted colors to the palette, each named in black marker on perfectly placed white tape. The final shelf featured mostly round canned goods stacked on top of one another, square scenic tins of Italian olive oils in a row like a travel advertisement, plus a section devoted to bottles: gin, vermouth, amari, brandy, rum. On the wall opposite the door Marlowe came in sat a formidable series of high-end refrigerator/freezers, microwaves, and more ovens. Police tape encircled sections of the room, which smelled vaguely of burnt butter.

Even considering the enormous amount of kitchen equipment, the best chef would have been hard-pressed to make a sandwich at the moment. Forensic people in white outfits, a handful of uniformed police officers, and one man in the far corner wearing white slip-ons over his shoes and a linen suit the color of green apples packed the room like sardines in a traditional tin. The suited man had short blond hair that would turn shaggily curly if grown out and a lean runner's body. Seeing Marlowe, he jogged around people, tables, and stools, stopping to pivot around obstacles as if around basketball defenders on a fast break.

Marlowe felt himself out of breath watching the man, who spoke breezily. "Detective Marlowe. Sir. Glad to see you." He reached out his hand to shake the older detective's, realized he had blue latex gloves on, and saluted instead.

"Nelson." Marlowe grinned. The young detective's boundless puppy-like energy never waned. "Sorry to bring you out on a Friday."

"Not at all, Detective Marlowe. Crime waits for no man, as they say."

He saw Nelson about to speak again and went quickly on. "Glad you are here. Morven said she sent you up. Liaising with the scientists? Did you get any specific information yet?"

"Yes, sir. Detective, I mean." Nelson hadn't been on the team long and tended to go formal when addressing Marlowe until reminded otherwise. "I talked to Sergeant Troy, and momentarily Doctor Peterson, who is at the center of the SOC. I also helped move the . . . witnesses. Or suspects. Or both. Either way, I helped get them settled with some uniforms."

"Solid work."

"Also," Nelson went on, as if worried he might not get every syllable out fast enough, "I asked one of them what happened more specifically." He pulled a small notebook out of his pocket, flipped it open. "Louisa Sweeney. Twenty-six. Shoulder-length auburn hair in a lob cut with bangs and a streak of pink. Cute red cat-eye glasses."

"Cute?"

Nelson blushed. "Not sure why I wrote that down. She was the co-teacher at the class tonight, assisting Douglas Small. Very broken up and in shock, but managed to give me her POV on what happened. She said they were working on the night's baking challenge, and that the classes over the past two nights, and tonight, had the same outline. Chef Small would give a short talk, demonstrate a technique or two relating to a specific pastry being made, then walk through how they should be 'flowing' the recipe. They would then, in pairs at this class, make the pastry or whatever. During a portion of that time, Chef Small would retire to his office down that hall." He made a vague gesture in the direction of an opening behind the main table.

"Every night, he'd stay in his office undisturbed for exactly forty-five minutes. Louisa would help the attendees during this time. Tonight, he didn't return on time. She went to check on him, but he didn't answer her knock. Two of the attendees followed her. One tested the door and it was locked. She came back and brought even more people. They broke the door down, finding Douglas Small slumped across the desk. She said someone ran downstairs to the restaurant, and someone else called 911. Sergeant Troy arrived, followed by more police. Not a perfect overview, as she started crying at that point."

"I get it. Can you head back outside on the landing and take down details—names, numbers—from the group. Try to do them solo. They'll be traumatized, but wrangle what you can. Lasso up a few more officers if needed. I'm heading back to the scene. Once suited up, that is. Don't want the scientists angry."

"On it right away, Detective Marlowe. Thank you."

"Thank you, Detective Nelson."

Nelson's eyes lit up like a kid in front of a candy counter, as they did every time he heard himself called detective from a senior officer.

Once bundled in a forensic suit, Marlowe's hefty figure appeared as if a very mobile cumulus cloud. Heading down the hallway, he ducked under another line of police tape, maneuvering past a few people also suited up. Two doors opened off the hall's right, and then further down, two on the left. The voice of Doctor Jones Peterson came out of the second on the right.

"Why, let the stricken deer go weep. The hart ungalled play. For some must watch, while some must sleep. So runs the world away."

Morven stood inside the doorway, aligned with the open door. She'd donned a full white suit and boots, managing to look athletic within it. Seeing Marlowe, she said, "Hold up, Doctor Peterson, Detective Marlowe has arrived."

Marlowe conscientiously stepped in the room, not wanting to contaminate the scene. A fairly basic office space, its muted walls, the color of peanut shells, were unadorned outside of a framed award certificate and bookshelves at the back. Culinary books packed the top two shelves, a few titles visible from his vantage point: *The Art of Eating, The Encyclopedia of Practical Gastronomy, Larousse Gastronomique, The Food Lab.* The middle shelf had three balloon whisks of different sizes, a small orange ceramic pot, and a number of knives. In the room's center sat a five-foot mahogany writing desk. On top of it were a dark-red rotary phone, pencils and pens flopped in a small copper saucepan, an adding machine, scattered notebooks, and a body slumped over.

A line of police tape separated the section of room the desk sat within. A few evidence markers and flags marked off places on the floor and wall, one near the doorknob. The room felt uncomfortably warm, as if attempting to balance the cold rain outside with a higher than normal dose of manufactured heat. Sweat already loosened the elastic of Marlowe's forensic hood. A compact man in a forensic suit crouched near the body, peering up at Marlowe and Morven through wire-rimmed glasses, one single strand of hair slipped out of his white hood, plastered to his forehead. Grinning, he stood. "Marlowe appears like Banquo's ghost at dinner. But visible to all."

"Doc." Marlowe waved. "Heard you were on the scene, so to speak."

"I was relaying that information as if on angels' wings to Detective Morven." Doctor Jones Peterson had been the City's head forensic pathologist for a fair stretch, and Marlowe and Morven were used to his tendency to dot his speech with Shakespearean quotes–or words and phrases that sounded like they could be Elizabethan. Marlowe wondered about it, once. He knew the man liked, as Sergeant Troy said earlier, amateur and professional theater. That was part of it. But he thought it was also a way to cope with seeing the aftermath of violent crimes, of being around so many unnecessarily dead. Maybe surmise on Marlowe's part. He'd read once something along the lines of all pathologists are born exhibitionists. That could be part of it as well.

"Sergeant Troy set me as sentry upon the tower, and I did my duty manfully, I can say without undue flattery. Think'st thou that duty shall have dread to speak when power to flattery bows?"

"Uh, no, Doc." Marlowe had gotten lost during the previous sentence's end. "And now we're here. Douglas Small I've been told."

Morven spoke up. "We haven't had a formal ID, but it's him."

"He is now an ill cook that cannot lick his own fingers." Doctor Peterson shook his head, causing the suit to rustle like leaves in a light wind. "A night of sorrow in Tolltown."

"Sorrow and rain. What a night." Marlowe eased closer, as close as he could without his belly breaking the tape. Douglas Small was face down on the desk, hands at his side behind it. Long hair was pulled back from his high forehead into a ponytail flopping off his left shoulder. From his vantage point, Marlowe saw the knife sticking out of Small's back. Its wooden handle was tan, with burgundy-shaded grain flowing through it in waves. Ironwood, he'd guess. A curious turquoise band was set between handle and blade, an inch or so of the latter showing cold silver against the victim's white chef's coat and the blood stain spread on it. Etched into the blade were three visible letters: DOU. A couple of greasy spots dotted the coat not far from the knife.

"Doc, this may be both obvious and too early to ask, but is that"—he pointed at the knife—"what killed him?"

"Give them meals of beer and iron and steel, they will eat like wolves and fight like devils. And surmising. I, Doctor Peterson, try not to surmise. However!" He gave a dramatic point. "You could be forgiven for thinking so. From the amount of blood, if I was a wagerer, I would wager he was still alive when the knife was driven into his back, but even that I wouldn't yet swear to in front of the bench of justice. He is dead, I can swear to that. I will know more later."

"Anything else stand out at this stage?" Morven followed up.

"There is a coffee cup, which contained more than just coffee if my nose does not deceive, back here that appears to have been knocked over. And a book near the cup entitled *Dinner with Tom Jones*."

"Fight perhaps," Marlowe replied, more statement than question.

"I know the answer not, and make no guesses." Doctor Peterson scratched his head with a gloved hand. "A couple more irons to your detective fire. Highlighted by Mr. Johnny Arris."

"Arris is here? Didn't see him."

Morven sighed. "Yeah. He was in the other room."

"He ask you out again?" Arris managed the forensic company the City Police often contracted with for suspicious deaths. The man maintained a major crush on Morven and had asked her out multiple times, always shyly respectful and a little awe-struck.

"Not yet." She changed the subject. "What were you going to point out, Doctor?"

"Hopefully not cold porridge," Doctor Peterson said. "You'll notice the door panel has been cracked. And on the floor resting to your left, a fundamental lock of the hook design. Above, a hole, minorly damaged."

"We heard the door was broken down. Makes sense." Morven crouched to look at the lock part on the floor, as Marlowe twisted to check the door. "Thanks, Doc."

Doctor Peterson bowed as deeply as he could without hitting body or desk, then replied. "I will have more, if not with the dawn breaking, as soon as my eyes allow."

"Okey-dokey. One or two quick questions."

"You have but to ask, and I will move the stars themselves if able."

Before Marlowe could ask, a faint plop interrupted as something splatted on Small's jacket. The noise startled the pathologist, who scuttered backward like a rabbit hearing a dog, bumping a large set of keys hooked to the victim's belt. The ceiling had wide wooden beams across it, and on one directly over the body was a shadowy mound. It could have been rectangular once, but the angles had faded.

"What is that?" Morven wondered aloud.

"I know not." Peterson's answer came out in a woosh. "I saw drops on his jacket, but they haven't been checked." He bent down toward the most recent yellowish drop stiffly, like a crane, and sniffed. "Is this butter that I see before me?" He leaned back, gazing at the rafters. "Dairy vision, fatal vision, sensible to feeling as to sight. Friends, this is odd. It will need testing, but I believe butter is melting from the skies."

"Butter in the rafters. That is decidedly a first. It *is* a cooking class. I've never heard of a dish made by dripping butter from above." Marlowe ground his teeth slightly, as if trying to taste a flavor long gone.

"Me neither." Even the hard-to-shake Morven's voice containing disbelief. "I'm not sure what that could mean. We need to be sure to get forensics all over that."

"Naturally. I'll be sure. Was that a question you alluded to earlier, dear friend Marlowe?"

"Wasn't, actually. Did Johnny, or you, notice any fingerprints on the knife?" He knew most criminals were well aware about avoiding fingerprints, but asked by force of old habit.

"Nothing yet. Perhaps they might appear, like gloss on faint deeds, but Johnny did take a brief look and wasn't holding much hope. Before you question further, time of death must wait, though you probably can get as much as I'll give from witnesses. A great man's last class. What memories are made of."

Morven still stared at ceiling. "Did you know the victim?"

Doctor Peterson put a gloved hand on the desk beside the victim's head. "Of him. There was never a great genius without a touch of madness. He contained both."

"Seems the consensus," Marlowe agreed. "One last one. Why is it so hot?"

"The heater was set to ninety-five degrees Fahrenheit when we arrived. Reducing, but still warm."

"Interesting. Important." The last mainly to himself. "We're heading out, unless you've more to tell."

"Nothing until I move him to a colder place. Love wounds with heat, and death with cold. I'll spend more time with our once fair chef here and there. Then expect me with news anon." He waved them out.

Marlowe and Morven headed into the hall, he motioning to the other doors. "Know what these are by chance?"

"Nearest on this side, a closet. Those across, bathrooms."

"Got it. Let's grab Nelson, do a rapid circling of the wagons."

Heading down the dark hall in the direction of the brightly lit classroom in their white suits, they could have been ungainly swans flying out of a storm into the sun.

John Arthur guided his black Honda Fit around a police car whose tail end jutted into the exit of the parking lot he'd chosen earlier, a block-and-a-half from the restaurant. Street parking in Tolltown on a Friday night was rare as drawing a straight flush or involved circling blocks for potentially an hour. Ponying up the six dollars per hour for parking seemed a fair price to pay for avoiding the hassle. Now he was even happier he'd done it, as much of the street parking nearer the scene was stuck due to police and emergency presence.

He turned onto 4th avenue heading north before taking a left on Emmett Way, a lengthy, curving road that eventually turned into 15th Avenue and took him into the neighborhood north of the city where he lived. The radio played, the deejay told him, Antonin Dvorak's Symphony No.7 in D minor. John tended to like classical music when driving, finding it calming amid the City's often stressful streets. Classical didn't interrupt his thoughts as much as provide musical background, accompanied by the routine swish-swish of wipers on windows, rain still coming down steadily. Deep clouds blanketed the sky, blocking out the stars and making the evening muffled, as if it had been swathed in layers of black cotton.

Quite a night for a murder, he thought. *Douglas Small, no less.* John tried to be humble, not thinking he was right every time he made a proclamation about a potential crime, but here, he thought he was right. The City's most celebrated chef, a leading light in the whole region's last twenty-year culinary revolution. A revolution paralleling the one worldwide, with a proliferation of celebrity chefs, more cooking and baking television series than could fit in a 1970s *TV Guide*, thousands of books, and social media accounts with millions of followers focused on food and drink in every manner imaginable—photos, videos, collaborations. Within the revolution, sub-movements abounded. Farm to table and glass. Molecular gastronomy and mixology. Organic and homegrown. A whole foodie and drinkie eruption.

Which meant increasing numbers of people going out and pushing themselves to cook more intricate meals at home, learning about ingredients from near and far, crafting their own food, from jams to cured meats to bitters, pushing skills. Sometimes by reading books, sometimes by watching the TV shows and videos, sometimes by taking classes like the one he found, after a quick search, was being taught by Douglas Small tonight. Murder at the baking class. Not a bad name for an episode of one of the British mysteries he adored. *I wonder what they were learning to bake?*

"Not surprising, in a way." John went from thinking to talking, his voice loud in the empty car over the low music. "There's been a whole shopping trolley's worth of episodes around chefs and culinary pursuits already." He unconsciously peppered his speech with British words and phrases, even when talking to himself. "Let's see, *Midsomer* has multiple ones; there's the one with Sharon Small as a celebrity chef, she's intense; the mill turned into a bakery episode; the one where the first victim is found in a vat at a microbrewery. I'm sure there are more I'm forgetting" His voice faded like a match that had run out of wood, then he continued his solo conversation.

"It's not solely the world's most murderous county, either. *Death in Paradise* has at least two celebrity chef episodes, one where the chef dies in his restaurant, and one where he dies while judging a competition for upcoming chefs, involving two different detective inspectors, Goodman and Parker. Probably others. The spin-off *Beyond Paradise* has an artisan chocolate poisoner episode. In *My Life is Murder*, lovely Lucy Lawless is an former police detective who makes her own bread, selling it to Reuben's café. And there's a celebrity chef episode, where the chef picks fresh herbs after calling someone an 'entitled snot stain.' The great *Whitstable Pearl* is set around a restaurant. Even slightly silly *Good Ship Murder* has a chef episode.

"Even shows that take place in the past haven't missed out on our appetite for culinary-minded murders." He laughed. "Appetite. I'll need to remember that word choice next time I talk to Marlowe about the case. *Earnest Endeavor* has a murder at a chocolate makers. Post-WW II *Father Brown* chef'd it up when a cookbook writer hosted a sort-of chef demonstration or festival in the tiny town of Kembleford. I should write these down. They're going to be important background for this latest case."

Driving up Emmett, surroundings transitioned from mid-level apartments looming in the dark night like square giants to a sparser spacing of buildings set off by gravelly vacant lots. Hooper's High-Speed Gas, Myers Mainland Multi-Level Storage, Tamzin's Top Shelf Pharmacy and Sweets, Wild Harvest Café. The signs blurred in rain. John drove this route so often he nearly knew them by heart. Soon, a sprawling outpost of the orange brick Whole Harriet's Grocery chain would pop up on his left like a ripe pumpkin. Full of organic veggies and fruits, pricy condiments, chocolate chunk cookies "homemade by hand daily," and wine, cheese, and meats made locally and from the globe's corners. Even on a dark and rainy night, the parking lot bubbled.

"Foodies never sleep. And I keep talking to myself. I don't even have Ainsley here to blame it on." The idea didn't seem to bother him. "I'm only remembering the tip of the murderous ice cube of food-and-chef television mysteries. I'll need to do some research if I'm going to help Marlowe. Makes sense. Mysteries, books and TV shows, have always been a mirror of the times they're created in. In the Golden Age, steamships and train rides, country house parties with corpses on all sides and Poirot sipping crème de menthe in the corner. Miss Marple solving the murder of a past maid. Back when everyone had maids. As sure as eggs are eggs, mysteries reflect contemporaneous events. Our current love of celebrity chefs, and bartenders too, seeping into favorite shows like blueberry juice through the edge of an undersealed pie crust."

Reaching the busier part of his own neighborhood, shops and stores began being crowded by, and then overwhelmed by, midsized apartments, the street becoming a stop-and-go affair, stoplights popping up as if holiday lights. Soon, he passed Lynley's Café, a favorite of Detective Marlowe's, and turned onto 80th as scenery grew residential with more single-family homes.

"Almost back, Ains. I wonder if it's too early to reach out to Marlowe again. He's probably busy. Maybe I'll give him until tomorrow."

He parked in front of his house, a passing jogger in a full lime-green hooded tracksuit giving him a wary look seeing John speaking animatedly in the car alone. In the City, even a heavy rain didn't keep the serious joggers at home. John waited until they passed to leave the car, breaking into a little jog himself as he went up the stairs to the white, cottage-style house with vivid lemon-yellow door. The blind on the window near the door had been smudged up, a dog's nose pressed against it. "Ainsley!" John's excited tone caused the nose to move up and down. "I'm back."

Marlowe, Morven, and Nelson huddled on the landing's far corner, white forensic suits off. Officers milled about, though Sergeant Troy wasn't in sight. Classroom attendees clustered in clumps across the landing, many talking to officers.

"Friday night." Marlowe's voice rumbled in a low key. "Not what we planned. What do we know?"

Morven's calm belied the surrounding chaos. "Douglas Small, chef and restauranteur, is our victim. Found in his office, where he had gone during the middle of teaching a baking class. Door reportedly locked from the inside. Body discovered by class attendees."

"Locked door. Could it have been suicide?" Nelson's voice was an enthusiastic whisper.

"Doubtful." Marlowe went on to quickly tell Nelson about the knife in Small's back.

Nelson gasped. "But the door was locked. That's wild."

"There are a few more wild"—she underlined the word with irony—"aspects. Butter in the rafters. Busy class. No screams or arguing heard. That we know about so far, unless more has turned up from interviewing the baking students." She motioned their direction.

Nelson whipped out his notebook. "Nothing like that. The interviews have been brief, sorry. They seem in shock."

"That's understandable, Nelson." Marlowe didn't want to undermine the new detective's confidence. "Hard to round up deep details in a situation this fraught. Did we get names and basic info?"

"Yes, that we got. Want me to go through them?" Both nodded. "I'm going to start with a name you'll recognize. Drogo Oates."

"Drogo?" Marlowe's voice raised above the din as he looked across the landing. One man, very thin, with grimy hair pulled up into a topknot, caught his eye for a moment before staring sheepishly at the shoes of the officer talking to him. Drogo's white top had Pollockian food stains on it, and his black pants only reached his ankles. He had been a suspect, then witness, in the last case John Arthur had helped them with.

Nelson went on. "Says he's a chef in training, but was in the back doing dishes."

"Odd. Go on."

"Right. Louisa Sweeney we talked about. She's really broken up. I can't believe she'd be involved, too nice."

"Maybe keep it to details, Nelson, less editorial."

"Can do, Detective. Next up, Kevin Holman and his wife, Claire Holman. She's a pharmacist. Both middle-aged. Not sure he has a job. They're sitting on the couch. Sarah Sykes. She seemed to think I should know who she is, but I didn't. Restaurant critic. Her husband, Chester Rowan, is here. Publisher of Gumberoo Books. They knew the victim. He's the stubbly one nearest us, she's next to him. Standing with his back to him is Martin Allen, bartender. Here with boyfriend, Flynn Will, a waiter at Joel Towell's restaurant With Bold Knife and Fork. Too much?"

"Perfect. Keep it coming."

"Jim Sean, tallest guy over there. Heaviest too. Salesman. Crying a lot. Olivia Sean, the woman with the barley-colored, curly hair, is his wife. Then we have Lucille Crow. She's imposing in a way, but friendly. Real estate agent. Here with her friend Madison Bernard. House photographer and artist. They take a lot of classes together."

"Nice overview, Nelson." Marlowe stretched his arms out. "From talking to them, were there any other people they saw, coming up from the restaurant or the hotel?"

"No, sir. At least none mentioned. Louisa—Miss Sweeney—said Chef Small didn't allow interruptions."

They were quiet for a moment, then Morven spoke up. "We have a room, locked from the inside. The victim in the room. No windows. Twelve people outside in another room, near each other. Through that room is the only access to the victim's room. It doesn't make a lot of sense."

Marlowe was having the same hard time getting his head around it. "We need to dig deeper into what happened this evening. And about the Chef. Not sure that lot is going to be helpful tonight." He knew after a tragedy victim statements were even more unreliable than usual. But letting them marshal stories could be unhelpful. It was a conundrum, and not the first time they'd had to deal with one.

He was about to make a decision as a statuesque woman approached the top of the stairs. She was in full dress police uniform, buttons shimmering, her appearance that of a resolute Margaret Dumont, the actor who played Groucho's comedic foil in many Marx Brothers movies.

"Captain Innocent." Marlowe couldn't rein in the surprise at seeing his boss at the scene. "Didn't know you were here."

3

Marlowe sat in the back seat of an unmarked black police SUV. Captain Innocent sat beside him, her back straight as if on a formal dining room chair and not a thread of uniform out of place. He slumped deeper into the seat, staring out the window at the rain that still came down as her police driver rapidly navigated streets. A bit too rapidly for Marlowe's taste.

They'd caught her up on the crime's details at the scene quickly, as there wasn't an expansive amount of information yet. She'd made an executive decision, as she called it, to send the class attendees home, told they'd be followed up with soon. Morven and Nelson were sent to the station to start doing background research on the victim, the attendees, and to liaise with forensics to try and put a rush on some of their reports. Marlowe knew it would probably take days or longer to get the information, however, it never hurt to deliver a tender spur to the scientists.

Innocent wanted Marlowe to come with her to give Douglas Small's ex-wife, Ruth Small, the notification about his death. It was hard for him to develop this particular picture, but it turned out his often formidable boss sang in a choir with Ruth Small that was dedicated to music of the 18th and 19th century. Innocent in a bustled gown and frilly bonnet belting at full volume? He couldn't see it. But given that connection to Ruth Small, Innocent wanted to be the one to give her the news. One reason why she showed at the scene. The second being the chef's celebrity standing in the City, and the whole country. Her appearance, she'd said, would let people know the police took the situation seriously.

Marlowe liked to believe they took every crime seriously, but felt perhaps now wasn't the time to voice that opinion. He wasn't sad for the company, even his boss. Conversations after a death were hard. You deliver horrible news, the worst news, to a person and then ask them questions. As the SUV blasted through a yellow light, then braked, screeching, for a turning car, Marlowe braced himself on the back of the seat. The officer drove at speeds that might suggest he was taking part in a cinematic car chase.

"A little fast for a rainy night," Marlowe mumbled.

Innocent's reply came slowly, as if she wasn't paying close attention. "Hmm? Were we going rapidly? Officer Hastings has driven me many times. We're in safe hands, Detective Marlowe. Don't fret. Instead, focus on how we can quickly solve this case."

He wasn't sure if her statement demanded a reply, and they'd just pulled up in front of a three-story, modern house, so he stayed quiet.

She brushed an imaginary crumb off her pants. "Inside, I can do most of the talking. But if she has any questions specific to the scene, you can answer. Do so in the vaguest way. Now, a quick walk up to the front door so we don't get too wet."

He'd been holding his hat on his lap and adjusted it back onto his head before following. She kept a brisk pace past a short white fence and brief, tightly cropped lawn before stopping under a metal porch roof jutting out a few feet. Marlowe kept two feet behind and could hear the tap-tap of rain on his hat brim as she rang the doorbell.

A five-and-a-half foot tall woman opened the door. Her short, almond hair was pixie cut, accenting the sharp lines of her chin, nose, and lips, a combination that would have been severe except for a mischievous light emanating from wide, sea-blue eyes. She wore a creamy silk top and lounging pants with matching slippers.

"Rebecca, is that you under the uniform?" Ruth's voice was surprisingly deep for her stature, reverberating like a subway underground.

"Yes, Ruth, and I apologize profusely for interrupting your evening. May we come in? This is Detective Marlowe."

"Of course."

As Ruth backed up, Marlowe noticed her original smile shifting warily. It was a look he'd seen many times when announcing himself as police at someone's door.

They walked into an entranceway with a small wooden rack for shoes on one side and hooks for coats on the other. It led into a hall painted the same shade as Ruth's outfit, causing her to blend in when stopping a few steps down. Doors opened either side, and the end of the hall seemed to flow into what he decided might be the kitchen.

"How about the drawing room. No need to remove shoes." Ruth led them through the door on the right into a spacious open-plan room. At the far end, the kitchen was visible, stainless steel appliances under dimmed lights like a play's audience. Nearer were two black-olive colored leather couches on shiny cherry wood floors around a low, dark wood table. A few side tables with curvy vases of flowers and a bookcase full of hardbacks decorated the room. The walls were adorned with a series of food photos, blown up while maintaining a high-def focus. One appeared to be a salmon fillet in a cloud, another an oyster with a sphere on it, another pale gnocchi swirled in a rich green sauce.

"Please, have a seat." She motioned to the couches. Marlowe sat next to Innocent on one, and Ruth sat primly across from them. "This can't be good, police showing up."

"Ruth, I am sorry to have to tell you this, but Douglas is dead." Innocent's tone was more delicate than Marlowe was used to.

The woman didn't reply, but stiffened. Her face drained of any emotion, as if it had become carved ivory instead of flesh and blood.

Marlowe started to stand. "Would you like a glass of water, ma'am?"

Ruth didn't reply, then shook her head at Marlowe as if seeing him for the first time. He sat back down, the only noise in the room his rustling on the couch.

After a minute, Innocent spoke again. “Ruth, first, my sincerest condolences. Would you like us to call anyone? Family. Friends.”

Ruth shook her head again, bowing it, then straightening to face them. “No. Thank you. Can I ask what happened?”

“There was an incident at the cooking school.”

“An incident. Does that mean Douglas finally irritated the wrong person?”

Marlowe spoke without remembering Innocent’s desire to lead. “Why would you think that?”

“Detective… Marlowe, I believe?” He nodded and she continued. “Rebecca here knows, but if you don’t, Douglas and I have been divorced for a number of years. While continuing to love him on one level, and never stopping being in contact with him, I divorced him for a reason. Multiple ones. But primarily because he could be very damaging to one’s nerves, very irritating. I feel bad saying it as he’s dead, but genius I suppose has its downsides. So was his death, uh, unnatural?”

“We’re following all lines of inquiry.” He trotted out the familiar line like he was riding a very tame pony. “But we are treating it as suspicious.”

She grunted in response. Innocent stayed quiet, so Marlowe felt he should go on.

“I hate to ask after such a shock, but can you think of anyone who might carry a grudge against your ex-husband?”

She looked him in the eye, the mischievous twinkle surfacing momentarily. “How long do you have, Detective?”

“Ma’am? Not sure what you mean.”

“As I said, Douglas could irritate people. Add to that, he was laser focused on being successful and wouldn’t let anyone stand in his way. If that wasn’t enough, he had, what’s the phrase? A wandering eye. The list I could give you of people who might have issue with Douglas would be long.”

"I see. If any recent come to mind, please let us know."

"I can try to put together a list."

"Very helpful. Up for one or two more questions?"

"Sure."

"Where did you and Douglas meet?" He felt getting some background now would only help later. And while the news had been a shock, she'd perked up, watching him closely.

"At a restaurant called Games. Sports themed. Seafarers baseball, Osprey football, you know. But nice food. He was sous chef, I waited tables. Love not at first sight, but at first drunken night, you might say. Before he became Douglas Small, capital letter chef, he was more fun."

"You worked there when you were married?"

Ruth groaned and smiled. "Oh no. We were kids. Douglas always wanted to open his own restaurant, and after saving and finding an investor, we opened Small's. It didn't light the scene on fire opening day, but then Douglas had what he always called in interviews his 'forest retreat.' A solo camping trip to the mountains. He said it changed his style of cooking. Maybe his whole style. It led to him changing the menu and then one extremely positive tongue-licking of a review. That review put Small's, and Douglas, on the culinary map. Then we got married."

"Very helpful background, ma'am."

Ruth's smile expanded. "No ma'am-ing, please. Ruth is perfect. Rebecca knows I'm not so formal."

Captain Innocent still hadn't replied, and didn't. She was gazing up at one of the pictures, entranced.

"Ruth it is." Marlowe's mustache tips trended up. "After Small's took off, you two expanded the offerings?"

"Not instantly, no. Opening places, finding the right real estate, concepting, takes a while. But more did come, starting with the first bakery and then Mansion Mess. I saw him less. Then books, his line of condiments, Douglas Small as brand. Finally, I didn't see him. And then we got divorced. Amicably." She drew the word out like reeling in a fish on a line. "There wasn't some knock-down, drag-out fight. We met up, I said we should get divorced, he agreed. The lawyers did up paperwork, we argued, they did up more paperwork, and it was done. He had so much going on, a string of successes, though this was before Behold the Stars. He'd moved on, and I realized I should do the same. Amicably."

"Behold the Stars? Not clear on that one."

"Not up on local culinary history, Detective?" Marlowe gave her a what-are-you-going-to-do look. "It was Douglas's last restaurant. A crowning glory, he called it. Very fine-dining spot. Pricey, upscale, white gloves, the works. A rare misstep, because the City isn't that. It cost nearly as much as a used Honda for a meal and wine."

"Not a destination on a cop's salary."

Innocent perked up. "We are very fair with salaries, Detective Marlowe."

"Yes, ma'am."

Back ahold of the conversation, she continued. "Ruth, again, I am so sorry. I'm sure we've taken up enough of your time, unless you'd like me to stay? Or call someone. These situations can be trying."

"Thank you for offering, Rebecca, but I have some calls to make. Unless you or the detective have more questions?"

Innocent stood, Marlowe slowly following suit. "I'm sure the detective is done." She reached out two hands, taking one of Ruth's, pulling the other woman up into the shake.

Marlowe felt even with Innocent's swansong he might ask one more thing. "Ma'am?" They looked his way in concert. "Ruth. These pictures. They're lovely, almost like portraits. Douglas's work?"

"The food, yes. The photos, I took."

"Quite remarkable, Ruth. I didn't know you were a photographer." Honey dripped over Innocent's words. "This one especially, I couldn't take my eyes from it." She pointed to picture of the salmon fillet.

"Salmon Altocumulus. Douglas's first signature dish. Pure in a way. Hard to master. A wild-caught king salmon fillet seared and topped with French sea salt, Tellicherry pepper, organic lemon, and a pine needle espuma. What do you think, Detective?"

"The photo is dandy. But I'm more fish-and-chips."

Back in the SUV, Officer Hastings driving at speeds that had Marlowe tightening his seat belt, Captain Innocent breathed out an exaggerated sigh.

"That went as well as possible." She ran a hand over her head as if to smooth it, though not a hair was out of place. She elbowed Marlowe's side, where his hefty belly bulged. "I felt you picked up my signal to get in some background questions nicely, Detective. We didn't want to rattle her, but do want to start solving this case. Team work, dream work, all that."

He wasn't sure what shocked him more, the elbow or unexpected jolliness. "Yes, ma'am." She might be jolly, but she wouldn't stay that way if he slid into calling her Rebecca. And he wanted to keep her happy, because he had a question and wasn't sure how it'd land. Thinking no matter how cold the water, it was better to rush in, he went on. "A question, ma'am. The culinary world that Douglas Small inhabited, we can agree it will probably be important."

"Agreed." He tone was like a teacher speaking to a pupil stating the obvious.

"Taking that into consideration, and admitting my fine-dining experiences are less than my campfire cooking experiences, I had an idea and would like to get your experienced opinion on it." It never hurt to add some sugar to the pill.

She cocked her head toward him.

"I believe our investigations would be helped by insight into that world from a civilian who knows it, and who knows Douglas Small. It could provide some lines of inquiry we might not discover immediately. Speed is of the essence, as you said."

"A civilian to help with the background and investigation. Not normal protocol."

"True, ma'am. Not normal. Douglas Small being murdered, also not normal." She nearly broke in, but Marlowe went on before the hurdle could be placed on the track. "We do have civilian contractors. Lots of them. For computer work, clerical, accounting, any needed services where we aren't always experts."

"I know that, Detective." Her voice scoffed on the edges. "I sign the budgets for most of them and spend many meetings on spreadsheets about this very topic. However. What you say may make sense. Are you looking for suggestions?"

"I have a person in mind." Here it was, the moment she'd blow up, laugh, or come on board. "John Arthur."

She was more shocked than amused. "*The* John Arthur? One-time suspect, two-time witness. British mystery obsessive who started showing up at the station multiple times. That John Arthur?"

This wasn't exactly accurate, as he'd only been a witness once, but Marlowe didn't feel correcting her was the best way to break this bronco of an idea. "Yes, ma'am. He has been involved in the industry, from the press side, for many years, writing about restaurants, food, and drink. Interviewed and knew the victim, and has taken classes at the cooking school. His insights are wordy, I grant you, but helpful. He knows the industry and the team."

Officer Hastings heavily braked, accelerated, and changed lanes around a truck that had *With Baited Breath, Seafood Suppliers* printed on its side under a green flying fish.

Innocent sighed once more. "John Arthur. Contracting with the police. But…" She hung on the word an extra beat. "It makes sense having industry experience. I'll find the money."

"He'd probably do it for free."

"Let's keep it professional. He gets hired to help with background and insider knowledge, but don't let him overcook the case."

Marlowe wasn't sure if he should laugh at the overcook. It could be hard to tell with his boss.

"Where can Office Hastings drop you?"

"Station would be ace-high. Morven and Nelson are there. But have him watch the speed downtown. Those roads get slicker than a dry gully after a hard rain."

Back at the station about five hours after originally leaving it, Morven and Nelson were hard at work. As always, their dedication and zest for the job impressed. The trio shared a corner within a vast, high-ceilinged detectives' room, a spot Marlowe had chosen due to its position out of the middle of the scrum and near to westward-facing windows. It never hurt to catch the sun setting. Currently, the room was mostly empty outside of a few detectives Marlowe waved abstractedly at in passing, taking a deep breath as he approached his desk. It was late.

Morven and Nelson had set up what John Arthur would call the murder board, a four-by-six corkboard on wheels. A picture of Douglas Small was pinned to the top-center of the board. In it, he stared fiercely frontward, hair pulled back tight from expansive forehead, stately nose, pursed lips, chef jacket on and hands crossed at chest level, one holding a balloon whisk and the other a chef's knife. Other pieces of paper and a few orange sticky notes with names on them filled out the board.

Currently, Morven and Nelson were looking at their laptops, sharing a single wooden desk as they had since Nelson joined the team full time. He was meant to get his own, but office supplies moved slowly at the station, as if traveling by steamship between continents instead of elevator between floors. Nelson's chair was pulled up along one side of the desk, filling the space between it and Marlowe's.

"Team." Marlowe made it to them without either noticing, moving surprisingly quietly for his girth. His voice caused Nelson to jolt, bounce out of his chair, and stand.

Morven swiveled around as she spoke. "Welcome back. Seems like a long time since we left this space."

"And yet it's the same evening."

"And yet it is. How was the widow?"

"Ex. We can still call her the widow. Shocked. Gave some background. Feel I'm getting to know our victim. You two appear busy." Tiredness draped over him like a thick antique quilt.

"Starting to be. Lots to do." Morven's adrenaline had kicked in, and she seemed well awake. "We've been pulling together background on Douglas Small and starting in on the people in the class."

"Give me your short victim bio. Nelson, feel free to sit back down and jump in as needed." Marlowe pulled his chair back, leaned it up on two legs precipitously, propping fawn-colored, dilapidated Oxfords on the desk.

"Douglas Small," Morven read off her screen. "Fifty-five years old. Single. Restauranteur and author. Media personality. First restaurant, Small's, opened when he was twenty-seven. Currently has six others: Bi Valve, Mansion Mess, Short's, The Ribery, Small Bakery, and Il Signore Piccolo, the restaurant in the hotel tonight. Actually, there are three bakery outposts currently. Books include *Douglas Small's Kitchen*, his first one, *Douglas Small's City Cooking, The Small Bakery Book, Small Plates*, and *The Small Bartending Book.* Has a line of branded condiments, Small's Sauces. Considered one of the preeminent regional chefs, also known nationally."

"Check. More?"

"Not too much. I scanned a few articles. Could be he's on the wane as a chef, if that makes sense. Once considered a cooking genius, now perhaps more a successful entrepreneur. We need to dig more."

"Agreed. What are his finances like? Any trouble in his past? Rivalries—business, culinary and personal. A deep hole."

She nodded. "And info from the scene itself. Forensic reports, Doctor Peterson's report."

Marlowe grinned. "The butter."

"The butter." Morven's words oozed incredulousness.

Nelson's hand shot up.

"No need to go classroom rules, Nelson," she said.

"Great." He still stood, then attempted to lean against his chair, causing it to knock into her desk. "Are we sure it was murder?"

"Not sure he could reach to put a knife in his own back." Marlowe stretched his arm backward as if to prove the point. "But point taken."

"Could he have somehow backed against it?"

"Not sure, again, Nelson. Let's agree to call it a suspicious death."

"Yes, sir, Detective Marlowe. If it is suspicious, the room was locked from the inside. Doubly. Who could have gotten in?"

"That's on us to track down. Which leads to the list of people nearby." He pointed at the board. A sheet of typing paper with the names of class attendees, plus Drogo, was tacked near the bottom.

Morven walked over to the paper, un-tacking it. "Are we positive it would be someone on this list? I believe so. But to play devil's advocate, could someone else have gotten in?"

Marlowe closed his eyes. "Doubtful. Maybe. Points back to the deep hole we find ourselves within. Need more information." He opened his eyes. "It's late, and we're floundering. Let's make a plan for tomorrow. Fresh eyes." Seeing their nods, he continued. "First interview, Louisa Sween—"

"I'll interview Miss Sweeney," Nelson interrupted like water unexpectedly cracking a dam. "Sorry, Detective."

"Appreciate the enthusiasm. Morven might be best." He felt Nelson might be too appreciative of Louisa in general to interview her alone. "But, Nelson?" The younger detective's face had gone from excited to crestfallen. "Could you solo interview Chester Rowan? He—"

"I can." Nelson perked up, standing straight again. "Sorry, excuse my interruptions."

Marlowe waved the apology off. "He was one of the first to view the body. And had a very long relationship with Douglas. As his original publisher, he should have more insights than most, so might be helpful at this early stage. See what he knows. We need to map movements of everyone there. Might need more help here, too."

"Beyond troop coordinating, what's your morning agenda?" Morven sensed Marlowe had something up his sleeve. After working together for so long, she read the palimpsest under the words he actually spoke.

"There is a matter I have on the morning docket, which will bring more help." He wasn't sure how to introduce John Arthur, police contractor.

"Another detective on the team?"

He took a yawning breath. "Not exactly. We're going to bring John Arthur on as a contractor."

Morven looked skeptical. Nelson gave a short fist-pump. His admiration of the older man from the last cases was hard to contain.

"Talked to Captain Innocent. She's okay'd. He'll provide culinary world knowledge, as well as insight on the victim, who he knew from interviewing him."

"Are you sure, Marlowe?" Morven said. "He can be distracting."

Nelson responded first. "Mr. Arthur is awesome. It's like Miss Marple said: 'There is no detective in England equal to a spinster lady of uncertain age with plenty of time on her hands.' Except we're in the City and he's a spinster man. Or widower. You get what I'm saying."

"He'll be assisting with background only, and we'll keep a tight rein." He didn't say it, but Marlowe was praying that was possible. "I'll go by his house first thing. Make sure he's up for it."

Morven laughed. "He'll be up for it. And quoting TV shows before you finish asking."

Rain trickled out of coal-gray sky when Marlowe left his house the next morning. He'd insisted they head homeward not long after dropping the John Arthur news, knowing they'd be better served in the morning after getting decent shut-eye. Once up, a piece of toast topped with peanut butter in one hand–*not a glamorous chef here*, he thought–his phone in the other, he'd called John. Didn't say much outside of asking if dropping by wasn't an imposition. He wanted to get John's response in person.

By the time he pulled up in front of John's cape-style home, the sun was out, with only a couple of water drops still hanging on leaves, shining brightly as if unwilling to believe their existence was going to be so short. The City's weather could serve as a dictionary's secondary definition of unpredictable. He wore his normal outfit of wrinkled white shirt and brown slacks. Today, his suspenders were also brown, with miniature gold highball glasses. He kept his blue baseball cap on, because he knew the rain could start back with a snap.

Before taking the first of four gray porch steps up to John's blindingly yellow door, he heard an oddly high-pitched barking coming from inside. A dog's face briefly appeared in the window, vanished, came back, then vanished again. Closer, he heard John from inside too.

"Ainsley, quiet." John's gentle command was accompanied by a laugh. "Quit jumping. Marlowe's gonna put you in doggy jail." The door opened. "Detective, welcome. Ainsley remembers you, as you can tell. Ainsley, calm down."

Ainsley was a curiously colored, sixty-pound Staffy. Brindled, but with a dried-apricot tan base marked by black, flaring highlights. A white streak like new lightning ran up one side of her neck. She had three white paws, too. As Marlowe bent over reaching out a hand for Ainsley to smell, her tail wagged as if stuck in a tornado funnel.

Marlowe scratched Ainsley's floppy right ear. "Morning."

"Detective." John beamed. "Come in. Ainsley, let the detective walk."

John also wore a blue baseball cap, his with two dogs on it instead of Marlowe's S, along with a red T-shirt with a dog nearing Ainsley in appearance in a field of sunflowers, sea-green shorts, and brown knee socks with manatees in teacups on them. The gold flecks in his clear glasses caught a twist of the newly returned sun. Pulling Ainsley gently back by the collar allowed Marlowe to enter and head left into the living room.

He knew the room well from the first time he'd been to the house to interview John after the man had found a body in a neighboring park. He sat comfortable on a near-to-the-floor royal blue couch under a five-foot by four-foot print of Dante's *The Divine Comedy* as John let Ainsley go, sitting on the smaller black and white couch beneath the front window. The dog bounded up next to Marlowe, giving him one of those peculiar dog gazes that says, "You're going to pet me, and don't pretend you aren't." He scratched behind her ear as they talked, she slowly oozing from sitting next to him to lying pressed tight to his right leg.

Light billowed through the windows, shining off an orange metal cabinet, a white coffee table topped with plants, an abstract-y painting of a green bottle and a red square, and the room's two huge bookshelves. Marlowe's gaze tended to wander their way whenever talking to John. Jammed with books antique and new of many sizes, widths, and subjects—cooking, Dickens and Trollope, history, mystery—the shelves also held snapshots of dogs and people, egg cups in the shapes of British queens, seashells, something called a cuss box, a four-inch Michelangelo's *David*, and other ephemera. Amongst the books, Marlowe particularly noticed a volume called *London Characters and Crooks*. John certainly did enjoy his chosen theme. Between the bookshelves was a canary-yellow pie safe topped with a TV.

John started as Marlowe gazed around. "I was watching *Endeavor*. You probably remember me talking about it. Spin-off of the British classic *Morse*. The second spin-off, as there was *Lewis*, which was about Inspector Morse's sergeant, now an inspector himself. All three taking place in Oxford, which with its legendary limestone university buildings, college greens, and Bodleian library, is a character in itself. *Endeavor* happens in the past, 60s and early 70s. Endeavor is actually Inspector Morse's first name, but no one calls him that. He's played in this show by the thoughtful if prickly Shaun Evans. Hard to fill the legendary John Thaw's shoes but—"

"John." Marlowe turned back his way. He knew John might lecture all day on his British mystery du jour.

John came out of his flow, confused. "Yes, Detective Marlowe?"

"Sadly, don't remember that one."

"You can't remember every show." The words carried a smidge of self-deprecation, like a person carrying a rarely used umbrella.

"True."

"You're probably not here to have me list my favorites, or to pet Ainsley."

"True. Though petting Ainsley is nice."

"You're here to ask my help on the case."

John could be uncanny. "Why would you think that?"

"First day after a murder is too busy for a social call." Marlowe shook his head but John didn't notice. "I wasn't this time at the actual scene, so not a witness. Ergo, you're taking me up on my offer to help with your inquiries, as they say."

"We would like to offer you a role as—"

"A consulting detective. The best in the City." He stood up and took a mock bow.

"Not a detective, John. A civilian contractor. To provide background on the victim and culinary insights."

"A contracting detective. Not sure of the ring to that."

"Civilian contractor."

"I'll take contracting detective."

"Don't take it out of this room."

John's chortle bounced around the couches, causing Ainsley's head to rise for a moment before she snuggled back up to Marlowe. "Very Marx Brothers, Marlowe. I get the message. Keep the detectiving down. Reduce TV mystery talk. Stick to food and bar talk. I can do it."

Marlowe doubted the complete honesty of the statement, but knew John would try. For a few minutes. "We'll pay you."

John put on mock disgust, as if he'd taken a bite of a peach past the sell-by date. "Arthur solves crimes for the betterment of humanity, not monetary gain."

"Part of the deal. Makes the books balance."

"You can give the money to Forgotten Dogs Rescue. They're super deserving. That's where I got Ainsley."

"Up to you," Marlowe replied, petting the dog in question.

"Let's get it going. Detective, what can you tell me?"

For the next fifteen minutes, Marlowe gave John an overview of what they knew so far. No paperwork had been signed on John's consulting, but he knew he could trust him. John rambled during conversations, but wasn't going to give out case details on a social site. Done, they sat for a moment, only Ainsley's breathing breaking the silence.

"Butter in the ceiling," John mused, half to himself.

"Indeed," Marlowe replied.

"'The one thing we can say is that he came to a sticky end.'" John adopted a voice he thought was close to a British private school accent, but was oceans away, before slipping back into his own. "Sorry to Douglas, that wasn't kind. And sorry to you, Marlowe. A quote from the *Endeavor* pathologist, DeBryn. Pathologists always have to have odd characteristics. His is dark humor, as it often is."

"Any thoughts outside of the quote?"

"It's a locked-room mystery, which I love. That's probably not what you're looking for. Douglas Small as murder victim is not completely surprising."

"Why?" John's comment reverberated in Marlowe's mind with Ruth's.

"'Frankly, he was an odious man. Anyone could have done it.'" The accent this time was higher pitched.

"Odious?"

Back to normal, John continued. "He could be. Could also be charming. And brilliant. And captivating. And funny. Often in the same five minutes. After interviewing him, I felt frantic and excited and worn out, as if I'd been on a Tilt-A-Whirl three times in a row. I imagine those in his immediate circle were the same. Can we stop by the scene?"

John's switch in subjects caught Marlowe off guard. Before he could formulate a response, John continued.

"As I've taken a class there, *you* might think I remember everything about the space and scene of the crime. *I* was thinking going back would spur the little gray cells." The last words slipped into a French accent. John could trot around Europe with accents in any short conversation.

Marlowe considered, decided it was worthwhile. "We'll take separate cars." He liked John and was glad to have him aboard, but not sure he wanted him along all day.

"Yes, chef. I mean detective." John bounced up buoyant as a helium balloon, causing Ainsley to jump off the other couch. "I'll bring Ainsley. She missed her morning walk while we waited for you."

4

Sadly, Ainsley did not get to make the trip. Marlowe considered the idea out of love for the dog. For most dogs. He no longer had his own, as pet ownership and a detective's hours weren't a healthy mix, so the idea of spending hours with Ainsley cuddled his mind. The scene continuing being gone over by forensics, however, and they probably wouldn't appreciate adding dog DNA. So, she stayed home. Which meant John had to take her on a walk first. Much as dog-ambling sounded enjoyable, Marlowe told John he'd meet him downtown in forty-five. This gave the detective time to pull up at his second favorite place in this neighborhood, Lynley's Café.

Discovered when working on the Case of the Nine Neighbors, Lynley's was a fairly nondescript café, one of hundreds their coffee-adoring city contained. He'd began thinking of it as *his* then, partially because the coffee was a cut above, partially because they had croissants baked at the outstanding nearby Renzo's bakery, and partially because he'd made café-friends with the owner, Nate. Walking in, shaggy black-haired Nate stood behind the counter making a cappuccino for a woman in orange running shoes, orange tights, and a black shirt that had a picture of a square-headed dog in a ghost costume and the words *Pit-Boo*. Halloween wasn't too far off.

Handing the woman her coffee, Nate saw Marlowe and proffered an exaggerated wave. "Morning, Detective, happy to see you. What's the proverbial poison today?"

"Americano please, Nate. And croissant. Thank you."

"Repeat that for me, would ya?" Nate had at one time been in a band, If Wishes Were Horses, whose amplified volume stood out even within the city's leagues of high-volume bands. They never quite surfaced from a steady regional following, but played enough in the past that his hearing loss led to order repetitions. Marlowe gave the order again, louder. Nate replied via an on-beat head bob and bent to the shimmering, steaming espresso machine.

Before long, Marlowe's coffee nestled in one hand, pastry in the other, legs stretched out long in front of the blue couch he'd sat on, a couch nearly as shaggy as Nate. He took a hot first sip, then a bite. *Strange*, he thought, *eating pastry before going to a classroom where they were at a baking class and where a murder was committed. Suspicious death*, he reminded himself. A violent death is always tragic. But the fact of it happening where people were learning to make delicious food, an activity usually done so you can then serve that deliciousness happily to others, who are then happier, added to the tragedy. He peeled the top, crispiest layer of stratified dough off, setting it aside, before taking a fluffy, buttery bite of the center. That top layer—the layering itself the pièce de resistance of pastry art—he saved to crunch at the end. Such a joy, surrounded by such sadness.

Morven got lucky, finding a parking spot directly in front of Louisa Sweeney's apartment building in the bustling Uppercase Hill neighborhood. Easing her Neptune-blue Kia Sportage into the tight space, two late teen girls in black leather jackets, jean shorts and Chucks provided mock applause, spikey haircuts bouncing. She returned a short salute, exiting the car and giving the apartment the once-over. Brick with white-paned casement windows dotting seven floors, the building had 1923 regally carved in block pale stone over the main entrance. Very classic. She scrolled the electronic keypad through the directory, hitting the call button when Sweeney came up. No reply flowed out the speaker, but the door buzzed and she went in and up the stairs.

Louisa's apartment was 601. Morven took each flight breezily in her olive-colored herringbone wool suit. She'd made the appointment earlier that morning, doing a brief bit of background, forgoing her normal dawn Muay Thai workout. Louisa Sweeney, twenty-six years old, had worked for Small in some way or other for five years. Currently listed as baker for the Tolltown Small Bakery. One article referred to her as his latest protégé, but there wasn't much else out there. Obviously, she helped in the classroom too. But was she deeply involved, or more fetch and carry? Finding herself at a cornsilk-colored door that could use a paint refresher, 601 nailed on it in red iron, she knocked, badge out in the other hand in case Louisa looked through the peephole.

After a moment, the door opened slowly, as if on tired hinges. Louisa wore baggy black sweats and a silver sweatshirt with arms raggedly cut off just past the shoulder. It had *Small's Team (Not a Small Team)* in black lettering on it. Her hair was tousled, nearly ratty, like she'd been gripping and releasing it repeatedly. Red glasses dangled from a gold chain around her neck, green eyes surrounded by bloodshot lines and dark circles. Overall, she seemed a wet towel recently twisted tight.

"Miss Sweeney." Morven gently moved into the apartment, causing Louisa to back up. "Thank you for agreeing to see me."

"Sure." The woman's voice was sandpapery.

"Should we sit down?"

Louisa gripped one arm in the other. "Yes, sorry. Just woke up. Wherever is fine."

She backed into the small apartment's main room, walls painted the same shade as the door, shiny oak floors, and delicately scrolled crown molding. A couch the color of an un-watered fern sat under the room's one wide window, two red metal chairs across from it, a third nearer the door. The far wall of the room served as the kitchen—generic appliances, laminate countertops, wood cabinets, and a two-person, wrought-iron, turquoise bistro table and matching chairs in one corner. Two doors led off the main room: Morven guessed bathroom and bedroom. She maneuvered around piles of books rising off the floor like paper stalagmites and sat in one of the chairs. Louisa took another, pulling a leg up under her, biting the nail of her right thumb.

"First, let me say how sorry I am. You knew Douglas Small a while."

"Yes." Louisa screwed her eyes up tight. "Five and a half years. One as a waitress, then I moved into working at the downtown bakery. I've been there ever since. I learned to bake there, from Douglas. He was— I can't believe he's gone. The body. It was, just, unreal. Do you know who did it?"

Morven knew traumatic experiences led to wandering thoughts. "We are investigating many lines of inquiry at the moment. How was working for him?"

She chewed her nail. "Wonderful. He is—was—a genius. He changed my life. I love baking now."

"Always wonderful?"

"Baking is hard, Detective, don't get me wrong. A science. And Douglas is a person who held very high standards, in baking, cooking, cocktails, restaurant experience, everything. Kind, too. But sometimes tough. Sometimes . . ." Words shifted into sobs.

Morven reached into a pocket and removed a white linen handkerchief, the initials TVM in silver stitching on one corner. She always carried it for these moments, and handed it to Louisa, who took it absently. Breathing deeply, she pulled the sobs in, rubbing the handkerchief over her eyes and cheeks. For a moment, it looked like a dove's wings fluttering.

She held on to the handkerchief. "I feel I've been crying so much that I would be out of moisture, like overbaked pastry leaking butter. But it still comes."

"It's expected, no apologies needed. You must have been close to Mr. Small."

"Very close." Louisa nodded, breathing in again heavily.

Morven decided to change the subject, to help stop the tears. "Let's talk about last night. It was a three-night class setup, correct?"

Louisa brightened. "A different cake every night. I might like patisserie best, or viennoiserie, classic French, but cakes are always fun. We started easier, a vegan Victoria Sponge with fruit and a buttercream, then a Swiss-roll style cake. Then last night was entremets, which are more than a simple cake, for sure."

"Now I'm hungry." Morven noticed a smile flash across the other woman's face momentarily, like a bubble surfacing in Champagne thought flat. "The same basic schedule each night, correct?"

"Yes. We'd start with an overview. Then Douglas would have everyone gather around his desk to demonstrate some cake point or filling points. Then people would get started and he and I would walk around giving advice as they worked on cakes, fillings, toppings. Very hands on."

"He'd leave at some point."

"He took a mid-class break, forty-five minutes, in the office. He works—worked—so hard. Like, I'm surprised he didn't take longer. Doing the class was harder than kneading five loaves." She chewed her nail again. Morven was surprised it hadn't started bleeding.

"And during this time, he was alone?"

"Always. His downtime. He hated being interrupted then. I would never open the door on him. He'd take his coffee back and relax. Deserved it. I wouldn't ever bother him. I watched over the class and gave instructions."

"You were more co-teacher than assistant."

"Yes. Not to say— I mean, he was the genius. But I'm a good baker." She blushed.

"Same attendees all three nights?" Louisa nodded, so Morven continued. "Could you let me know who sat where?"

Louisa reached for a notebook. "Can I map it out? I think visually better. It'll only take a second." She started sketching before Morven responded.

"Sure. Whatever is easiest."

In a few seconds, she handed over a single sheet with a rough sketch of the desk layout, names next to each table. Giving it a quick look, Morven said, "Did any of them know Mr. Small beforehand?"

"You don't think…"

"Just getting background."

"Oh. Some did, for sure. Chester Rowan from Gumberoo books, that's where Doug's first book was published. Not sure they are close anymore, he didn't seem too friendly to Douglas. And Sarah Sykes, the writer, Chester's wife. She's a little frightening, just such a popular writer and catty with her comments. People usually come in twos and share a table, so you expect couples. Martin—he used to bartend at Mansion Mess—and his partner, Flynn. I thought I overheard a guy named Jim Sean and Douglas talking as if they knew each other, but when I asked Douglas, well, he told me in no uncertain terms to focus on the class. His wife—Jim's—was there too, Olivia. She's pretty, but what a flirt. Like an over-sweetened cherry tart. She tried to flirt with Douglas, but he told me not to worry about—" She cut herself off as if she'd mistakenly started across the street when the walk light had changed to stop.

"Anyone else?"

Louisa shook her head, raising the handkerchief to eyes again as Morven went on.

"Was it a good class, do you think?"

"Yes, fun group, enjoying the baking. I'd done a few with him."

"Did anyone leave their desks, do you remember, during that forty-five minutes last night?"

"I don't know for sure, I was busy." She leaned her head back as if stretching her neck. "But I do think people left the room. Going to the bathroom. Maybe to take dishes to Drogo, the dishwasher. Got up to get ingredients. It gets a little frantic. People want to finish their cakes and time is tight. Nearly everyone was up at some point. But they're all so, so nice. They couldn't have done it, right?"

"Any specific issues with any attendees during the class?"

"Not that I recall. Sometime Douglas can be tough, like I mentioned, and maybe that rubs people the wrong way on occasion. Kevin Holman, another attendee, seemed to take some comments poorly. But most know it's just his way. Doug's a lovely man. Was." She started crying, quieter, tears tracking down cheeks, eyes pointed at the wall as if taking in the endless view off a ship's deck in the middle of the ocean.

Morven felt a twinge of guilt but had to ask. "Louisa?" The woman looked back at her. "Were you and Douglas Small more than work associates?"

Louisa tried to appear shocked, but it didn't last, fading into acceptance. "Yes. I guess so. I'm not sure. He never said we were like dating, but we did, you know, we did that. First time, we had taught a class and stayed to have some drinks together afterward. He talked a lot about my career, what he could do for me, what we could do together. Next thing, it happened. I felt ashamed. He never said anything specifically about what happened that night. It happened a few more time, like that. He said to keep it between us. He always kept pushing me to work harder. Pushed hard. He could be mean, even. It was to make me better. But then he'd be sweet, maybe a touch or glance, you know? I think he meant we'd be together more like a couple one day."

Morven had heard that story from women before. "Did you feel taken advantage of?"

"No. I think he meant it. Maybe."

"Did he use your ideas?"

"In the bakery, or the class? Sometimes. I probably came up with most of the new bakery items the last few years. Some made it in his bakery book. I know he was going to give me credit eventually. He said he was. The next book. And I was going to run the whole bakery. He promised."

"The chocolate blackberry tart at Small's Bakery. It's amazing. Was that one of yours?"

"Small's Chocoberry Curiosity." Louisa's gratefulness to talk about pastry instead of her painful relationship was evident. "Silly name. Doug came up with that. But the tart itself, that was one of my first bakery inventions. Nothing cutting edge, but the combination—fresh local blackberry mousse, pâte sucrée crust, almond feuilletine, dark chocolate cardamon dome, with a white chocolate coin on top. Fun."

"That tiny hint of earthiness with the berry's creamy tang and chocolate richness—tasty. Well done."

"You got that earthy part! That's my secret. A very light addition of nettle reduction in the mousse. Don't tell. Douglas thought I was crazy, but loves it. Loved it." She started crying again, and Morven decided that was enough for this interview.

At the doorway to Small's Cooking Classroom, Marlowe and John paused to put on white booties and blue gloves. Forensics had put in hours of work, but a few technicians remained at the scene taking samples and making notes. The landing was empty, outside of what Marlowe assumed was a tired technician completely covered by a blue blanket on one of the couches. It felt like the night after a very poorly thought-out party.

"I can't believe I get shoe covering and gloves." John's animated tone neared cartoonish. "This is quite a day, Detective. At the scene. Forensics. Arthur. Marlowe. Criminals beware. This is my métier."

"Uh-huh."

The body on the couch shifted and sat up at John's loud voice. The sheet covering it slipped down like a ghost costume, revealing a ponytailed man.

"Drogo Oates," Marlowe said with a frown. "You're still here."

Drogo stood up and wriggled his skinny frame like a dog shaking off water. He'd ditched the white coat, but black pants remained. His long T-shirt was tie-died a convoluted red, orange, and green spiral.

"Yeah, I'm here. You police kept me all night." He looked John's way. "Are you police now? I thought, you know, you weren't."

"I'm a consulting detective." He noticed Marlowe's eye roll. "Civilian consultant, I mean."

"Whatever. Shamus. Police. No dog?" Drogo, like most, had fallen for Ainsley when he'd met them previously.

"Not today, sorry. What are you doing here?"

"Man, this is my job. I'm a chef. Or a dishwasher. Gonna be a chef. Currently, probably a dishwasher."

"Drogo." Marlowe reined the man in. He knew Drogo, like John, could lose the trail quickly. "Everyone from the class was told they could leave."

"Maybe I missed that. Or I'm an important witness?" He noticed their incredulous looks. "It was raining? No? It could be that I am currently un-housed. Today. Hopefully not tomorrow. Zara—you remember my girlfriend and like fourth cousin? She is currently my ex-girlfriend and kicked me out again. I've been sleeping in the back, but your scientist pallbearers moved me out here."

"Did Douglas Small know you were sleeping here?"

"Chef high-and-mighty? Yes. Well, not exactly. I tended to tell him I wanted to stay late and clean more, then stayed."

"Why'd you leave the concession business?" John asked.

"You know, after the reverend's murder—"

"The Case of the Retired Reverend." John couldn't skip the chance to give out his name for that past case.

"Retired? He died, not retired."

"In baseball, when someone is out they often say retired, like retired the side. So it clicked for me as a case name because the murder, or murders, happened at a baseball field."

"If you say so. After that, the concession biz, I couldn't do it. Too freaky. And it's no long-term career, if you get me. Chef? That's impressive."

"You helped solve that case when we talked on the bleachers. Key insights."

"Did I? I did. Yeah, you said I was a genius. Getting a job shouldn't be so hard for a genius. But it was. So here I am."

Marlowe felt the conversation current pulling them away from the river at hand. "We have work to do, John, less reminiscing. Drogo, before we go in, did you notice anything different last night?"

Drogo scratched his armpit. "No, detective man. Lots of dishes. The same as—Wait, there was something. One guy, sandy haired, droopy, came in and threw a glass in the sink and broke it. What a mess. Swearing about the modern world and people should get what's theirs. Most people at class don't break things on purpose. Oh, another guy, black hair, muscleman, came back and slammed a pint of vodka behind the dishwasher. Didn't think I saw. The chef himself was snuck behind the dishes kissing some hottie. No one thinks about the dishwasher."

"Thanks. Did you like working for Douglas Small?"

"Sure. I mean, sure I didn't. He was . . ." Drogo scratched his head as if trying to remember a word.

"Imperious?" John prompted.

"Nah, he was a Sagittarius, I believe. He called me a degenerate dishdog with the taste buds of a slug when I didn't like some pie he made. I told him I didn't like pie. I'm cake. Louisa's cool. She'd give me snacks. He treated her not so well. Jerks, man, why do they become famous?"

Marlowe though he'd let that deep question slide. "Thanks, Drogo. Get some coffee, call Zara, get a shower. Take her breakfast."

"Sure. She'll probably let me. Or not. I suppose I can't stay here."

Marlowe's unsmiling face as he and John walked into the classroom gave the answer needed.

Nelson partially reclined in a Milano Red Honda Civic his cousin Gavin lent him two weeks ago when leaving to visit relatives somewhere in England called Fletcher's Cross. It was a fortuitous lend, as Nelson didn't currently own a car and getting a police-issue one on a weekend in a rush might cut into the time used preparing his I-POA, or interview plan of attack. Being his first serious solo in-home interview as a detective, the I-POA wasn't as neat as he'd normally like. A few jitters before a big game, he told himself, weren't a bad thing. "Focus that energy," he whispered.

He'd done research, learning that Chester Rowan's wife, Sarah Sykes, was a well-known food and restaurant critic who wrote for the local rag and a few nationals. A publisher and a critic. Power couple in the food industry. Digging deeper, he uncovered a blog post saying that Chester's company, Gumberoo Books, hadn't had a solid seller in a few years, and that Douglas Small's first book remained their biggest hit. An older article he'd found by Sarah praised Douglas in a manner almost sensual, intimating they were close without undermining her, as she'd written, "impartiality."

Taking a sip of a peppermint tea he'd picked up on the drive, Nelson leaned way over the passenger side seat to avoid a single drop falling onto his slim-fit, heather-blue suit, slightly darker blue tie, or white shirt. Picking up I-POA sheets, he opened the door, stepped out, and instantly had to lean back against the car as a man in a black trench coat and black wool cap zipped by on a green electric scooter, nearly hitting him. For a moment, Nelson thought about going after—that was some unsafe scootering—but the opening bell was about to ring on the interview.

An updated old Tudor, the Rowan-Sykes house was pistachio-colored with white windows, two sets of steps leading up to a postage-stamp porch, garage a level lower to the left. The garage door had been replaced with two French swing-out doors, probably, he guessed, changing it from parking space to usable sitting space, like so many in the city. Taking the second set of steps two at a time, he raised his hand to knock on the white front door, which opened before he could knock.

"You must be officer Nelson," Chester said.

Nelson remained silent, confused by his near knock. The man in the door wore fuzzy bronze-shaded corduroys, a chestnut fisherman's crew sweater, and thick gray socks. Just over five ten and probably 165 pounds, his short, straight hair was the color of a Dickensian gruel, and visible stubble showed he'd skipped shaving that morning. A firm chin and straight nose might have been handsome except for very small eyes, which seemed to have made a scared retreat into his head.

Nelson made a fist in one unnoticed hand. "That's Detective Nelson. Thank you for seeing me. Should we . . ." He motioned through the door.

"If you think it'll take long." Chester's eyes flicked side to side, as if watching for neighbors.

"Just a few questions, sir."

"All right then. Not sure how I can help, but come on in."

The open-plan main area the door led into was well laid out: family room with matching mid-century brown leather sofas spilling into a kitchen with stainless appliances, cherry cabinets, and glass doors that opened to a back deck. There were wooden bookcases of various sizes on every wall in the family room, jammed with books, hardbacks and paperback. Between the couches, a glass-topped table stood, more books stacked on it like un-roofed Doric columns.

Chester backed against a coat rack flush with jackets, hoodies, and rain slickers, not saying anything else, so Nelson moved toward the couches. "Shall we sit here, Mr. Rowan? Is your wife around?"

"What?" Chester seemed strangely apprehensive. "The couches are fine. Do you need to speak to her?"

"It would be best, sir." The formality didn't disguise command. Nelson may have been nervous, but he was a detective. Time to take charge.

"Give me a moment. She's in her office."

Chester walked off nervously enough that Nelson considered him fleeing the house a legitimate possibility. He browsed the top books on the table as he waited: *A Perfect Day of Northwest Hiking, Finding Fantastic Edible Funghi,*

Doing the Doughnut Dance. All published by Gumberoo. In a few minutes Chester returned, trailing a woman Nelson knew was Sarah. She wore a pleated black skirt, black turtleneck, and black leather boots polished to a shine that would have made a plate fresh out of the dishwasher jealous. Pale skin, thin nose, intelligent eyes the shade of a stormy ocean, and pinched cheeks offset by full lips painted ruby red. Oval wire-frames settled low on her nose.

Nelson stood to take Sarah's outstretched hand. "Mrs. Sykes, thank you for meeting with me."

"I wasn't sure I had a choice. Chester seemed worked up. But he makes every possible moment a flambé. Shall we sit."

Nelson sat back down, not completely sure about the flambé. They sat across from him, Chester fidgeting, Sarah cool. Nelson's I-POA sat on his lap.

"Again, thanks for meeting." *Stay on target, Nelson*, he told himself. "I have a few questions."

"About last night." Sarah looked at him over her glasses.

"Indeed. You were both there." They nodded. "Did you notice anything odd?"

"Besides Douglas Small's death?" The stern look she gave Nelson reminded him of one an English professor he'd had in college had given him when he'd asked if a semicolon was really necessary.

"Before that, if you please."

"Nothing odd outside of the class being a little underdone. Raw dough in parts."

"What do you mean, exactly?"

"Douglas could be a sinfully amazing cook, and a well-risen baker. But honestly, he gave over too much of the class to his sidekick."

"Louisa Sweeny."

"Was that her name?" Sarah sneered.

"Mr. Rowan, did you notice anything?"

Chester started at hands, clenched in his lap. "No. Nothing but what Sarah said."

"After Mr. Small left the room, did anyone else leave the room?"

"I see," Sarah said. "You want to sort of *mise en place* the scene before pouncing on a suspect. I was busy with my entremet—mirror glaze, to die for honey custard, decadent chocolate genoise, raspberry mousse. Chester is only marginally helpful." As she talked, Chester's eyes seemed to sink even farther back into his head. "Not much time for watching others. I did notice a few people leave the room. Probably to go to the bathroom. Martin, his partner Flynn, the loud laughing ladies at the front left table, whose names I never got, Kevin, Holman that is. I think they all left at one point. Maybe the big man, too. Everyone could have. As I said, I was coddling my cake. No time for watching."

She certainly seemed to see a lot for not watching. "This is helpful." Nelson took notes as he spoke. "Did either of you leave?"

"It's a long class, Detective, breaks are necessary."

"So both of you left the room at some point?"

She nodded.

"Thank you. When it appeared Mr. Small had been gone longer than usual, what happened?"

"His little assistant seemed worried, so she went to check. She came back and asked for help, but I was harried by my entremet. The two loud ladies went to help, then came back to ask for more help. A few of the men went with them and broke the door down."

"But you stayed."

"That level of, shall we say, artisanal cake demands attention. Like a souffle, you can't walk away and expect perfection."

Nelson had never had a souffle, so took her word for it. "Mr. Rowan, you were one of those who went to help."

Chester ran a hand through his hair, then sat on it before answering. "Yes."

"Tell me what happened then."

"The girls came back yelling for help. Kevin and I and the big man, Sean his name was, went back to his office with them. The door was locked. It was a tense moment. Together we managed to knock it open. Douglas was slumped over his desk. There was lots of yelling, but he didn't move. I went to shake him and saw the knife. Then Sean ran out, we all ran into the hall, someone called you all. That was it."

"Poor darling Douglas." Sarah sighed.

"Darling." Chester spit out as if it were a sip of sour wine. "That's rich."

"Chester, be quiet. Apologies, Detective."

Nelson felt there was more to tell with the *darling* and switched tactics. "Did you like Douglas Small, Mr. Rowan? You published his books." Even though he knew the publisher only put out Douglas's first book, Nelson adding the "s" like a fisherman adding an extra worm to the hook.

"I only published one book of his, though we'd originally planned more," Chester said angrily. "It's probably bad luck to speak ill of the dead, but where Douglas is concerned, I'll take the risk. I thought he was a pompous jerk, a philanderer, and famous because of others, not talent. I'm not happy he was killed, but—"

"Chester, enough," Sarah cut him off. "He's like overcooked Wellington, en croute cracked crust and tough beef. Douglas switching publishers after that first book rankled, but it was best for his career."

"Oh sure, his career. We'd agreed on more. And that's not solely why I didn't like him." Chester glared at his wife.

"Is there more, Mr. Rowan?"

"What?" Chester seemed as if he'd forgotten Nelson was there. He looked at the detective, then over his shoulder out the bay front window as if expecting a fleet of patrol cars. "Sorry. I didn't hurt him. I didn't like Douglas a lot for reasons." He glanced back at Sarah. "But that's all."

"Mrs. Sykes, you're in the middle of the City food scene." She again looked over her glasses at Nelson, smiling like a cat with a fresh bowl of cream. "Did Mr. Small have any enemies within it?"

She looked now like the cat that had finished the cream. "Douglas was a legend, in his way. You can't become a legend without chiffonading a few along the way. And Douglas had vast appetites. When you take lots of bites from many plates, someone goes hungry. So, enemies yes. But to kill him? I can't think of someone. Maybe his wife."

Chester rolled his eyes, caught Nelson watching, and then began scratching behind his ear.

"Thank you, this is very helpful. One final question. How did Douglas Small appear that night?"

"Like a well-baked truffle-onion gratin. Rich, satisfied with himself, flavorful enough to overwhelm any pairing."

Nelson stood, walking to the door before turning. "Thank you again. We will probably have more questions. I'll be in touch." As he spoke the last sentence, Chester's left hand began shaking.

5

John and Marlowe stood together in the back corner of the classroom. They could see over the desks to the hallway beyond. The room was chaotic, still a tornado of half-used baking tools, ingredients, and forensic markers. "Same basic set up as when you took classes here?"

"Yes." John gazed intensely over the room, empty except for two men in full forensics suits nearer the top right table. "Douglas lords it at the front table, attendees entranced at class's beginning, then gathering round as he or his assistant demonstrate technique—his words—then back to individuals or duos at the tables making whatever is on the menu. For someone who liked celebrity's distancing effect, he also liked people watching him up close. I can remember being right next to him as he pounded bread like he was hitting the strength tester at a county fair. Caused his coffee to spill out of the cup and keys to rattle."

"Did he always swill the Arbuckle?"

"That's cowboy slang for coffee, correct?" Marlowe nodded. "Bet your grandfather taught you that." Marlowe nodded again, wishing he had another cup of coffee. "I'm pretty sure Douglas's coffee was routinely laced with an amari of some kind." John tapped his nose. "Arthur knows. Had that smell. That and his keys were omnipresent. Like totems."

"Both found in the office."

"Not surprising."

"I'm thinking a bread-making class was one you took."

"You are a good detective."

"Could be. You took another."

"A cocktail class, Shaking and Stirring Northwest, it was called. Emphasizing cocktails using locally foraged ingredients, leaning in to some of the recipes from his restaurants."

"Cocktails? Weren't you already an expert, having written books and articles."

"Perhaps an odd choice, as I used to teach cocktail classes myself. But you can always learn more, even at my age."

"I can always learn more about John Arthur, it seems."

John laughed, causing one of the forensic team to glance.

"I suppose I chose that class because I'd had a few drinks at Mansion Mess I thought were really intriguing. The lead bartender from there was assisting, Martin Allen. He has amazing cocktail chops. That helped."

"Martin Allen. Interesting. He was here taking the class last night."

"That is interesting." John accented the "is" with a dollop of dramatic intrigue. "He left the Small empire a while back. Unexpected, as he was a sort of protégé of Douglas, or seemed such. Then gone. There's a story there. I'll stir up the mind palace and get back to you."

"Helpful."

"Can I get a list of attendees, by the way, and can I browse the tables?"

"What for, exactly?"

"Clues." John's eyes could have belonged to an eight-year-old in front of a Christmas tree spread above a stack of presents.

Well, they were here. "Let me ask the scientists." Marlowe went over, got the okay, gave John a thumbs-up. John started at the top table, pulling drawers out, flipping a few sheets of paper on the table over, bending down to better view stubby table legs.

"Forensics"—Marlowe said from directly behind John—"does a solid job."

John raised quickly, knocking a wooden spoon whose handle was over the table's edge off with a clatter. "I'm sure they do. Just getting my thoughts mixing."

"Useful thoughts?"

"As the masterful actor Bertie Carvel said when playing Inspector Dalgliesh, 'They're all useful thoughts.'" John moved to the next table and browsed the detritus on the table's top. "Entremets. Not a snap class cake. I suppose it was the third day, the crown of the cake menu. This one's pretty complicated." He held up a piece of paper with writing on it.

"How so?"

"Lots of layers, two mousses, white and dark chocolate, multi-berry coulis, rum-infused crème brûlée, genoise, homemade feuilletine, raspberry marble glaze. This table knew what they were doing. See." He raised a finger as if giving a stump speech. "The classes usually get harder as you go, but each class takes the same amount of time. You learn from chef, then make your own dish, which you must plan out before coming to class. *Bake Off*-y, in a way."

"Indeed." Even Marlowe, who liked to eat baked goods way more than watch someone make them, had heard of the *Great British Bake Off*.

John rooted around the drawer. "Curious. A little clay back here."

"Probably dirt, flour and all," Marlowe said.

"You know me. I'm like Thursday said of Morse: 'I'd find something suspicious in a saint's sock drawer.'" John wasn't above making fun of himself. He'd moved on to the next table in the first row. "This is odd." He held up a lipstick he'd pulled out of the drawer. It was a deep crimson color. "Seems a little flirty for a baking class. Maybe I'm too old. Also, this recipe is really simple. And why so many knives in the drawer?"

Marlowe wasn't sure whether John was talking to himself or the room. He let the man keep looking while he went to ensure the forensics team was all over those knives. Upon returning, John had moved on to the next table.

"Uncovering more intriguing recipes?" Marlowe leaned on the top table, watching John intently reading a piece of paper he'd picked up from the table. Even though he had forensic gloves on, John held the paper in a flower patterned oven mitt.

John set the paper down. "Nothing advanced here. Strangely, they've written in pencil, 'what an ass,' and 'see how he treats her,' and 'someone should stand up to him,' with replies like 'someone will someday' in a different hand. As if the two people here were talking back and forth on the paper so no one would hear. Two questions." John could change directions in a sentence like a running cheetah. "Do we know who sat where? And— Wait, what's this?" John pulled an empty pint bottle out of the drawer. It had a picture of two buck deer, antlers locked, and the words Stag Night Vodka. "Way in back. Not the highest-end local distillery. Empty."

"Closet drinker."

"You never know, but in my favorite British TV mysteries, some small clue ends up being the case clincher. Usually one noticed in passing."

"This isn't a television mystery, John."

"But you can—"

"Learn a lot from TV."

John moved to the next table. "Another interesting recipe. Messy table however. I think they spilled butter in the drawer. And got some on this Seafarer's oven mitt."

Marlowe felt they might be getting far afield. "Probably going to have to speed it up. If it helps, we will find who sat where. Your other question was?"

"Guessing all this will be bagged and tagged, as they say, and taken back to the station? It'd be good to check these recipes."

"We are thorough, John. It's not our first rodeo."

"Sorry, I know. Excited being here." He'd moved to the next table, the final one used for the classroom. "Also, who showed up first to class, who was last, who knew Douglas in the past, and who decided— Whoa, look at this." He pointed to red stains on the table, beside which were some evidence markers. "I always wanted some of these marking tents to add to the bookshelves, maybe in front of the Agatha books. This is blood?"

Marlowe ambled over as John talked. "It is, perhaps. Forensics will tell us."

"People could get cut in a cooking class. Less in a baking one. Not sure about this recipe. Scotch bonnet chilies with a white chocolate mousse. That would destroy the chef's taste buds."

"Did Douglas taste the bakes?"

"Always. Then make grand pronouncements. He liked to judge people, then send them packing."

"Enough table time."

"For now. But I may need to revisit the scene. There's almost always a scene revisiting in a mystery. Speaking of scenes."

"You want to see the office."

"I do." John's smile matched the earlier kid at the Christmas tree one, except now it was wider, as if the kid just opened the gift atop of his Santa list.

"Follow me." Marlowe led them back. Douglas's body was long removed, but the forensic tags and tape remained. "Don't sit on anything."

"Detective Marlowe, you insult me." Mock indignation infused the words. "I'm not a junior *Midsomer* sergeant. Here it happened. The crime. *Crime passionnel* perhaps. Douglas Small was passionate. Or a deep-seated revenge finally opened. Financial misdoings. So many options. And the butter was?"

Marlowe pointed up to the beam. "Strange as a two-headed calf, that butter."

"Was it?" John mused as he bent down near the desk. "Coffee cup. Faint laced aroma." He rapidly straightened, moved to the door, nearly knocking into Marlowe. "The locked room. Hidden Depths."

"In Douglas Small?"

John now bent over to look at the lock on the floor. "Hmm, what was that, Detective?"

"Hidden depths."

"*Midsomer Murders* episode. Man locked in a cellar and murdered. Though this might be more "Ghost of Christmas Past," where a man locks himself in to supposedly commit suicide. It's never what it seems. Douglas did shut the door every time he went back for his break, and demanded not to be disturbed. He did sometimes have one-on-ones back here, at other times, to give personal insights. I think you had to pay more. Or chef's prerogative I suppose. He always had an assistant to help with the class during his break. This door was broken in, the door directly in front of the desk. But he was stabbed from behind. Curious."

"Agreed. Why—"

John finished the thought. "Would he let someone behind him, especially if they had a knife. Or let someone in at all during his break."

"Yep."

"That's strange. The butter is strange. The locked room is John Dickson Carr strange." He saw Marlowe giving him the 'what are you talking about' look John had come to recognize. "Carr was an American but lived in Britain, grouped with the British Golden Age mystery writers. Master of the locked room mysteries. Not always my cuppa, but legendary."

"Seen enough?"

"For today. Mind if I take some notes?" John had pulled a small notebook from his back pocket. It was nearly identical to the ones Marlowe and team had.

"Quickly."

"It'll help take my mind off the fact Douglas Small was killed here. A person I interviewed, who had his faults, but was remarkable. Focus on the puzzle, not the tragedy. Is that what helps you and the other detectives?"

"Nothing helps make it easier, if that's what you're riding toward. You do the job because it has to be done. Do it best you can, for the victim and those near to them. Might be a rough ride, but as my grandfather said, he who rides slowly gets just as far, only it takes longer."

"Grandfather tended to be right."

"That he was, John."

They left the office and walked down the hall, John scribbling in his notebook.

Driving to the station from the scene was nearly a straight shot for Marlowe. Johnny Cash's classic "Don't Take Your Guns To Town" played, and he wouldn't have heard the more than a few verses if nearly every block didn't end in a red light. John headed the other direction, back home, after a solid five minutes of wavering in front of the hotel. He'd wanted to accompany Marlowe to the station. He also knew he should go home and let Ainsley out. Marlowe finally convinced him the station wouldn't fly off into the clouds like a crow, which led to John spending another five minutes telling Marlowe about the crow that recently had taken to trotting alongside him and Ainsley on walks, and how he'd started giving the crow treats, calling him Heckle. The man could couple on clauses as if his sentences were a very long train.

Finally, after promising John he could visit the detective team later, they drove opposite directions. Marlowe pulled into the big station parking lot, curving up floors crowded tightly with cars, and thought about John. What a curious man. Obsessed with his television mysteries to the point they flowed through his conversation like vermouth through a Martini. Carrying a deep loneliness, only occasionally shown, since his wife died. Insightful but easily sidetracked. Was their visit to the scene helpful? Not yet. But could John eventually pull the murderer out of his mystery magician's hat via some small detail seen, maybe one not even yet mentioned? He'd done it before.

Finally, on the top floor of the lot in a back corner, Marlowe found a small free space. Johnny's raspy grittiness singing, "and wondered at his final words," as he turned the car off. Would anyone ever know what Douglas Small's final words had been? Had he had time to formulate any, even? Marlowe shook his head. No time to sit here and ponder like a philosopher sitting under the stars. It was time to get inside and keep working.

Not an easy job, he found. He'd had to back the Matador out once to straighten it enough to fit the tight spot. Smooshing his wide frame between two cars, almost sticking at one point, twisting left and right, he finally managed it. When twisted like a walrus in a straightjacket, he'd caught a bit of graffiti in the shadowy corner, sprayed on with orange paint. "Have a cracking day, copper!!!" Three exclamation points. He decided walking to the elevator that it was meant friendly, and took it as a positive omen.

Morven and Nelson sat at their desk, putting in interview notes, suit coats flopped on chair backs. "Top of the morning to you," he said, walking up.

Nelson didn't move, but Morven rotated and replied. "Barely morning, Marlowe."

"Too true. Time flies, they say." He shucked his sports coat and tossed it over his chair.

"Do they still say that?"

"Somewhere. Nelson have the volume up to 11?" He'd noticed the young detective had headphones firmly in place and still hadn't noticed Marlowe.

Morven grinned. "Nelson decided with John Arthur coming aboard it was time for him to restart his British mystery education. He's listening to an Agatha Christie audiobook. Nelson." She smacked him on the arm.

Nelson jumped, headphones pulling out. "What? Oh, Detective Marlowe. Sorry, didn't hear you."

Marlowe headed to the board. "No fretting, Nelson. Flying at it, I see. Shall we gather."

"We shall." Morven joined him, Nelson a step behind as he untangled himself from the headphone cord. She continued. "How was Mr. Arthur?"

"Excited as a hog at a trough, you might say."

"He would probably say as a British detective at tea time."

"Might at that. Digging in. Gave some helpful details from past classes. Thorough view of the scene."

Nelson made it to the board, grabbing a yellow stress ball with "Luther's London Gym" printed on it. He squeezed vigorously with his right hand as he talked. "Did Mr. Arthur have any idea who did it?"

"Early days, Nelson. Even for our British TV lover. Tell me about your interview."

"It was—"

Marlowe gently interrupted. "Sorry, Nelson. I know we need to get a wiggle on, but hearing about your interviews and catching up is bound to be thirsty work. I don't suppose . . ." he trailed off.

"Coffee." Morven knew Marlowe's tendencies and knew he enjoyed the station's coffee, which she thought tasted as if it were made from pencil shavings and bracken.

Nelson dropped the stress ball. "I'll go," he said, already heading toward the exit.

"Detective Nelson." Marlowe's lassoing voice caused Nelson to pivot. "Two cups for me, please."

The detectives had spent the last hour catching up on interviews and scene revisits. Marlowe tipped back the last drop of the second coffee Nelson had returned with, set the cup down, and picked up a carved olive-wood bowl which sat on his desk. Made of eddying dark and lighter wood tones and about the size of a softball, the bowl had been bought in Assisi on a long-ago trip to Italy he'd taken with his ex-wife. Holding it to his nose, he inhaled deeply. The wood still delivered an echo of hillside groves and olive oil, transporting him for a moment to a daydream of sunshine splattering painterly over the valleys of Umbria. Once when talking to John, who had spent a lot of time in Italy, the older man had quoted a poet Marlowe couldn't remember, who said, "Italy is a dream that keeps returning for the rest of your life." He could believe it.

But he couldn't return there now, so he set the bowl back down. "That's a lot of wagons to circle, make no mistake. Hard to tell diamonds from dirt."

When getting coffee, Nelson also got himself an energy drink called Chief Bright's Bouncy Brew. It contained a mountain-high dose of caffeine, and the young detective currently leaned to the right of the board, doing push-ups off of the window sill. Morven had stuck to water, and sat pushed back from her desk, legs crossed in front.

Standing, Marlowe circumvented Nelson with a short eye roll at the push-ups. "This map of who sat where." He pointed at a piece of paper stuck to the becoming crowded board. "Handy to have, or not important? Everyone could have left the room, so we've been told, so does where they sat make a difference? Or what cakes they made?"

Morven replied. "Not just plain cake. Entremets. We have layers to deal with, just like they did. Motive, means, opportunity. Which to focus on when."

"What do you mean, Detective Morven?" Nelson paused his push-ups, his words sauced with confusion. "I know about motive, means, and opportunity. But don't we focus on all three?"

"Yes, we do." She walked over to where they stood. "Fair point. But in this case, so far, it's hard to know exactly which to hit first. There are inklings of motives, I suppose. Usually that comes as we investigate more. It appears that everyone theoretically could have had the opportunity, if we're positing the murderer came from the group of class attendees, plus Louisa and Drogo. But the room was locked." The two men nodded. "Unless there's an undiscovered entrance we don't know about."

"Secret passage," Nelson whispered.

"Seems unlikely," Marlowe replied.

"Right." She went on. "Then there's means. We'll get the final report from Doctor Peterson, but seems likely Douglas Small died from a knife in the back, while sitting in a locked room. How did that happen? How did the means of murder take place? Often we have one leg of that three-worded stool to devote time to; here we have three."

"Laid out well, Morven. It's a hard broomtail to break. We need more information, like a cowboy needs a firm saddle."

The other two didn't exactly parse Marlowe's cowboy saying, but the gist was clear.

"Next steps. Finish talking to other cake makers. One had to have seen something out of the ordinary. Get on forensics. What can they tell us. Doc is probably a few miles out, but hopefully we hear from him soonish."

"Sounds like a plan." Morven leaned closer to the board. "Specifically, I think we talk to Lucille Crow and Madison Bernard first. They were at what we're calling table one, providing a view of the hallway opening. No connection to the victim that we know of."

"Smart, Morven. I'd say Martin Allen is up high on the list too. Table three. Used to work for Douglas Small. Either he or tablemate Flynn Will wrote those odd notes on their recipes. And that bottle—closet drinking. Seems important. How about I take him, you two take Lucille and Madison."

"Agreed. You up for that Nelson, or need more push-ups?"

Nelson had started up once more, but sheepishly stopped. "Definitely, Detective. Might need some water, and a snack. And work on my I-POA."

Marlowe sat on the edge of his desk, knocking off a coffee cup, which he ignored. "Food first for all. Need more background too. Let me see if I can wrangle another officer." He picked up the phone, with the other detectives moving back to their desk, opening laptops. Holding the red rotary-style desk phone handset in one hand, pointing toward the opening of the big room with the other, he instructed, "Computers down until we've fueled up. Could one of you grab me a sandwich?"

Morven and Nelson sat in her Kia, parked on the western corner of a block in the Hallingcord neighborhood's main street, 45th Avenue. She'd managed to get a hold of Lucille quickly, and it turned out Madison was with her.

"A second interview in one day, Nelson." She gazed out of the front window as she talked, checking to see how far they were from Lucille's real estate office.

"Definitely ready. More than ready. It's like the second race of the day at a track meet. I feel completely warmed up, loose, ready to rock." He gripped a sheet of paper in one hand and a small green notebook in the other.

"Let's go then, but don't rip your I-POA."

Nelson gave the paper a frightened check as they excited the car. They'd left Marlowe back at the station before making the twenty-minute drive, and Morven hoped he'd had some luck tracking down Martin. He'd made a few calls to the number the man had given the police the night before, but no pick-ups and no returning of messages. Marlowe did get a hold of Captain Innocent, who happily assigned another officer to him to aid on some research.

Lucille's real estate business, Sourdough Home Sales, sat in the middle of the block, between Reuban's Reubens and More Sandwich Shop and Gabi's Gorgeous Bubble Tea. The office's glass front windows were covered with printed sheets detailing homes for sale, mirroring real estate shops worldwide. A yellow and black "Closed for Lunch" sign hung on the door's inside, but when pushed, it opened readily.

"Hello," Morven called out, walking in with Nelson behind.

"The detectives are here," a brisk woman's singsong voice called out, following it with, "Come in, detectives."

They entered into a basic square room with two desks on one side, a computer on each alongside black vertical file holders plump with papers and magazines, pencils and pens scattered around. On the room's other side, two plush periwinkle barrel chairs sat around a short oak coffee table covered in issues of *Home and Garden* and *Better Homes and Gardens*. The office walls were painted a matching shade of blue, mostly barren except for a yellow neon sign that said, "If you can dream it, you can own it."

A late-twenties, African American woman walked toward them from behind one of the desks, hand outstretched. She wore heavily flaring pants boldly patterned with bright daisies in various shades of orange, an orange button-down, long-sleeved shirt, and black Chelsea boots. She had finely etched features, an Afro puff hairdo that added inches to her height, and an infectious smile. It was so friendly, the often serious Morven found herself grinning back, offering her hand.

"Detective Morven and Detective Nelson." As she spoke, Nelson gave a little hop to get around her and also shake hands with the woman. "You are Madison Bernard, correct?"

"Yep, that's me." She half-turned, yelling back to a door opening off the office's back wall. "Lucille!"

Before the door completely opened, a deep woman's voice rumbled, "On my way. Can't a woman go to the bathroom." The person the voice belonged to followed. Mid-forties, a stitch over six foot, two inches above Morven's own five ten, and probably thirty pounds heavier. Well-proportioned, she carried her imposing body casually as a lioness. She wore a single-button black blazer over white T-shirt and black slacks. Wavy, shoulder-length hair surfaced auburn roots under blond streaks. Substantial brown eyes took in the detectives with a honed glance.

Unlike Madison, Lucille didn't reach out a hand, but gave a curt wave. "The police have arrived, Madison. Lock up your loose lips. Why are you here, by the way?"

"Lucille Crow, correct?" Morven knew it was her, but wanted to put the interview on a we-ask-the-questions footing. Lucille nodding, she continued. "As I told Miss Bernard, I'm Detective Morven and this is Detective Nelson. We have a few questions. To start, how is it that you both happened to be here?"

The women both started talking. "I'm usually here," Madison said, as Lucille said, "Having lunch." They stopped, looked at each other, and laughed. Madison pointed at Lucille. "You go."

"Sure. We are both right. Madison is a real estate photographer and artist who helps me out a lot and often shows up around lunch, as I don't like to eat alone. Speaking of eating, apologies for the state of me." She pointed at a fading yellow splotch on her pants. "Rueban makes delightful sandwiches, but isn't shy about the mustard."

"I hadn't noticed."

"Me neither," Nelson chimed in, feeling left out from the conversation so far.

Morven shot him a quick side glance. "You both were at the cake class last night, and had been there all three nights." They nodded simultaneously. "It was a traumatic experience, I am sure. Did you notice anything out of the ordinary before Douglas Small was discovered in his office?"

"Bad entremet making," Lucille replied.

"Lucy, that's not what they mean. Not all the cakes were bad. I didn't notice anything, Detective. It was much as most nights. Chef and Louisa demonstrated mousse making and talked about genoises, then everyone was busy, busy, busy."

"Did anyone specifically leave the room?" Nelson asked.

"Specifically?" Lucille had a way of making every line the teeniest bit sarcastic. "Maybe not specifically, but I'd guess unspecifically everyone left at least once. Four plus hours is a long time. Nature calls."

"You did two nights before. Did anyone leave the room last night longer than normal?" Morven wanted to try and pin them down.

"Normal is different for different people. But I see what you mean. I don't believe so. Madison?"

"Nope. When we're in baking mode, it's hard to pay close attention, as you're rushing to finish. And last night was the toughest class. Lots to do, so anyone could have left. But then they wouldn't have a well-made entremet, and during the chef's review might get called out. No one wanted that."

"Why, was Douglas Small difficult?"

Lucille's eyes glistened, but Madison spoke. "Difficult is right. He had a way of calling out the smallest imperfections in the final cakes. Not that we had many."

"Are you good bakers?" The cake talk was making Nelson think maybe he hadn't had enough lunch.

"Lucille is awesome. Our cakes ruled. Everyone was jelly," Madison gushed.

"We're both okay," the other woman said. "We've taken some classes together, and so work well, and have picked up a few things."

"Other classes with Douglas Small?"

"No, our first with him. Other culinary classes—yeasted breads, croissants, French macaroons, Indian street food—"

Madison took over. "Roman pasta, farmers market meals, Tex-Mex tacos, and non-food classes like ceramics, floral arranging, gouache painting—"

"That was a little gauche," Lucille cut back in. "A lot of classes."

"Was the cake class more difficult than most?"

"On the difficult spectrum, high up, yes. Lots to do. But as we said, we work well together. Part of it is planning too. I had a fortune cookie once that said proper prior planning prevents poor performance, and have tried to follow that rule."

"Smart," said Morven. "Over the three days, did anyone seem to take offense at Douglas's criticisms or have any outward problems with him?"

"You really think someone at the class killed him over cake criticism?"

"We're just getting background."

"Very policelike. I don't think anyone did. It was part of taking the class."

"Wait, Lucille," Madison energetically said. "We walked in on night two and the chef and Kevin and Clair were arguing. How'd you forget that?"

"I didn't forget, just didn't think it was important. Probably a cake fight. Neither of them were much at baking."

"We'll decide what's important," Nelson firmly said.

The woman smiled faintly. "Yes, sir, Detective."

Morven followed up. "You didn't hear what it was about?"

Madison and Lucille said "no" and "sorry" at the same time.

"Anybody else acting odd?"

They thought, before Madison spoke. "Mostly a nice bunch, as people are at cooking and baking classes. It's food, should be fun. Martin seemed a little intense, but Flynn balanced him out. Martin's been our bartender before, maybe he's always intense."

"You think?" Lucille said sarcastically.

"Ha ha, Lucille. Do you remember more?"

"Classes with a famous chef are the same no matter the subject. There are the awestruck ones, the flirty ones who think the teacher might date them, the serious ones, and the hungry ones. It's a bit like Black Forest gateau."

"A what?" Nelson's stomach growled.

"It's a cake that has layers. There may be slight variations, but it always contains chocolate, cherries, Kirsch, and cream."

"Are you a serious baker, Mrs. Crow?"

"That's miss, Detective. And no, just a class baker."

"What did you think of Douglas Small, Miss Crow?" Morven was starting to believe the older woman was insightful, if hiding it.

"God, the famous chef. He had technique and knowledge, but not sure he was an amazing teacher, and not always a nice human. Listen, don't take it the wrong way, but it was probably his fault he got killed."

Madison bobbed her head, the usually present smile vanishing like chalk erased. "Agreed. He was a legend, but Louisa did more teaching. He treated her sorta shamefully. Right, Lucille?"

"I suppose. I think there was something weird between them. He'd order her around like an army private, then pat her behind." Lucille's tone was playful, but her hands curled into tights fists, like bird claws gripping onto a fence in high winds. "Could be wrong, of course. But I'm never wrong."

"Louisa went back to check on Douglas when he didn't return from his normal break, correct?" Morven prompted.

"That break he demanded every night, after charging a ton for the class. Yes, she was worried, then came back screaming. Before you ask, we were the ones who went back with her to knock again. And then Sarah. Louisa's a nice kid, very talented, and was very upset then. We wanted to help."

"Makes sense. The door was locked."

"Completely." Madison made a knocking motion. "We were knocking like hungry hippos. Nothing. Louisa was yelling, freaked-out at that point, making it chaotic. Then we went for more people, and a couple came back and broke the door in. It was wild. I… it's hard to put all the pieces of what happened into place in my mind, sort it out."

"Traumatic, I'm sure. Mrs. Crow, remember anything else about that moment?"

"Madison covered it like meringue on a lime tart. Sorry, that's flippant. It was a confusing time."

"Moments of crime often are." Nelson sounded a bit teacherly himself. An intonation undercut by his stomach growling. He took a peek at his notes. "You mentioned Martin had bartended for you before. Did you know anyone else previous to the class?"

The women looked at each other questioningly before Madison spoke up. "Nope, can't recall meeting anyone before. I mean, we both know who Sarah and Chester are, just being into food and food books. Not sure they loved the class. Felt like Chester was put out by Douglas's manner in some way, you know. Cool they were there, however. Everyone met at the beginning of the first class."

"Got it. What about Drogo Oates?" Nelson's question caught even Morven off guard.

"Drogo. Nearly forgot about him. Oops. I didn't know him much, but one of his cousins is a friend of mine. I'd met him. Lucille didn't, unless I'm confused. Drogo was funny, helpful mostly, in and out picking up dishes."

"Is your friend Nikola Cassian?"

"Nope, should I know her?"

"No, past case, just checking."

Lucille unbuttoned her jacket, scratching her side in a move reminiscent of a dog. "Sorry, this shirt is itchy—crumbs. I must have eaten my chips in a rush. Are we done?"

"I believe that should wrap it up. Nelson?"

"No more for now. But please be aware we may have more questions later, and contact us if you remember anything else."

"Sure, detectives." Madison's affable smile was back in place.

Lucille held open the door for them. "Take care out there. And Detective Nelson? Get some lunch.

6

Marlowe had given up waiting for Martin to return his calls. The wait hadn't been excessive, but he didn't have time to sit and being desk-bound like a wounded horse this early in an investigation went against his nature. After a short search online, he'd decided to visit Martin's current place of work, a restaurant called With Bold Knife and Fork. It wasn't many blocks from last night's classroom in Tolltown. The restaurant was owned by a chef named Joel Towell, who could be considered Douglas Small's main rival, as he had a series of restaurants and was branded a "name" chef.

From a brief search of LinkedIn, Marlowe saw that Martin took a bartending break after leaving Mansion Mess. Seemed he'd had a period of unemployment, though you never knew if what you found online was accurate or only as permanent as writing in dust on a windy day. For a while, Martin manned a security guard role for a place called Line of Defense, before recently starting bartending again. Marlowe was shuffling into his sports coat to head out when a uniformed officer approached the desk.

"Detective Marlowe," she said, her voice smooth and slightly low-pitched. A muscular five foot four, her nearly black brown hair would have been gently wavey, except it was pulled back into a bun at the back of the neck. She held her hat under one arm, and a laptop in one hand.

"Yes, officer . . ." He left the question hanging.

"Natalia Weber, sir. Sorry to interrupt, but I was told to report to you to help with background checks around the recent Douglas Small incident." While her voice matched pursed lips in officiousness, her eyes shimmered excitedly. A few rogue freckles splattered her clear, light cheeks.

"Perfect." In mulling Martin, Marlowe momentarily forgot he asked Captain Innocent for more help. "Are you okay setting up camp here at my desk while I'm gone? We can find a better hitching post later."

The corners of her mouth snuck up into smile for a moment at the hitching post, before becoming formal once more. She seemed to have a way of balancing seriousness with a hint of hilarity. "Fine, sir. Were you leaving?"

"About to. But let's chat a spell. Are you interested in the case?"

"Yes, sir, very much. Also, I'd love to learn more about being a detective. I enjoy the uniform and the various posts, but always thought I'd try for detective eventually. When this opportunity came up, I reached for it."

"Do you know the basic outline?"

"I believe so, sir. I quickly read up on the notes taken so far." Her drive to impress was apparent. While she wore the earnestness in tone like an overcoat, her hazel eyes remained smiling

"Smart shooting, Officer. We can use the help. The rest of the team's out. Mosey this way." He moved to the board, pointing at the list of class attendees. "If you could burn the breeze on background information for these people, plus Douglas Small and his ex-wife, that'd be ideal. Whatever you can discover online, databases, anywhere."

"Happy to, sir." She leaned in slightly to get a closer look at the list. "Have we requested cell phone checks, access to banking records?"

"Not yet. Can be a struggle, judge's orders and all. Let's see what you can discover. Go from there."

"I'm an adept surfer, sir."

"Surf away, Officer Weber. Call me as needed. Detective Morven too."

"Yes, sir." She set her laptop on his desk, flipping the lid open.

"Officer Weber, one more note."

Looking up worriedly, she said, "Yes, sir?"

"Sir spooks me. Detective Marlowe is dandy."

"Sure, si— Detective Marlowe." The smile winged down from eyes to her mouth like a flitting butterfly as he walked away.

Finding a parking spot directly in front of the restaurant, he paralleled the Matador into it. The sky's profuse clouds lay low, making it seems as if buildings were covered in a thick layer of exhaust. Not a sliver of sun or blue sky broke through. No rain either, at the moment, so he left his cap in the car. *Probably pouring by the time I leave*, he thought, ambling up to the glass front door placed between fifteen-foot glass windows, curtained. With Bold Knife and Fork was italic'd in gold on the door, right above the hours. Currently closed, he wondered if he'd have to utilize the loud knock police unleashed at times. But pushing on the door, it swung open easily.

Directly in front of him was a black host stand—*maître d' stand* they'd call it in a place this high end—a few short maroon-cushioned benches along the windows, a matching heavy maroon curtain blocking the restaurant from view. About to push through a slot in the middle of the curtain, he nearly smacked a man walking through at the same time.

"Sorry," he said as the man neatly ducked, swerving behind the stand. Nearly as tall as Marlowe, but lean as a whippet, he wore an immaculate white T-shirt and black jeans. His ash-blond hair was combed back over his head. To Marlowe, he looked a bit like a young Bing Crosby.

"I'm sorry, too," the man said helpfully. "We're currently closed."

"Not here for chow, sadly." Marlowe held up his badge. "Detective Marlowe. You're Flynn Will." He recognized him from the night before.

"Guilty as charged, Detective. You're here about that awful business last night."

"I am. Hoping to talk to you and Martin Allen. If he's here."

For two seconds, Flynn seemed to consider, then replied. "He is, as it happens. We're both on shift tonight. I'm waiting, he's bartending."

"Won't take much time. Guessing you're busy."

"Restaurants are still open even after Douglas . . . well, you know." Flynn moved to open the curtain. "Come on back."

He followed Flynn into the dining room. It was shotgun style, deeper than wide, with a wood-paneled bar running along one side. The atmosphere was dark: dark wood walls twinning the bar, curved ceilings giving what they probably thought was an atmosphere of coziness but which felt claustrophobic, cork-covered tables. Hanging oblong Edison bulbs above the bar and a copper lighting feature undulating along the walls like a snake provided scant illumination.

Behind the bar watching them walk up, Martin Allen stewed, arms crossed. His black hair was trimmed short, small eyes intense as a crow about to dive. Under black shirt and lime-green vest, biceps popped, but his overall musculature felt fading, like an athlete who stopped exercising six months ago.

"Marty," Flynn called out as they approached. "This is Detective Marlowe. Here about last night."

Martin didn't move, just nodded as the two made their way to standing in front of him at the bar. Marlowe couldn't help taking notice of the deep selection of spirits and liqueurs lined up behind Martin on glass shelves. On a back corner, he noticed a bottle of Amaro Braulio, an amaro he'd recently had at Gary's, his favorite bar. Its herbal spiciness—he'd picked out cinnamon, nutmeg, mint, and sage—combined with a solid bitter undertone enthralled. For a moment, he didn't say anything, staring at the bottle.

"You need a drink, Detective?" Martin asked with a sneer.

"Not yet. Thanks for taking a moment. A few questions."

"Why question us?" Martin's voice rose. He had a habit of adding an implied exclamation point ending to every sentence, like a carpenter who believes a nail always needs a final smack even if it seems driven in completely.

“Getting background as we continue our investigation.”

“Martin.” Flynn’s voice came out like he was codding a toddler.

“Didn’t want to get the third degree while setting up the bar.”

“No third degrees.” Marlowe tried to lighten the mood. He hadn’t even asked a question yet. “Getting the scene, so to speak.” As neither responded, he continued with the basics. “Did either of you notice anything out of the ordinary last night before the incident?”

“Nothing on my side, Detective,” Flynn said. “I was focused on cake.”

“No. Douglas being Douglas. Before the incident, that is.” Martin lingered on incident as if sucking a hard lemon candy.

Did Martin smile for a moment as he said the last sentence? Marlowe couldn’t tell. “What do you mean by Douglas being Douglas.”

“Nothing,” Martin’s voice went up, then relaxed. “I’m sure you know I worked for him in the past. He hadn’t changed. Always the celebrity. And always the ass.”

“Oh, Martin. Detective, you’ll have to forgive him. Douglas was hard to work for. His personality as he got more famous could be difficult.”

“How so?”

“Authoritarian, might be the word. We weren’t important outside of being part of his fan club, or retinue, or admiration society. If you weren’t fawning, he was dismissive, or plain mean.”

“Damn right.” Martin slammed his hand on the bar, causing some glassware to clink edges.

“Why take the class?”

“Why not?” Martin shot back. “It was open to all.”

Flynn covered one of Martin’s hands on the bar with one of his own. “Relax, Martin, it’s a fair question. Here’s the story, Detective. We both used to work for Douglas. Same as here, Martin ran the bar, I waited table. We adored it. Then there was a bit of a falling out, I suppose. We decided taking the class would show there were no hard feelings.” He smiled. “And anyway, I like cake.”

Marlowe appreciated how Flynn balanced Martin. “Me too.

Makes sense. Anyone else at the class have any unfriendly interactions with Douglas?"

"Not that I noticed," Martin brusquely replied.

Flynn considered before speaking. "We knew a few people there already, Sarah and Chester, food universe folks. And had seen at least Kevin and Clair and Lucy and Madison before. They're fun. I didn't notice any specific arguments, but none of those first four to me seemed, oh, happy. Growly, even. Jim and Olivia we didn't know, but talked to. He adored Douglas. She too, maybe, but she was one of those gorgeously flirty types. Guessing she watched a lot of *Sex in the City*. Everyone got along."

"Notice anyone leaving the room during last night's class?"

"Not outside of the norm." Flynn said. "People would take small bathroom breaks."

Martin just shook his head.

"When you arrived, was everyone there?"

Flynn perked up. "Chester and Sarah were there. We arrived same time as Lucy and Madison."

"Did anyone spend time with the chef in his office, last night or on one of the other nights?"

Flynn wiped a hand on the bar. "Alone?" he asked himself. "No, I don't remember that. Maybe Jim or Olivia, once. We would go back, usually in twos at times, to talk about our cake creations. Usually later in the class, or after even."

"Did you two have a meeting with Douglas any of the nights?"

"We did, the second night."

"How was it, with your history?"

"How would you think!" Martin flared up.

Flynn gave him a pat on the hand. "Marty, it was fine. It *was* fine, Detective. Douglas didn't even reference the past; it was more like he didn't know us, most of the time. He said our Victorian Sponge was overmixed and showed us with a spoon how to mix. Gracefully, he told us, pantomiming. Hilarious really. Then something about rolled cakes and cracking. Nondescript."

"Until the last shot, the ass."

"What last shot, Mr. Allen?"

Flynn replied, not Martin, who just gripped the bar, knuckles white. "Douglas being Douglas, said something like, 'Don't lean on my bar shelves.' Just his way of reminding us he's the important one."

Marlowe felt he should push them more and read from his notebook. "I saw the notes you wrote each other on your recipes: 'What an ass. See how he treats her. Someone should stand up to him. Someone will someday.' Can you explain them?"

"Are you tapping our phones too?" Martin pulled his hand out from Flynn's and raised it.

"Marty. Take it down." Flynn's voice could have calmed an angry bear it was so placid. "We should have known you'd ask. We were just conversing between ourselves on paper, nothing serious. Douglas could be an ass, we've admitted that. It was just couple talk."

"Who was the 'her' referenced?"

"Louisa. Like most of his many protégées—though the respect implied by that term probably gives Douglas too much credit—he treated her poorly. A roller coaster—up one minute, down the next, yelling then praising, cuddling then cold. She is a way better baker than he was. Everyone knew that."

"Persistent behavior on his part?"

"You could say that." Martin's voice dripped anger like hot honey. "He was like an abusive spouse. He'd had accusations in the past, but nothing would stick to him. He was far too slick."

"You thought someone should stand up to him." Marlowe pretended to read his notes.

Martin turned around, pulling a bottle of vodka off the shelf, Flynn's hand on his arm. After he set the bottle back down, Flynn replied. "We did. But that did not lead us to kill him, of course."

Seeing the bottle grab, Marlowe said, "We also found a bottle of vodka in your desk."

Before anyone could speak, a voice laced with irony came from over Marlowe's shoulder. "What's this? Taking a bottle to the cake class?"

Marlowe turned to see a man walking up, hand outstretched. He had square, black, wire-frame glasses over sarcastic eyes, a pugnacious head on a stocky body, close-cut hair and beard the color of an oyster, and wore a slate-blue apron over white T-shirt and jeans. His face seemed to be that of a man who was, before all things, self-centered.

Marlowe took the proffered hand, which had an uncomfortable oiliness. "Detective Marlowe."

"Detective. Chef Joel Towell. This is my restaurant. You aren't interrogating my staff, I hope. You know, here and at my other award-winning restaurants, my philosophy is about keeping it simple, using fresh ingredients, and allowing the food to do the talking. Not the staff. We have lawyers for that."

"Nothing formal, a few simple questions about last night, but a lawyer could be present if requested."

"And one had to do with drinking at class. I could see how having Douglas as a teacher would lead to that. But Martin, I hope you weren't sipping too strongly. We at Towell Restaurants believe that the City, and the world, is a happier place when we gather around a table, not a bottle. Though we also like better-made drinks, naturally. So what gives?"

Marlowe rarely disliked anyone immediately, but Joel Towell might be one. That oiliness from his hands dripped over every word like a salad with too much dressing. Martin's heavy breathing during Joel's speech was audible, Flynn gripping his arm throughout. It was the latter who spoke.

"Joel, it was nothing. A long class, that's all."

Joel whistled in mock shock. "A long class with Douglas. The longest, I'll bet. Not that I want to speak ill of the dead."

"Did you know Douglas Small well?" Even if he found Towell slimy, the man was prominent within the City food scene.

Joel smirked. "Naturally. Though we were very different, as restaurant owners and chefs. Between us, he wasn't much of a chef recently.

In my opinion, chefs in a restaurant kitchen are craftspeople, not artists. I'm just a simple craftsperson, who happens to be winning awards for his craft. Douglas thought the opposite, acted like he was some Picasso or Michelangelo. All ego. We didn't get on. I'm happy to provide a home for those he puts out like the trash, as with Flynn and Martin here. Provided they don't stray too far into the bar, right boys?" He gave a wink.

Marlowe's ability to stomach the chef's words, which brought up the taste of overdone ham in the back of his throat, had been filled. With the customary, "We will possibly want to talk to you later," to Flynn and Martin, he left the restaurant.

On his drive home, John was a wee bit giddy, as if he'd sampled each cake made the night before. The looming clouds above like a fleet of battleships waging war in the sky didn't reflect his mood. Called in to help the police *and* he got to visit the scene of a crime. In his mind, even if Marlowe's mustache would have drooped down at the phrase, John could call himself a contracting detective. The sound of that title wasn't nearly as memorable or as literary as consulting detective, maybe was even a bit goofy, as if a detective on a weight loss plan. But he still relished the idea of it, savoring the phrase as he said it aloud. Helping the police in an official capacity after reading and watching so many armchair or amateur detectives was a dream come true.

All that watching and reading he'd done should give him some insights into the processes, the clues, the arranging of facts. As well as into crimes and criminals. *Not that I want to be like Poirot in The Veiled Lady and commit a crime or break into a house*, he thought, bumping the curb slightly as he parked. *"Ma foi, they even employ me when they themselves fail.'"* The voice he heard in his head while walking up the steps belonged to legendary English actor David Suchet, his favorite Poirot.

As he reached the front door, the blind on the nearest window scooted up, impelled by a nose on the glass and accompanied by Ainsley's high-pitched barks. "Hold on, *mon ami*," he said, in a poor imitation of the Poirot actor he so admired. "Papa Arthur is nearly home." Door opened, he crouched down to scratch the excited dog behind the ears. Whether he was gone for ten minutes or three hours, Ainsley acted as if he'd been absent days, exuberantly wagging her tail, running into the living room next to the front door, then back to be petted, then into the dining room on the other side, then back again. It certainly made him feel welcome, which was a blessing, as walking into the house, empty of another human presence since his wife died, would be depressing without the joyful dog.

They went into the backyard first thing, both so Ainsley could go to the bathroom and so they could play fetch with a neon-orange ball. It was a curiously set up space, with a curving deck against the back fence blocking off the alley, a scraggly yard between deck and house, sidewalk winding through it on the way to a gate in the fence leading to the driveway. A side yard and sidewalk ran alongside the house's north side, partially taken up with a curious collection: plants, weeds, cobwebs, three bison statues—one white, one black, one metal—a green iron frog, broken shards of colorful clay and terracotta pots arranged artfully, a ceramic bird waterer, a stool missing one leg, and more curiosities. Marlowe called it Mrs. Havisham's garden, a name John enjoyed.

The other part of the side yard was grass, an ideal spot to toss the ball, as Ainsley loved pouncing through the grass searching. John stood on the deck, throwing the ball and chasing her when she returned, before grabbing it out of her mouth to throw again. Ainsley liked the tugging as much as the fetching. Between throws, he texted with one hand on his phone, looking somewhat like a baseball pitcher reading signs from the screen instead of a catcher. Ainsley didn't mind as long as the game continued.

Which it did for fifteen minutes, until she didn't chase after a throw, happily panting but giving him the I'm-done-with-this-game look he knew well. "Enough is enough. Let's go inside and mull things over, get some water. We have to keep the brain hydrated. While pounding the pavement, swinging ferocious fists, and loudly swearing might be the modus operandi for some detectives, at my age, I'm probably more the thinking type." If his neighbors thought it odd that he talked to the dog, they had long gotten used to it. For him, it had become natural, filling the space that once had two humans conversing.

Both of them snuggled into the couch near the front window, Ainsley having made a stop at her water bowl on the way, John taking sips of water from a quart-sized mason jar. Petting her randomly, he thought over everything he'd seen at the classroom, jotting occasional phrases in the police-sized notebook he'd picked up. After a while, he realized he'd just been doodling the last few minutes, swirls and lines looking like a madman's line-drawing of a croissant.

"Ainsley, it's time for me to head to the office." He patted her now-sleeping form. "Been a long time since I've thought that, but I should meet Marlowe and the team, get to consulting. Hastings may have wanted to kick Lavington down the stairs in his own home, but to solve this case, I'm going to have to leave our home." Ainsley woke up when he said "leave" and gave him sad eyes. "You dogs have a language peculiarly your own, Ains, and can give a person ten kinds of guilt with your eyes. Better than any human. But we've got to help Marlowe, so you'll have to tough it out."

He got up, going into the kitchen to a moveable wooden island set against one wall. There, he cut up dog treats into smaller treats, talking as he cut. "Don't worry my doggy friend, I will be back soon. First, I have to stop in at your friend Gary's, who will be very sad to miss you. Maybe he will have one of those sausages you like that I can bring home." She now stood at his feet, giving him a different look, one he took to mean, "you'd better." He scooped up the treats, managed to pull on a gray and black striped hoodie without dropping any, grabbed his notebook off the couch, and opened the door. Before leaving, he scattered the treats across the geometric rug covering the wood floors. "I'll be back in a few minutes," he called out as he always did when shutting the door, leaving the dog behind.

John made it downtown in record time. While skies remained an imposing hefty gray, no rain snuck through the clouds, helping keep traffic moving. It was a continually amazing phenomena that drivers in the City were slightly paralyzed by rain, considering that it rained on probably three-quarters of a year's days. Maybe not a hard rain, thunderstorms as rare as hen's teeth. But rain in some form, and when the drops came down, traffic seized as if water rusted gears. Parking in front of Gary's bar in the popular Settler's Square neighborhood in downtown's southwestern corner, he knocked on his car's dashboard. "Let's keep the luck rolling. Easy traffic and front-row parking. I'll take it."

Exiting and locking the Honda Fit after paying to park via an app on his phone, he walked into the bar. He'd visited Gary's for the first time many years before once and liked it, but hadn't returned until meeting Marlowe. It was a stretch too far for a quick stop, and going out solo wasn't his favorite. But Marlowe loved Gary's, and so John had become more of a bar semi-regular. The space was a thin rectangle, wooden booths on one red brick wall, a few wooden-topped tables in the middle, and a fifteen-foot, L-shaped oak bar with red vinyl barstools and a big mirror behind it on the other wall. Unlike many spots that seemed to fear blank space, the walls were mostly bare except for a few framed black-and-white European liquor ads: Campari, Fernet-Branca, Chartreuse, Strega, Underberg.

Settler's Square brimmed with bars of all types: sports, pick-up, dives, speakeasy, mixologist fine-drinkers. Gary's didn't fit into any category directly; it was just a bar that served well-made drinks at well-lower than average prices. Cozy without being tight, currently medium busy, with two booths and one table full. One booth held a group of four men in outlandishly rainbowed golf plus fours, pom-pom hats, and vibrant polo shirts, the other a couple holding hands across the table. A group of twentysomethings in shorts and punk band T-shirts was playing Uno at the table. Only one bar stool was occupied, by a woman in a pink cashmere sweater sipping a drink that matched the sweater in color, reading *Bleak House*. The Zombies song "She's Not There" played in the background, not too loud but noticeable.

Behind the bar stood Gary himself. The bar's owner was originally raised in England, still carrying an accent that wouldn't have been out of place in a countryside English pub. He'd worked at this bar first for seven years, then bought it eight years ago. Marlowe once said Gary reminded him of what St. Francis would have looked like if he'd tended bar: fifty-ish, lean, brown hair trailing nearly to shoulders, a tiny goatee streaked gray, wearing his normal outfit of black jeans and white shirt buttoned to the collar. He absentmindedly wiped the bar with a towel, gazing over customers to check drinks, nodding to John as the door closed behind him.

"John Arthur in shorts on a day that would chill a badger."

"Gary, how goes the day?" John sidled up to the bar, sitting on the stool nearest the door.

"Fair to middling to begin, my friend. Calm before the storm, perhaps. What can I pour you?"

John really came by to chat, but not having a drink in Gary's seemed sinful. He felt he'd stop by the station later, so didn't want to wade in too deep. "Italian red if possible."

"Cracking choice under the clouds. I have a red blend from Vecchia Cantina. Umbrian, which I know you favor."

"Bella, bella."

As Gary pulled a balloon wine glass off the shelf, setting it on the bar, then reaching for a bottle, John said, "Mind if I ask you a question?"

"Would it be related to the death of one famous chef?"

"How'd you guess?" John's surprise popped out of the phrase.

"Your predilection for showing up around a crime wouldn't be out of place in Midsomer. Big name, I'd be gobsmacked if your question wasn't Douglas Small related. However." He set the wine down in front of John. "You know Marlowe doesn't appreciate case talk in the bar."

John took a sip. The wine was the color of almost-ripe blackberries, with a berries-and-leather flavor and dry finish. "Wonderful wine, thanks. I know we shouldn't talk the case, but I need some bar background. I'm consulting. Officially." He couldn't help grinning as he said the words.

"Consulting detective, you don't say. Sherlock style."

"I shouldn't say consulting. And I'm no Sherlock. Civilian contractor. Helping the police with their inquiries."

"Your dream realized."

John surprisingly tried to be modest. "Just background around the culinary scene. Nothing too serious."

"That sounds quite accomplished. Television mysteries sprung to life." Gary had picked up on John's love of his home country's detectives from his last few visits. It was hard not to.

John took another sip, rolling the wine around in his mouth. Gary gazed out over the bar, catching the eye of one of the golf-attired drinkers. "Hold on, John, must deliver a round of Suburban Caroline Noisy Neighbors to the go-away golfers. Show up on the regular dressed to the back nine nines. Don't actually golf. I think they're pharmacists." He reached down into a cooler tucked behind the bar, pulled out four bottles in one hand like a magician pulling a pack of rabbits out of a hat, and somehow managed to open each with the other hand within seconds without even setting them down.

John sipped wine as Gary delivered the beers, coming back with four empties he tossed in a recycle bin.

"Beer dispatched, glasses topped or near, back to Detective Arthur."

John's cheeks reddened, either from wine or the Detective Arthur moniker. "A question or two."

"Softly, softly." Gary leaned over the bar. "Don't want to turn this into a house of gossip."

Pitching his voice lower, John went on. "I was trying to remember more about Martin Allen, the bartender. He was at the scene, so to speak."

Gary nodded, so John continued. "I was texting Andrew—"

"Bohrer."

"Yep."

"Favorite of mine. Best bartender in the City, when at it."

"Agreed. I wanted to get the inside information on Martin and Douglas's split. They once being thick as restaurant thieves, to be colloquial. Andrew said he wasn't 100% sure, but thought it had to do with Douglas's bartending book. Gave me some insight, but said I should double-check with you."

"Did he now? I'll rap his knuckles." Gary picked up a cherry wood muddler and pretended to swing it. "Lots of bartenders come here when not slinging, so I do hear the odd rumor. Martin included. For the record, this isn't on the record. Concur." John nodded. "Martin developed the signature drink recipes at Mansion, very terroir centric, heaps of homespun items, pine syrups, thimbleberry bitters, the like. Then Douglas signed the contract for *The Small Bartending Book*, which boasted those recipes. No credit for Martin, no cut of the dosh. Got Martin's knickers in a right twist. Boyo could drink for England normally, this took it to another level. Removed, shall we say, from his job for being pissed. Stint in rehab. Heard Flynn, his partner, sold his condo to pay for that. Quite a smashup for Martin."

Twirling the last ounce of wine in the glass, John spoke quietly. "Interesting. Thanks. Seems Douglas might 'steal the fat off your bacon,' as an intense Adrian Dunbar said when playing retired detective Alex Ridley in the show of the same name. What did you think of chef Small, by the way."

"He didn't stop by but once. Not his favorite free house. Wanted regal treatment, but here even the king gets served same as everyone else. Speaking of, the mooning couple over there looks dry."

Gary headed out onto the floor as John jotted down a few words in his notebook. By the time he was done, the bartender was back, shaker in hand. "Drinks to make, my friend. Another wine?"

"Nope, but thank you. For the wine and information. I'm heading to the station." He laid a bill on the counter to cover the wine and tip, stood up, slipping into his hoodie, which he'd draped over the stool. "One more. This will just take a moment, as the family liaison officer in *The Bay* always says when trying to get a silent suspect to talk."

Gary began putting ice in the shaker. "I'm a suspect now?"

"Never. But Andrew mentioned Douglas may have had some, shall we say, claims brought against him by staff—sexual and other harassment. You happen to hear anything along those lines?"

"Not to grass, but shady things in Douglas's past. From overheard chatter here, let's say he could have kick-started the Me Too movement. One victim of his even had a breakdown, rumor went. Nothing proven in Old Bailey, however. Between us, mind."

John patted the side of his nose. "Completely. Thanks, Gary."

"Consulting Detective Arthur, on the case."

John couldn't help chuckling as he walked out the door, waving over his shoulder.

7

It was late afternoon, the day after Douglas Small's death. Marlowe returned to his desk to find Morven and Nelson standing near it, chatting to Officer Weber. He could hear Morven as he walked up.

"Glad you're here. We can use the help."

"That we can." Marlowe's baritone echoed in the cavernous, nearly empty detective room. "It's quite a stampede. More wranglers the better."

The two detectives turned in unison as he spoke, with the uniformed officer standing up quickly from the desk, looking a little shocked at his sudden appearance. His soft walking while carrying an XL frame took some getting used to. She'd let her hair down from its bun, and it was surprisingly long, cascading over blue-suited shoulders. All three spoke at once.

"Marlowe, welcome . . ."

"Detective, you're back . . ."

"Sir, sorry I . . ."

He held up his hand and they quieted. "I suppose we're going to have to take turns."

Before anyone replied, the phone on his desk rang. Office Weber began to reach for it, then remembered it wasn't her desk. "Sorry, sir. Detective. I suppose you should answer that."

He trotted around the desk to grab the phone on the third ring. "Yes, this is Marlowe. Got it. Be down in a minute." Hanging up, he said mostly to himself, "Now another shows. Gonna need more horses." Seemingly re-noticing the other three, he spoked louder. "Sorry. Looks like our civilian contractor is here."

"John Arthur arrives. Figured he couldn't stay away." Morven gave Marlowe a you-get-what-ask-for face.

"The many, the merrier." Noticing Weber's blank look, he said with a grin, "Can you two give Office Weber the John Arthur background. He can be, well, you know."

Morven shooed Marlowe toward the exit on the other side of the room. "We know. Enough to say you'd better get him before he derails the officer at the front desk."

"He'll probably have them singing." Marlowe walked off, remembering one of the last times he'd met John in the station's lobby.

Opening the door off the lobby's back leading into the station, Marlowe saw John was indeed deep in conversation with Officer Coleman, who was sitting behind bulletproof glass at the lobby's main check-in point. A massive 6'5" and 300 pounds, Officer Coleman sported a handlebar mustache that rivaled Marlowe's for size, though one that had seen more consistent trimmings. He often worked the lobby, as his combination of size and friendliness made him ideal for the more random public interactions that often happened there.

Marlowe heard John's voice, this time adopting a British accent that would have gotten him thrown out of many pubs, as he approached.

"'A copper's a copper, first, last and always.'"

"That so?" Marlowe's words caused both men to turn.

"There you are, Marlowe. I tried to get Officer Coleman to let me in to meet you, then when he wouldn't, to give me a badge, figuring I'd need one. But he, rightly so, said he'd better check with you. Even though we go way back."

Officer Coleman's voice rumbled like a subway. "Detective, I didn't know John was part of the force now. And we should always follow protocol."

"Not part of the force. But he is a contractor."

A smile sailed across the officer's face, so glowingly genial in nature it was easy to see how he'd gotten a reputation for being able to calm the most hectic visitor. "John, that has to be a dream come true."

"It is." John beamed back. "Consulting detective Arthur."

"Civilian contractor Arthur," Marlowe corrected.

"Contracting detective."

"That doesn't sound—"

"Very positive, I agree," John smoothly interrupted. "I still get a badge, right? To help with the contracting."

"Sadly, no badges for contractors."

"Could I get my own?"

"Like a kids' sheriff badge?"

"I suppose that wouldn't hold up."

"Probably not even for the most nearsighted suspect."

Officer Coleman leaned back far on his chair, hands locked behind his head, beatific smile remaining on his face as he watched them talk rapidly, like tennis players hitting forehands across the net.

"So, no badge. But then, Sherlock went badgeless."

"I could get you a lanyard with an identification photo."

"Which one might call an identification badge."

"I wouldn't. But you could."

"Deal."

"Coleman." Marlowe knew the officer well enough that the lack of officer prefixing wasn't frowned on. "Can you request a contractor's badge for Mr. Arthur. Or put an officer on it."

"Not a problem in the least. Might take a couple days."

"In that case, I might not need it for this case. We'll have solved it by then."

"Optimistic." Marlowe put a hand on John's shoulder, moving him in the door's direction, giving a nod to Coleman.

"Oui," John said loudly, in a terrible Belgian accent.

Marlowe led John through the detective room, the older man pausing multiple times to stare awestruck at everything from a detective typing up a report to a poster on the wall reminding officers to take their annual health exam. On the elevator ride up, Marlowe told John that another officer was currently helping them, on the team for the first time, in hopes of John reining in the British TV quotes. *A vain hope*, he thought, but one worth attempting.

Morven stood by the incident board, the movement of their approach catching her eye. "Marlowe. And Mr. Arthur. Welcome back and welcome to the station." As she spoke, Nelson and Weber stood to greet the other two.

"Team," Marlowe drawled. "Officer Weber, this is John Arthur. The civilian contractor we mentioned."

John introduced himself to Weber and said hellos to Morven and Nelson while moving closer to the board.

"The traditional murder board. Remarkable. This sketch of the tables and who sat where is handy. Do you put string on the board tying suspects to victim? I've seen that before. Quite a collage. Of crime." The last sentence he said as if the narrator in a 1920s radio serial, expecting a cacophonous organ to play as he hit the period.

"John." Marlowe drew the name out into two syllables, pulling other man's eyes from the board as if a trout on a slow reel. "Let's not get too distracted."

"Yes," John exclaimed. "I have information, gathered while detectiving."

"Detectiving?" Weber unexpectedly spoke up. John's curious ways tended to confuse the uninitiated.

"While doing research as a contractor, is what John meant."

"Naturally. Research, interviews, you know the drill."

"John, you weren't interviewing actual suspects?" Marlowe was trying to reassure the rest of the team, and himself.

"Sources, not suspects. Not without you or an actual officer present. I know better."

"What kind of sources?"

"I believe police never reveal their sources."

"That's reporters, Mr. Arthur," Morven reminded him.

"Is it? Either way, I'm no snitch. Industry folks, bartenders I know, that kind of thing."

Marlowe guessed Gary might be on that list and didn't want his favorite bartender dragged in. "Fair enough, consultant, let's hear what you know." He held his hand up. "But you aren't the only bird with a song to sing. Morven and Nelson have been on the trail, me too. It's time for a—"

John couldn't help himself. "Team conference around the murder board. Every police show has one at some point in an episode. *Brokenwood*, *Midsomer*, all of them. Even with *Father Brown* they gather round the rectory kitchen table. Maybe we need tea."

Marshall Dillon help us, what I have unleashed, Marlowe thought. "Easy, John. Tea, and more importantly, coffee, later. Your report first. Without TV talk."

"Stay on target. I can do that." As John began to talk, Marlowe wondered if that last statement was true.

Once John, Morven, Nelson, and Marlowe gave overviews of their various research and interviews, they took a collective deep breath, followed by silence descending on the corner momentarily. It was like the moment after an important political speech before the dam breaks with reporters' questions.

Marlowe finally spoke, typically laconic. "Interesting."

"Does it get us to who killed Douglas Small?" Morven shook her head. They were standing in a half-circle around the board, one broken by Marlowe's desk, where Weber still sat.

Nelson beat John to speaking. "Closer, for sure. We know Douglas had issues with staff and caused a very angry Martin to not only lose his job, but his partner's home, or that's how he sees it. He was drinking heavily at the class too. Pushed over the edge. All the way to murder."

"That's dramatic." Marlowe said, undramatically. "Not sure it proves guilt."

"And when did he do it?" Morven followed up.

Nelson answered, a little smugly. "Faking a bathroom break. He's strong enough to overpower the chef. Then stabs him."

"With that much drinking, you'd think his bathroom break would be real. How did he do it with the door locked? And overpowered him without causing a noticeable noise? You may be correct, but not sure I'm sold, Nelson."

"Madame How and Lady Why." John finally got a word in.

"What's that, Mr. Arthur?" Morven asked.

"John is fine, Detective Morven. We are colleagues. It's a line from a Cyril Hare book I've been reading. Fantastic British author, he—" Marlowe's upturned hand cut him off. "Sorry, Marlowe. On target. Just thinking that the why with Martin may be there, but not the how. And why that butter?" They nodded as he continued. "Martin almost seems too easy. It's never the obvious choice."

"On TV," Marlowe said. "Here in real life, it often is. Martin's a suspect, make no mistake. More facts are needed, like more spice in a bland stew. Which leads us to Officer Weber's background work."

Weber didn't look shocked to be called out, instead more like an expert student thrilled for her turn to read aloud in front of the class at a new school. She'd been taking notes as the others talked and clicked a few buttons on the keyboard of her open laptop.

"Yes, Detective Marlowe. I've been doing some digging into backgrounds, starting with the victim."

"Smart."

"Douglas Small. I'll skip his restaurants and books, as you know that. Local legend, but one article I read points to his star having faded some lately. No awards in years, fewer TV appearances, not the most massive social presence. One restaurant failed, other new ones mentioned but never actually opened. Nothing specific on financial trouble, though he did sell an expensive house a year and a half back, downsizing to a downtown apartment. Farther back, rumors, as mentioned, of harassment and sexual misconduct allegations, never proved, no trials."

"Lots of smoke, no arsonist booked."

"Correct, Detective Nelson. More years ago, I found multiple mentions referencing the article written by Sarah Sykes, now forty-nine, the one kicking Douglas Small's career into overdrive, and an ancient blog post making it seem they were an item, during which time she was married. As was Douglas, to now ex Ruth Small. Sarah is still considered a top food writer—articles in national magazines, as well as locally. Three books of her own, published by Gumberoo Books, owned by her husband of twenty-five years, Chester Rowan, age fifty-four. Gumberoo's biggest seller remains Douglas's first book. At one point, he and the victim were very close—'as beef and pork in a bolognaise,' one article remarked—but Douglas choosing not to publish his following books with Chester's company nearly led to a court case, until they settled. Gumberoo was almost purchased by a conglomerate, but some trouble when the finances were dug into had it called off. Not sure I'd say Gumberoo was failing, but not in a strong position."

"He could still be mad at Douglas leaving and having an affair with his wife. Double motives." Nelson had a hard time solely listening on occasion.

"Fair point, Detective." Weber nodded diplomatically. "Moving on to some other guests. Kevin Holman, age fifty-two. Hard to get a grasp of what he currently does, as he's had a number of careers. Restaurant owner. Marketing gigs in the local tech industry. Real estate agent, working for the company that sold the building the crime was committed in if that's interesting. Car sales. Nothing seems to last. Could be unemployed currently. Downsized homes recently."

Nelson leapt over that last fact like a high jumper. "Did you know that 39% of people move for more storage space?"

"I did not, Detective Nelson. Here, as they lost a lot of square footage, perhaps money problems. But most intriguing was a potential connection uncovered when researching the victim. When opening his first restaurant, Douglas Small's partner was one Richard Holman. I believe Kevin Holman's dad. Kevin's wife and class co-attendee is Claire, forty-nine, a pharmacist. Long-term at the same pharmacy."

The others were intensely concentrating on Weber as she spoke, which meant they were startled by Doctor Peterson giving a profound mock cough from a few feet behind them.

Marlowe spoke first, stepping over nearer the bespectacled pathologist. "Doc Peterson, you caught us like a cowboy caught stepping on a rattler. Unexpected. Late for you on the weekend."

"What majesty should be, what duty is. Why day is day, night night, and time is time. Which is to say, Marlowe, you are right, but, colloquially, duty calls. I answered. Who is there yonder at your desk? Not the normal crowd of front row faces."

"You're correct as usual, Doc. Officer Weber is assisting us, and John Arthur is also assisting, as a civilian."

Weber gave a wave from behind Marlowe's desk, but John walked over, reaching out his hand. "You must be the famous forensic pathologist. It is an honor."

Shaking John's hand emphatically, Doctor Peterson glowed. "I am indeed. I've heard tales of you as well, Mr. Arthur. A great help to Marlowe. Some are born great, some achieve greatness, and some have greatness thrust upon them in the form of new teammates."

John blushed, but stayed quiet, his normally effusive manner seemingly overshadowed by Doctor Peterson's Elizabethan staginess, like a robin in front of a peacock.

"What brings you so soon, Doctor Peterson?" Morven knew the normal waiting times. "We wouldn't expect results from you or forensics quite this quick, though happy to have information if and when available."

"Ah, Detective Morven, as focused as the gaze of a queen, with a voice like the nightingale in Trafalgar. It was a day of unswerving hours on the pathological boards, if I may be bold in speech, that I spent with Douglas Small. One that led me here with a few items, hopefully helpful."

"Any information at this point is helpful, this nightingale believes." Morven wouldn't let many call her voice after a bird, but the doc was the doc.

"Taking pains to be perfect, admitting I will continue to work, let us begin. Douglas Small was in decent health for his age. Drinking might have become an issue, if he'd lived, but overall, in the pink as they say. The cause of death, as you might conjecture, was penetrating trauma coming from the back into the mediastinum and heart. I would mention there are stranger things in heaven and cooking classes, as the saying goes, but fairly certain instantaneous death. Said trauma caused by a seven-inch tapering blade, found at the scene. But you surmised such."

"Pretty simple surmising," Marlowe admitted. "Any specialized knowledge needed?"

"Not necessarily, especially with a weapon of such size driven in with force."

"Doctor Peterson. Does that force mean we are looking for a man?" Nelson's cautious tone sounded somewhat like a student who rarely vocalizes in class.

Doctor Peterson caught Weber's slight eye roll. "Though she be but little, she is fierce. No, Detective, at the angle and considering the extreme sharpness of the blade, any adult could have done it. More on the wound?" As no one spoke, he continued. "Onward to a second item. We found that he had either taken or been given a fair dose of a benzodiazepine, possibly temazepam, though continuing to test that."

"Enough to make him woozy?"

"If riding into the hazarding a guess hurricane, yes, Marlowe. More than. Not enough to kill him, but put him asleep or nearly. He wouldn't have been concluding the class with eating cake. Golden sleep wouldath reigned."

"Enough to kill him if he hadn't been stabbed?"

"I would say no, only enough for Morpheus's gentle embrace."

"Do you know how it was administered?"

"Not conclusively. Take this as a gift while waiting for final results. He had consumed coffee with a heavily herbal spiritous liqueur, which could have been the vessel for the drug. He hadn't consumed much else recently, and no marks of ingress dotted his body. One tattoo did, a set of chef's knives, crossed on his right arm."

"Drugged. That adds another aspect to the crime." Morven considered. "Probably made it easy to approach him. Once getting through the locked door. With no one noticing."

"As your imagination bodies forth into the forms of things as yet unknown, I make my adieus. Unless more questions."

"I don't—"

John cut in. "Doctor Peterson, I have a question. Sorry to interrupt, Marlowe."

Marlowe smiled at the older man. It was the first 'sorry to interrupt' he'd gotten from John today, he thought.

"Mr. Arthur, speak." Doctor Peterson waved his arms as if cajoling a flock of pigeons to fly.

"Was there butter in the wound?"

"The mysterious substance. A favorite of you mystery buffs. I will not say yet, as tests are ongoing. But to assist the newest arrival, I will give an opinion that, yes, butter had dripped in, but not deeply, as well as nearby. Our friends in forensics promise to provide definitive substance answers. Plus more I am sure."

"Any word yet from them, Doc?"

"Marlowe, they are beyond my ken as the stars. So far. Reach out to Arris."

"Can do. Thanks, Doc."

Doctor Peterson walked off, thanks echoing as if in chorus from the others. John, closest after shaking hands, heard the doctor say softly, "When we do meet again, why, we shall smile, as this parting was well made."

Quiet descended over the group like a door suddenly shutting, each in their own thoughts about the case. Marlowe finally cracked it.

"Doc's thrown more fuel on the campfire, make no mistake. Stopped Officer Weber's detailing, however. More to come officer?"

Weber transferred her attention back to her screen. "I believe I told you most of what I know so far. Martin and Flynn—nothing outside of what has been gone through by you and the other detectives. And Mr. Arthur. A few things on Jim Sean and Olivia Sean. He is a kitchen equipment salesman, a job he started the same year the victim opened his first restaurant. The two grew up in the same small town north of the City called Cement, due to a cement plant being the main employer for many years. She is apparently younger, and harder to track down. Nothing at all under that name until their marriage five years ago. Has been working as a buyer at local clothing chain, Vêtements Pas Chers, for the last three years."

"Helpful background." Morven sat on the desk's edge. It'd been a tiring day.

"Thank you, Detective. Not much more. On the other attendees, Lucille and Madison, you and Detective Nelson covered what I've found. Drogo Oates was apparently involved in another case." She glanced round the attentive faces.

John got there first. "He was indeed. The Case of the Retired Reverend. Helped solve it, unknowingly."

"The Case of the Retired Reverend." Nelson made a motion with his hands like an umpire calling out a close play at the plate. "I didn't know you'd named that one yet, Mr. Arthur; the baseball connection with the victim is great. You know, I've been meaning to get—"

"Nelson," Marlowe grumbled. "Let Officer Weber finish before going down a side gully."

"Sure, Detective." Nelson was new enough that his nervousness showed if he thought he'd made a misstep. "Sorry, Weber."

A friendly smile lit up her face. "Not a problem. I've covered the salient points discovered. Drogo's facts seem well known. Oh, two more items. Jim and Olivia do have a child, a son, also Jim, middle name Douglas. Four years old. Only couple with kids. Finally, did see that Joel Towell, owner where Martin and Flynn work, and the victim had a few very public fights in the past. One involving physicality."

Marlowe ambled back up to the board. "Chefs in a brawl. I'd figure they'd want to protect their hands. Lots of information, Weber, thanks. More is needed. Can we keep you on the team longer?"

"Yes, sir. I can do more tonight."

"Let's mull that. Getting late." Marlowe knew the first days, hours even, after a major crime were extra important, but felt that working when you were dog tired never led down the trail to better results. That balancing act was one police had to become adept at. "We do have a list of jobs stretching from San Fran to San Antonio."

Morven agreed. "That's fair. Here's where I see the next steps. Initial interviews with Kevin and Claire and Jim and Olivia. Follow-up interview with Chester and Sarah. Down here, formal." Marlowe nodded as she continued. "We need to track down any CC TV around the hotel. Alley if possible."

"Thinking there might have been someone breaking in from the outside? Like scaling the wall?" Nelson made what he thought was a passable scaling the wall gesture, but which appeared more as if he was scratching someone's back.

"Not necessarily, Nelson. Reviewing it for any abnormalities. Need to meet up with Chelsea Hinkley, the victim's PA. With her being in charge of most of his communication and schedule, she's got insider knowledge.

Plus, maybe we can get a look at cell phone activity, if any, and emails without getting a court order. More background, whatever we can find. That's a start. Marlowe?"

He stared at the board. "Nope. You covered what I was thinking." The two had worked together for many years, so he wasn't surprised. "Let me give a whirl at breaking it down. Tomorrow, we hit up the two couples ASAP. You and Nelson take the first, I'll take the second. Then I'll try and get Chelsea. Weber, you get after CC TV, forensics, and keep backgrounding."

"Sounds like a plan," Morven replied for the three other police.

John had been quiet, walking back around the desk to stand in front of the board. Marlowe noticed the man had his notebook out and was penciling furiously.

"John, whatcha drawing?"

"What?" John replied, then he switched to a British accent. "'I write everything down, rule number one of good policing.'" Switching to a different, Indian-tinged British, he continued. "'I thought that was catching the bad guys.'" Weber backed away from her desk a step, wondering if he was having some sort of episode, then saw Morven's bemusement as John switched to his own voice. "Bit of Mrs. Sidhu for you. Making a copy of the seating plan. Seems important. I was still listening." He patted Marlowe on the back paternally, a gesture that caused Nelson to cough in surprise. "Attentively. Enough that I heard no assignment for Arthur. I figure I can tag along with you. Then if they try to slip in a culinary faux pax, I'm there."

Marlowe considered. It couldn't hurt. "As long as you keep the TV talk in check."

John held up three fingers. "Scout's honor."

"No posting about interviews or sketches on your socials, Mr. Arthur," Nelson kidded. While Morven was more wary of John's involvement, Nelson was fully in awe after the past two cases.

"Socials. I think you're confusing me with a younger man, Detective."

"Oh-kay." Marlowe singsonged the word. "Plan is set. John, I'll call you first thing tomorrow. Morven, you arrange interview times. Nelson, don't break a leg working out tonight. Officer Weber, our thanks. It is"—he pointed at the institutional black-and-white clock on the wall above them—"quitting time. Let's clip this case tomorrow."

Outside, night had taken hold, but as if by a sainted miracle, clouds once as imposing as vengeful mythological figures had vanished, the sky's Prussian-blue singularly dotted with stars above and streetlights below. Inside, the incident board stood alone, filled with photos of Douglas Small, the class attendees and tangentially involved people like Joel Towell and Chelsea Hinkley, set off by article cutouts, sketches, and Post-its in various handwriting. Marlowe's scratched scrawls, Morven's regulation printing, neat as if graphed, Nelson's high-school cursive, and a single one with BUTTER written in bold marker by John Arthur. Once the center of attention, the board was currently like the last guest at a party wondering how it ended so quickly. A sole detective sat across the room, finishing paperwork before heading home, not even glancing its direction.

Being in the same position in the past, Marlowe sympathized with the detective when walking out. He'd originally thought an amble down to Gary's for a quick drink filled his dance card, a way to shake the case from his mind for a few minutes. Once back at his apartment, the tenacles of Douglas Small's death would encircle his thoughts like a giant octopus. *So, why not Gary's to derail the thoughts for a short time first*, he considered, standing in front of the station, teetering on the decision.

From Settler's Square, a few blocks below, music could be heard breaking through the cloudless night. Somewhere a baby wailed, raised voices an indistinct collage of sounds, crying, laughing, talking, horns honked in unison and solo, a deep throaty dog barking happily. Saturday night's tapestry rising up in joy at the vanished clouds, at the lack of work for most in the morning, at the fact they were alive. But Douglas Small wouldn't have another Saturday. Marlowe turned away from the noise and the bar, walking his way toward the station parking lot.

John Arthur was already halfway home. Knowing Ainsley missed him, he'd been the first to exit, his car only a block from the station as parking luck continued, combined with upper downtown's usual lack of weekend traffic, most buildings quiet as dawn. Office workers instead at soccer games, friendly dinners, new release movies, and sprawled napping on couches. Stopped at a red light, fingers tapped out the beat to the song "I'm Henry the VII, I Am" by Herman's Hermits. Being at the station left him a bit breathless and a lot exhilarated. And his first in-person interview tomorrow. Hard to believe.

He thought of Poirot at interviews, able to get suspects to talk by a combination of at-times motherly caring and foreignness. Sherlock distant and insightful as an ice pick. Father Brown forgiving, Mike Shepard curious and unthreatening. Vera with her hat pulled tight, unafraid to push people while calling them pet. A phrase from *Inspector Morse* popped into his head: 'Watch the mouth. It gives away what the eyes try to hide.' Then traffic moved.

He found himself on the same melancholy seesaw as Marlowe, one he'd ridden when embroiled in past cases. Douglas Small, a man he'd known, had been murdered. Perhaps he wasn't the nicest, perhaps even criminal in a way, but still, did he deserve a knife in the back? Douglas had friends, many who looked up to him; a host of hosts, waiters, bartenders, chefs, bakers, dishwashers depending on him, his name and culinary and business acumen for jobs. What would happen to them? Watching TV mysteries, the credits always rolled, never giving a view into the fissures emanating out into the world for many moons after the murder was solved. Nearly at the door, high-pitched barking broke into his thoughts. Ainsley wanted her Saturday night pig ear. The case and its stretching ramifications would have to wait.

By this time, Morven was lying on her back, one muscular leg pulled straight above her, toes nearly directly above nose, other leg bent at the knee, a pink yoga mat underneath as she stretched hamstrings. Luther's London gym hadn't received any message about clearing out for Saturday night. The gym nearest the station and favored by officers as well as downtown denizens, it had multiple classes happening, two rooms three-quarters full of people utilizing machines—treadmills, rowing machines, ellipticals, and strength training machines—like a sort of cyborgian future come to life,. Plus rooms with every sort of dumbbell, adjustable lifting bench, chin-up bars, and one with punching bags, speed bags, and uppercut bags.

She and Nelson were in the latter. They both wore slate-colored running shorts, T-shirts—hers a plain emerald green, his orange with "Sheldonian Sixteen K" in black on it—and white workout shoes. Morven was a contest-winning Muay Thai practitioner, Nelson a willing novice, and she'd been training and taking the younger detective to classes lately. Tonight, they'd been practicing a range of kicks using the heavy bag, doing many repetitions and occasionally stopping for Morven to demonstrate technique or for stretching before taking it up again. Over and over, teaching the muscles how to effectively strike in different ways, how to approach with different opponents, different situations.

Her mind wandered for a moment as she now held the bag while Nelson practiced high kick after high kick—thunk, thunk, thunk. Being in a match was a little like solving a murder case. There were routines you had to follow, paths you took on every case—forensics, interviews, the scene, the background—and as you experienced more cases, the better you became at knowing those routines. But every case was different too. If you approached each exactly the same, you got your wheel stuck in a gully without being flexible enough to navigate out of it. When that happened, there'd be a time where you couldn't move the case further, couldn't solve the case, or the opponent. Murders weren't solely routine. *Wheel stuck in a gully*. She laughed to herself. Next I'll be dropping cowboy metaphors routinely like Marlowe. *And Nelson's dropping his back leg too deeply.*

Nelson listened attentively as Morven demonstrated, then began kicking again. The case didn't currently cross his mind. Not that he hadn't or wouldn't think more about it tonight, but at the gym, he kept his mind militarily on the gym. Especially with Morven here. He didn't want to disappoint the detective he looked up to. Kick, kick, kick. The case wouldn't go anywhere.

Weber, exhausted physically, emotionally, and mentally after working on her first case with members of the detective branch, rode her black Yamaha Vino scooter home from the station. She lived in a one-bedroom apartment in a thirty-unit Brownstone-esque building on the Uppercase Hill neighborhood's far eastern slope. It was neatly arranged with storage containers full of art and crafting supplies—paints, canvas, sewing equipment, glue sticks and gun, fabric scraps, thread, markers, and more—all tucked under a mohair fluffy couch covered in a patchwork quilt, a turquoise wingback chair, and even the small glass-topped dining table pushed against the wall near the kitchen.

She'd changed from police uniform to loose-fitting black pajama pants with the Marvel logo on them and white tank top. After a quick sandwich, sprawling on the couch, she ignored the book she was reading, Sue Grafton's *A Is for Alibi.* The idea of solving a case with actual detectives took over every time she started a sentence. She'd worked patrol for years, different roles, different neighborhoods, different types of people brought together, woof and warp. You'd think such varied policing would be like a vaccine against getting overly excited by any new type of police work. But she was. After rereading the same page multiple times, like memorizing a speech that refused stubbornly to take root in the brain, she set the book down.

Taking a hearty sip of the tropical-flavored hot tea she'd brewed earlier, she replayed the day in her mind, bringing up case facts and considering them like jewels unearthed alongside ones she'd heard related by the rest of the team and Doctor Peterson. And the consultant, John Arthur. Kindly, but with a TV-driven way of looking at things that was decidedly odd, like a stitch slightly out of place. Such a monumental day, she decided, a ripple of joy at being part of a detective team flowing through her reclining body before causing her feet to flutter stretched out over the couch arm. What might tomorrow bring?

Marlowe reached the office at eight a.m., croissant in one hand and coffee in the other, both picked up at his favorite coffee stand, Sampson's Sips, on the way in. Weber already sat on the opposite side of his desk, laptop open, head down, having pulled up her own chair leaving his free. Morven and Nelson were in place at the desk they shared, she on the phone and he on his laptop. He couldn't help but be proud of the team. They'd crack this murder. A hearty hello sure to cause Nelson to jump caught in his throat as the phone on his desk rang. He reached to grab it.

"Yes, this is Marlowe. What? I see. Yes, on my way."

Noticing the concerned grimace he wore, Morven gently spoke. "What is it, Marlowe?"

"Chester Rowan. Sarah says he's missing. And she found blood on their driveway."

8

By the time Marlowe pulled his car into a space about half a block from the Rowan-Sykes Tudor-esque house, the police presence was already in full effect. Multiple marked cars parked in front of the house, the driveway had been taped off, and officers milled about. It wasn't the bees on a blooming lavender bush in summer buzz that had occurred outside of the hotel when Douglas Small died, but it was enough that onlookers stalled on the sidewalks during morning dog walks, and more than a couple of faces pressed close against neighboring front windows.

In a twist of weather fate that so often happened in the City, yesterday's gloomy skies were replaced by a crisp, sunny fall palate where blue skies and sun dominated completely. A wisp of a breeze trailed through neighborhood trees, causing the occasional leave to drift down like a small ship letting a mild memory of current decide its fate. A beautiful day.

He'd decided to come alone, leaving the rest of the team focused on the interviews talked over the night before. Douglas Small's murder couldn't be backburnered. If Chester Rowan's body was found, that might change. This might just turn out to be a domestic squabble that led to a husband taking a night off, or it could be a missing person. Or it could be worse. He'd called the forensic company they often worked with, though they hadn't showed yet.

As they'd planned meeting up that morning, he'd called John Arthur to let him know their schedule changed. John, in his gentle garrulousness, picked up on the fact of Chester's possible disappearance. Marlowe originally tried to dissuade him, but John insisted on meeting the detective at the Rowan-Sykes house. "It's just down the street," John argued, making it sound as if they were practically neighbors. "I've already walked Ainsley. Won't take me a moment. Quick as trotting across the Midsomer Florey village green." Marlowe relented eventually. John was contracting with them, might as well take advantage of his offer to help.

Opening the Matador's door, Marlowe pulled on a sports coat the color of dried cantaloupe over his white shirt and green-and-gold checked suspenders. A red Vespa scooter reminding him of those thickening the streets of Florence pulled up, backing in in front of the car. John nearly jumped off the scooter, putting down the kickstand and removing a black helmet, his slightly less bald than Marlowe's head sparkling. He had on a black and white striped hoodie, blue shorts, and green knee socks with pictures of foxes in boxes on them.

"Marlowe." John said. Turning the scooter key, he popped the black seat up, revealing a storage compartment under it. Pulling hat, cell phone, and wallet out of it, they were instantly replaced by his helmet and a pair of tight black gloves he'd been wearing. "Thank you for inviting me. Even if it's not a jolly occasion."

Did I invite him? Marlowe thought, before replying, "Didn't know you were a scooter person."

"Felt it'd be quicker to the scene, easier to navigate around cars and gawkers. Following the rules of the road naturally."

"Naturally. Hope the trip wasn't for nothing."

"Chester hasn't turned up, has he?" John didn't give space for an answer. "I doubt it. Him missing like this, probably points to this being more of a two-murder show."

"Real—" Marlowe began, but the enthusiastic John cut him off.

"Life, not TV, I know." He smiled, tucked his blue baseball cap over his head, and pulled a notebook out of his pocket. "Shall we visit the scene of the crime. Or possible crime."

"We shall." Marlowe couldn't fault John's energy. He hoped he'd have the same at John's age.

A white forensics van pulled up while they were talking, blocking half of the street. Marlowe saw an officer head that way, so kept shepherding John toward the house. The whole yard was blocked by one line of tape, the empty driveway another. Walking up to the tape directly in front of the house, an officer he didn't know came to stop them.

John waved. "Morning, Officer. Don't worry, we're like the police."

"We are," Marlowe's voice bellowed, a bit like a tired bull, "actually the police. Or I am. Detective Marlowe. This is John Arthur, a civilian contractor aiding us currently."

"Yes, sir." The officer saluted. He had a deep cleft in his chin, as if someone had gripped it tightly. "Officer Warner. First on the scene."

"Any word of Mr. Rowan?"

"Not yet, Detective. We're doing some door-to-door. Blood was discovered on the driveway; we'll get forensics on it. Mrs. Sykes called it in."

"Got it. Nice work. Is she . . ."

"Inside, Detective."

"We'll head that way. John, you coming?" He'd noticed John inching in the direction of the activity on the driveway.

"Right behind you. After one more question for Office Warner. Any cars missing?"

"No, um, sir. We checked with the wife. All accounted for."

"Thanks." John pulled up the tape they stood in front of. "Shall we?"

As often when he thought John wasn't paying attention, Marlowe realized his error. "Onwards." Marlowe ducked under the tape, followed by John. For being in his sixties, he managed to maneuver under the tape smoothly as a gymnast, while still holding it.

They passed another officer at the bottom of the stairs leading up to the porch, and had nearly reached the door when it opened. Sarah stepped out onto the porch.

"Are you the detectives? I could have proofed maritozzi in the time it took you to get here." She wore a black housecoat with orange tigers over black lounge pants and black flats, hair pulled back achingly tight, wire glasses on, but with a visible smudge on the right lens that must have made the view blurry.

"I am Detective Marlowe, ma'am. I'm sure this is a stressful time."

"Wait." Astonishment permeated her voice like air in meringue. "Aren't you John Arthur?"

John made a mock bow. "Guilty as charged."

"I've read some of your drink writing. Not too bad. What are you doing here?"

"Drink writer by day, police—"

"Civilian," Marlowe muttered.

"Civilian police contractor by night. Or vice versa."

"John is currently assisting us, ma'am. Hopefully it's okay if he's here while we talk."

"Whatever works." Her grip on the door whitened knuckles. "I just want to find Chester."

"Shall we go inside?"

"Can we not? Feels empty as a bakery at three inside. Maybe he'll just walk up."

"Maybe. When did you notice he wasn't at home?"

"This morning. Got up to make coffee, which usually wafts into his room, waking him. Before you ask, we sleep in different rooms. He snores. Doesn't mean anything." She gave both a glare. "I checked his room, nothing. Bed was cold. Still made. Whisked the house, he wasn't anywhere, or in the yard."

"Ever happen before, him going out early?"

"Chester sleeps solidly. Even when stressed. He'd bake until noon if left to his own devices. I can't imagine what happened."

"When did you call the police?"

"At first, I wasn't too worried. Maybe he decided to take a walk. Rare occurrence, but with Douglas's death and us being at the class, we're out of sorts. Outside, I noticed a stain on the drive. That got me worried enough to call. What if someone is killing local culinary luminaries? I could be next."

"Can you think of anyone who might want to harm Chester? Or take him?"

"No, not in the least. He could be crunchy, but sweet inside. Like a lemon drop."

"Anywhere particular he might go?"

"Go? Leaving a pile of blood?" Sarah's dismissive tone cut sharp as a recently honed blade.

"We have to look at every possibility."

John stopped taking notes. "What did you have for dinner last night?"

The question caught her off guard. She paused before speaking in a less angry tone. "Not much. Too wrung out from the other night, you know. Some caciotta al tartufo and bufala mozzarella, castelvetranos, a baguette from Lake Coyote bakery. Glass of Ackerman grenache. Raspberry, cherry, little white pepper. Decent wine."

Marlowe wasn't sure of the menu items, but was glad John had diffused her. "How did Mr. Rowan appear last night?"

"Upset, as you'd expect. Nervous, oddly pacing around."

"Any calls or messages he received that seemed bothering?"

"Nothing like that rose up. I would have smelled it."

Marlowe nodded, as John spoke up. "It was common knowledge he and Douglas had a falling out."

Sarah glared. "Common knowledge. Journalist fodder. What are you trying to shake up, that he had something to do with Douglas's death?"

"Sorry." John backed up a step.

"We have to ask hard questions," Marlowe continued, "to discover what happened. Did you and Mr. Rowan have any recent arguments?"

"Am I suspect here?"

"Let's just say you're helping us with our inquiries." John's voice was low-pitched, but audible.

"You aren't even police."

Marlowe held up hand in a pacifying gesture. "Fair enough. But he is aiding us. And we have to ask questions."

"We're wasting time here on the porch. You should be out finding Chester. No more questions." She started backing in, shutting the door, but Marlowe reached a firm hand out.

"No more for now. But we will need to talk—"

"I'll bring a lawyer then," she interrupted. "We'll see about your grilling continuing." She shut the door.

John smiled. "I thought that went well."

Morven, Nelson, and Weber were at the station discussing the news.

"Another murder, and one of the class attendees." Nelson whistled.

"Not so fast." Morven felt that phrase could be used with Nelson a few times a day. "We don't even know if a crime has been committed. He could have left voluntarily."

"But the blood," Nelson protested.

"Might not even be his. Never assume. Especially this early in a case. Or cases."

"Got it, makes sense. Cases. I guess it could be unrelated. Though in a Miss Marple, they're always related."

Morven let that lie. One John Arthur was enough. "The possibility," she stressed the last word, "does mean a change up for today. Here's a new plan." She'd been sitting at her desk, stretching legs out, her chrome-colored, lightweight wool suit's creases sharp, but now walked to the board. "I'll go interview Jim and Olivia Sean. Nelson, you are on Kevin and Claire Holman. We have to stay on top of the Douglas Small case while Marlowe is out. Officer Weber, pretty long list for you." She gave the officer a questioning glance.

"No problem, Detective Morven." Weber sat at Marlowe' desk, pen poised over notebook like a raptor about to plunge.

"Can you try to reach Johnny Arris, forensics. Number in the system." Weber's head was down as she wrote, but she nodded. "We need to get some data from the Small scene, see if it helps both with our killer and with the locked office. Ask for a rush on the blood found at the Rowan house. Plus check on CC TV as mentioned, but around Rowan's too. If you can contact the officer in charge there, see if door-to-doors have turned anything up. Continue class attendee backgrounding. If that wasn't enough, track down bus routes that go near Rowan's."

Weber stopped writing. "That last one is interesting."

"Agree with that," Nelson chimed in. He had unbuttoned the coat of his sharkskin navy suit and was doing desk dips, fox-red tie flopping over on one side.

"There's a possibility Chester just left, maybe trying to avoid responsibility for his part in Douglas's death, and didn't take his own car."

Nelson jumped up. "Wait, you mean you think he is on the run because he killed Douglas and is faking being taken?"

"We need to stay open to every possibility. With information, we can theorize fully. Follow the facts."

Both replied, Nelson's "makes sense" overlapping with Weber's "got it" like synchronized swimmers with slightly different choreography.

Turning back to the board, Morven said over her shoulder, "Let's get to it."

"On it right away. I'll have my I-POA rapidly, not forgetting the ACP."

Not looking, Morven tossed back, "ACP?"

"Alibi confirmation protocol. Now that last night is part of the frame, want to check those appropriately."

"Smart, Nelson."

As they'd been talking, Weber walked over to Morven. She talked in a whisper only they could hear. "Detective Morven, a moment?"

Morven matched her volume. "Yes, Officer?"

"I, well, it's a lengthy list. I can do it, everything, but worry on timing, and on reaching out to many higher up than me. I don't want to let the team down."

Morven considered. "Officer Weber, you're doing a good job. Being in the police as a woman is tough. Being in the police in general is tough. You wouldn't have made it this far, be here helping us with this high-profile murder case, if you weren't a solid police officer. One competent and successful at her job. Don't let anyone, especially yourself, tell you you're going to let the team down. We need you to help solve this case. Or these cases. Believe in yourself."

"Thanks, Detective. That's exactly what I needed to hear."

"You're a part of the team. We support each other. Like layers in an entremet." She looked down at the slightly shorter officer seriously, then a wide smile surfaced. They both started laughing, loud enough to startle Nelson into dropping his pen.

Nelson pulled a police-issue brown Buick he'd checked out into a parking space in the lot fronting the Ovation Apartments. A mighty, sonorous name for an unobtrusive, fairly dingy concrete and steel block of eight units in the City's Second Hill district, perched on a slope between downtown and Uppercase Hill. Painted a red once probably meant to mirror a candy apple, the shine was washed-out to the point where it was closer to fruit dried by being in the sun too many days. A cement and rust walkway hovered creakily in front of the units on the second floor, a lone metal staircase leading up to it on the south side. Two units had potted plants in front, a colorful dotting of marigolds and petunias providing a lonely vibrancy to the run-down urban landscape. Another had two tricycles in front, and as he navigated around them to Number 8, the farthest unit on the top floor, he heard a baby burbling inside. Nothing was in front of 8's metal door, not even a welcome mat.

Nelson took a hearty breath, double-checked that his suit coat buttoning was perfect. With two cases, or if not two cases two suspicious happenings, he needed to be even more on top of his game. These two, Kevin and Claire, were suspects; everyone at the class had to considered in that category. His job was to win the interview, find out if they were the criminals. He climbed the stairs, then knocked on the apartment's screen door like he was hitting the hanging bag.

The chipped, red-painted door behind the screen opened, but the mesh top of the screen door, combined with the darkness behind, made it hard to see more than a vague outline. He held his badge to the door.

"Detective Nelson, City Police." He kept his voice firm.

"Right, you called. Come in, please." The voice was female, cultured. Obviously, Claire. She opened the inner door fully, unlocking the screen so he could swing it out and walk in.

She continued as he moved. "How about we chat here in the living room. It's a little crowded, but comfortable enough. We moved here only recently and are still in the process of unpacking."

The room she gestured to was much nicer than you might assume from the rattier building it sat within. Polished oak floor, recently painted walls the color of tanned leather, a color which nearly matched the buffed loveseat and recliner combination. Three canary-yellow pillows added flair, a bookshelf half full of books and half full of what appeared to be lab equipment—glass beakers, flasks, a Bunsen burner, test tubes—sat against one wall, a low-hanging, glass-topped coffee table in the room's middle, and two abstract painting slashed with reds and oranges hung on another wall. The paintings were eye-catching, and as he went to sit, they made him think of a thunderstorm lit on fire.

"One moment, Detective Nelson, let me gather Kevin. He's in the office." She walked off down what seemed a short hallway. Probably just under five and a half feet tall and 130 pounds, Claire's jeans were slightly worn, offset by a basic white corded sweater. Tightly bobbed blonde hair jogged toward gray, while evenly spaced features were highlighted by midnight-blue eyes. Her overall prettiness was offset by abundant worry lines carved into her forehead and eyes' corners.

As she returned to the living room, Nelson stood back up. Something about the intelligent way she carried herself demanded respect.

"Sorry, Detective, here we are." She walked into the room, followed by her husband. He also wore jeans, torn in one knee, and a polo shirt the color of a green fish seen through dirty water. There was a classic matinee idol handsomeness in his overall appearance—squarish jaw, head, and mouth line, full hair a rich brown—but it was if he were weighed down by double the gravity of a normal person. Shoulders sagged, the jaw that once must have jutted sagging like a sentence trailing into an ellipse, mouth pulled to a frown that never went away. He had Band-Aids right beneath knuckles on two fingers of his right hand. There was a curiously furtive or hunted air about him

"Kevin Holman, I'm Detective Nelson."

The man only nodded, but Claire said, "We can take the couch, Detective, if you don't mind the chair."

They sat, Kevin's eyes surprisingly attentive as he slouched into the couch, Claire teetering on the edge. Nelson pulled his notebook and notes out, balancing the latter on his knees. "Thank you for seeing me. We are looking into the incident of two nights ago involving Douglas Small, and wanted to ask a few questions."

"Not sure how we can help." Kevin's voice held the rasp of a smoker. Past, Nelson rapidly surmised, not seeing any ashtrays or smelling any residual smoke.

"We are happy to help if we can." Claire's smile didn't have any feeling behind it.

"Thank you. First, did you notice anything out of the ordinary that night?"

"Nothing. We were prescribed the type of cake to make before the class, received some instructional tips, then went to baking. Everyone seemed to be doing the same. Until the emergency, that is." As Claire spoke, Kevin's eyes stayed unnervingly focused on Nelson.

"And you, Mr. Holman?"

"I noticed nothing at the class. The chef was his normal blustering self."

"You didn't like Douglas Small?"

"I didn't."

"We didn't." Claire followed Kevin's short statement quickly. "Dislike him. We didn't know him, not really."

"You did know him before the class."

"A little."

Nelson nearly replied with another question, but held it back. He'd learning since joining Marlowe's team that you sometimes had to let silence do the questioning.

After five stretched seconds, Kevin spoke again. "You've probably uncovered this anyway, but quite a few years ago, my father opened a restaurant with Douglas. We knew him then. Knew, not know. Again, it has been some years."

"Your dad, Richard Holman."

"I knew you know that."

"He partnered with Douglas on his first restaurant, but that was the only one. What happened?" Nelson's inner cop sense was twitching.

"Small stole it from him, plain and simple. Not that you lot did anything."

"Stole a restaurant?"

Kevin didn't say anything, waving his hand in front of his face as if brushing off a fly. Claire replied. "They had been friends and coworkers when they decided to open that restaurant. Richard took out loans, helped design it and the menu, did construction, did everything outside of cook, put his life into it. But Douglas had a clause in the contract where he could buy him out for his original monetary contribution; a clause Richard had missed or didn't understand. When the restaurant took off after that review by Sarah Sykes, Douglas got lawyers involved and ended up with the restaurant. It destroyed Richard."

"He stole it, the crooked cook crook," Kevin snarled.

"It's the past." Claire's tone soothed. "Leave it there."

Nelson's curiosity pitched his words slightly higher than normal. "Why would you sign up for a class if you held such a grudge?"

"To show that we didn't hold a grudge, I suppose." Claire was wistful. "I somewhat wish we hadn't, but the class was fun most of the time. Douglas could be like a prescription that tastes icky, but then leads to feeling better, if that makes sense. When he wasn't preening, making the cakes was very enjoyable."

"Did you enjoy the class, Mr. Holman?"

"Wasn't my favorite. Claire made excellent cakes. Douglas was hard to stomach."

"You mentioned Sarah Sykes, do you know her?"

"She helped him steal the restaurant from my dad. That review of hers, and how she preened in the press over Douglas, gave him the ability to take it. I swore then and do now that if they hadn't hooked up, it never would have happened, and life would have been different." Instead of the anger Nelson had been getting used to, Kevin looked deflated.

"We didn't know her exactly, Detective," Claire said. "Of her, yes. She didn't know who we were."

"You both arrived early the second night and argued with Douglas. What about?" Nelson thought a quick change of direction often startled out more truthful responses.

"You pulled that piece of information out too," Kevin said like a hissing cat. "I've told you; he stole that restaurant. I wanted to call him out on it. He owes my dad, and so owes us. We should be paid."

"We happened to be early, and Kevin did dispense a little anger Douglas's way. Douglas laughed it off, and I got Kevin to calm down."

"The night of the incident, Mr. Holman, you helped break the door down to the office. Can you describe the events before and after."

Claire beat Kevin to speaking. "Louisa, sweet kid, realized Douglas's break had gone long and went to look for him. She came back worried, and the two women went to help. Then a couple of them came back, Louisa a deafening mess, almost in need of a sedative, I thought. It got confusing. A group trailed back and broke the door down. Kevin was one of them."

"Why, Mr. Holman, would you go to help someone you didn't care for?"

"Hoped to catch him doing something he shouldn't. As he probably was. He probably caused his own death."

"You said trailed back, Mrs. Holman. What did you mean?"

"What?" She was confused. "Just a word. I suppose not everyone went back at once. But Kevin and the big man, Chester, all went. Maybe others. Like I said, it was confusing."

"Did either of you visit the office earlier in the evening?"

They both shook their heads, but then Claire spoke. "We didn't visit the office, but we both went past it when visiting the facilities during cake making. I did stop for a moment at the open office right when he went back and said a few words."

"You did what?" Kevin started to rise, flopped back down.

"I wanted to apologize for the night before. Douglas seemed to have forgotten about it. He appeared to me sluggish somewhat. Insisted on me shutting the door."

Nelson's note-taking was the only sound outside of Kevin's raspy breathing. After a moment, he said, "Do you know the time of that visit?"

"Not exactly, sorry, Detective. Shortly after he went back for his break."

"See any other person back there?"

"I passed the glamorous woman, I can't recall her name, on the way to the bathroom, but that was it. Are we almost done? I think Kevin is tired. We recently had to move, and you know how unpacking is a heavy dose to swallow."

"Just another question. You mentioned Chester Rowan. Do you

know him?"

"He's married to that woman who helped Douglas. Not sure why," Kevin spit out.

Claire followed him up like a mother after a destructive child. "No, Detective, We didn't. Outside of having a few books from his press and class talk, small talk. I once thought about pitching a pharmacy book, but it didn't pan out. He didn't seem to mix well with Douglas, from the tones I overheard when they spoke at class. Is that all?"

Nelson headed toward the door before turning in a move he hoped mirrored the TV detective Columbo, a show he watched growing up when staying with his grandmother. "Just one more thing. Where were you both late last night and early this morning?"

Kevin shot out an answer. "We were here. Unpacked, slept, had coffee when we woke up." Not once in the interview had Kevin shown the vestige of a smile.

"All night?"

The man didn't reply, but after a moment, Claire did. "All night. Kevin took a walk to get some air later in the evening, as he sometimes does. Why?"

Nelson ignored her question to ask his own. "Where did you go, Mr. Holman?"

"Around. Walked around, nowhere specific."

"Did you see anyone?"

"Lots of people, here and there. Didn't talk to anyone. Just saw them."

Nelson knew that was all he'd get at this time. "That's all for today. We probably will want to talk to you again in the future."

After they'd left the Sykes-Rowan house, John convinced Marlowe they absolutely had to visit the nearby Rosellini's bakery, which baked, he would swear on his badge when he got one, the best croissants in the city.

Taking advantage of the clear weather, they sat outside of the bakery at the table farthest from the door. Marlowe had to admit John was right.

"This may be the finest croissant ever." He took another bite. Crispy outside, tiny bit of caramelization underneath, unbelievably feathery buttery soft inside. If there was a bakery at the afterlife watering hole, this is what they'd serve.

John peeled the crispiest top ridge of croissant off the top. He, like Marlowe, tended to save it for last. "They never disappoint. I'd eat one every day if my waistline would allow it. Though there are a number of rotund detectives. Poirot's egg shaped. Hathaway's a pear. The good Father Brown's never turned down a strawberry scone. Even Morse likes his real ale enough to keep him from being called slim."

Marlowe took another bite, savoring each crumb, saying nothing.

John managed to take a bite while talking. "Wonder what they would make of this morning's work. Sarah herself a suspect."

Marlowe didn't reply. He only had a third of his croissant left. He held the remaining bite in front of his face, as if missing the part he'd eaten.

"Perhaps," John continued, half to himself. "Without a body, it's hard to nail down. Chester could be a suspect, on the run. That blood. That locked room, still niggling at me. Could be there's an extra set of keys. Who might know that?"

Marlowe pulled his eyes from the croissant. "Chelsea Hinckley could."

"She could, at that. Louisa?"

"Not a bad thought. Need to talk to her again. Everyone we've talked to, actually, with last night's disappearance straying into the case. If it has."

"Has to be related. The second crime in a show is always related to the first."

Marlowe took his last bite, then sighed as if he'd heard bad news about an old friend.

John went on. "I know someone's been brutally murdered, but I'd really miss doing this, talking over the case. And Chester *was* connected to Douglas. Sarah too."

"We're just fishing."

"As Doctor DeBryn said in *Endeavor*, 'Love and fishing. Sooner or later, it all comes down to the same thing. The one that got away.'"

"If the cows are lying down, the fish will not bite." Marlowe could obscurely quote too.

"That's deep, Marlowe. Not sure what it means."

Marlowe pushed himself up away from the table. "I might not either. Maybe if we need the fish to bite to ensure our perpetrator or perpetrators don't get away, we'd better stop eating and hit the trail again. Though I may need another croissant. Gonna be a long day."

9

Morven parked in front of the condominium complex where Jim and Olivia lived. A gleaming white building in a neighborhood southwest of downtown, not far from a massive church a past case centered around. The Case of the Retired Reverend, as her now-teammate John Arthur called it. The condo building was broken into ground floor units with small patches of yard, and units above with brief balconies either covered in plants or with three-legged barbecue grills and chairs. The Sean unit was a ground-floor number, with white fence matching the condo itself in brightness squaring the yard. Tucking a stray strand of hair back into the bun pulled tight to her neck, she walked up to the gate, a "swack, swack, swack" noise echoing as she approached.

Peering over the fence to try and ascertain the source of the noise, she saw an immaculate lawn, grass like a green carpet in the day's unexpected sunshine. It was broken only by a sidewalk in the middle leading up to a black metal and glass front door, a single Magnolia tree on the side, one the same height as the door. A rainbow ring of chrysanthemums and pansies encircled the tree. Or partially encircled it, as currently a boy, probably five, with brilliantly blond hair was knocking off blossoms methodically with a stick. The boy wore shorts the color of the sky, a plain white T-shirt stained with what appeared to be raspberry jam, no shoes. He'd managed to destroy about a quarter of them when Morven gave a knock on the wood fence. The noise caused him to quickly drop the stick and jump back from the tree, exclaiming, "I didn't do it."

"Hello," Morven replied. "I'm pretty sure you did. But I'm here to talk to your parents."

The relief on his face was obvious. "They're in there." He thumbed in the direction of the door, then yelled, "Dad!"

She reached the door as it opened, the boy skipping around the other side of the tree to pick up his stick. A man filled most of the space where the door had been. Six foot four, pushing 250 pounds carried in a pear-ish shape, he had thinning hair the color of a baby deer, the balding contradicting a surprisingly boyish face. Pudgy cheeks, thin mouth slightly open with expansive teeth, runny nose, and light-brown eyes, currently reddened as if he'd been crying. He wore gray sweatpants and matching sweatshirt with emerald-green sandals.

Stretching out a plump hand, he said, "Detective Morven, correct? I'm Jim."

She shook his hand, which was dry as paper. "Correct. Thank you for meeting with me. I have a few questions."

"Come on in." He lumbered back. "Olivia's here." He didn't say a word to the boy.

She entered into an open-plan space, the nearest section a living area, the farther section a kitchen-diner, the whole room starkly modern in appearance. In the living area, white walls surrounded black furniture that included two couches in the center and one against the front wall, a pair of sparsely populated bookcases, and an abstract sculpture much like a mutated jellyfish in appearance on a square pedestal. A picture of what seemed a salmon steak in a cloud hung on one wall. From what she could see, the kitchen glimmered with shiny high-end appliances and silver fixtures surrounded by granite countertops that may have cost as much as a car.

She was surprised by the lack of family pictures. Not a one that she could see. And by the lack of toys, an absence contrasting with most houses she'd been in that had a child as a resident. A woman lounged on one of the couches, legs pulled up under her. She didn't get up as Morven moved nearer, but did give a smile, then spoke.

Her voice purred. "Detective. I'm Olivia. Forgive me remaining seated. I've the most delicious spot and don't want to ruin it. Please, sit opposite." She motioned to the couch across with surprisingly lengthy, tapering fingers that would have easily encircled most hands. Wearing designer jeans, a cashmere sweater the color of oak leaves in fall, and no shoes, she gave off a luxurious resting impression. Amber-hued hair hung down straight past her shoulders, framing an oval face with full lips, high cheekbones, slightly pointed nose, and blue eyes so light they were nearly white. There was something peculiar about her. Pretty, but peculiar. It took Morven a moment to realize Olivia had a slightly larger space than most between eyes and eyebrows, the latter sculptured very thin, a purplish eye shadow between. She also was not the sort of person who was unable to look others in the face, instead staring as if trying to read their innermost thoughts.

Morven sat, as Jim moved to stand behind Olivia, who said smoothly, "Lovely suit, Detective. Who knew the police had such style."

"Thank you. And thank you for talking to me about the incident the other night."

"It was awful," Jim nearly wailed. "I still can't believe he's gone."

"You'll have to forgive Jim. He knew Douglas, in the past."

"A tragic event is very difficult, I appreciate." Morven decided to ease into the night itself. "You grew up with Douglas Small, Mr. Sean?"

He wiped a hand over his eyes. "We knew each other since we were nine or ten. Together we climbed hill and trees, and learned of love with our ABCs."

Morven wasn't completely sure, but she thought he'd just quoted an old song. "Had you stayed in touch?"

He sighed. "I always told him to think of me and I'd be there, but we didn't see each other as much as I'd have liked. I got into selling kitchen appliances for Minus-1 and knew he'd end up in the industry. That brought us back together. But not too much wine and not too much song for us lately. Now he's gone."

"Mrs. Sean, did you know Douglas Small previously?"

Olivia played abstractedly with her hair. "Not really. I met him a few times here and there. And then once Jim and I got together, we went to his restaurants. Had a few cocktails."

"How did you end up deciding to take the cake class?"

Jim began crying, so Olivia replied. "It was Jim's idea mostly. He thought it would be a good way to see Douglas, spend some time together."

"Did you enjoy it?"

"Enough." The woman said it as if the class had been a chore one was destined to do. "I'm not devoted to baking. But one has to pass the time."

Jim wiped tears away again, replacing them with a wan smile. "Olivia is a great baker. I'm all fumble fingers. Awkward as a mule. When we used to play as kids, I'd end up with the skinned knees and Douglas the skinned heart."

"What do you mean?"

"He was always the favorite with the girls we grew up with. Guessing that never changed. Handsome devil, my friend Douglas." He seemed about to cry again.

"Did either of you notice anything strange the other night at the class before the incident? Or at previous classes?"

Olivia blew on the nails of one hand. "Nope. Solely nights of mixing batter."

"I talked to Douglas a bit that night," Jim said. "He was doing a great job, great teacher. Made everybody bloom in their baking, like spring was in the air when he was around. I can't . . ."

"It is difficult, Mr. Sean, I'm sure, but we can use your help. Did either of you spend time with Douglas in his office, that night or previously?"

"We suspects, Detective?" Olivia didn't seem bothered by the idea.

"Just getting background information."

"Naturally. I believe we both had been back to discuss cakes. Everybody did. Carried in the cost of the class."

"I would have paid three times as much for more time with Douglas." Jim smacked his hand for emphasis. "We had joy, we had fun." Morven was now completely sure he was quoting. "But now he's gone. I went back to talk with him every chance I could. Without interrupting his downtime. He deserved that, working so hard."

"Did you notice any friction between Douglas and any other students?"

Olivia's voice was playfully low. "Friction? Guessing you mean unfriendly friction. To be honest, not sure everyone liked Dougie as well as Jim. The bartender, the publisher and his wife, the ex-partner's son, even the dishwasher, all seemed, shall we say, glary toward him at some point."

"That's interesting. You must have spent some time watching the others Mrs. Sean."

"Olivia never misses anything. She's got a sharp eye. That's why she's an amazing designer."

"Thanks, Jimbo. But making cakes isn't too difficult, and a girl's gotta stay entertained somehow." Olivia's voice became higher, girlish, near the sentence's end.

"Goodbye to you, my friend Douglas." Jim turned toward the kitchen, crying again.

"Forgive my husband. He's emotional." They were an odd couple, him crying, her as calm and cool as a cat. "I don't believe either of us saw anything. I made cake, Jim mooned over Douglas."

"Just a few more questions. Mr. Sean, you came downstairs after?"

Olivia replied as Jim was crying. "He did, haphazardly in a way. Like a boy who has seen a car accident. Looking for an adult. Which I suppose the police stood in for."

"What about you?"

"Me? There was so much commotion, hard to recall. I eventually went back to see in the office. Tried to keep people out. Felt a cooler head should direct traffic."

"The hills we climbed as kids in all seasons are just memories in the sun." Jim cried hard as he talked, then removed a dingy handkerchief that had probably once been white but was now shaded to used dishwater and blew massively. Morven wasn't sure she'd ever seen a witness cry quite as demonstratively.

Olivia leaned toward Morven, whisperingly conspiratorially. "Maybe we tailor this convo for today. Jim is so blustery, it's giving me a headache. I can walk you out." She stood as she finished.

Morven followed suit, knowing Jim would be useless and wanting to take advantage of the chance to talk to Olivia alone. By the time they reached the front door, Jim had moved to sprawl on the couch, a pillow over his face. Outside, the two women walked to the gate. Morven saw the boy again, hiding behind the tree.

"Not sure if you saw him, but I believe your son is over there."

Olivia appeared confused for a moment, then snapped her fingers. "Little Willie. Hard to keep track of at times." Turning, she caught his eye. "Head inside. Upstairs." Willie zipped by, swinging the door shut behind him and saying nothing. Nearly all the flowers were missing blooms.

Olivia opened the gate, backing out of the way. "Energetic kid. Hopefully we answered your questions."

"Most," said Morven, pausing. "I have one or two more for you."

Olivia didn't blink as she held Morven's gaze.

"First—"

"Was I having an affair with Douglas?"

"Were you?" Even the steady Morven was thrown off balance by Olivia's blunt interruption.

"No," she replied wistfully. "I'm guessing the dishwasher saw us kissing. Probably wished it was him. But kissing was it, though Douglas was chasing after me like a hungry dog, if that's not too insulting to dogs. Maybe we were in a nearly serious clench once or twice in his office, but nothing scandalous. A girl's gotta keep herself entertained, you know."

Morven always felt that real, hard selfishness was written on someone's face if you were attentive. But with Olivia it was hard to tell. "There was nothing between you and Douglas before the class?"

"Nothing more than the same. I crave fun sometimes. I have to do what's good for me." She licked her lips. "Not sure that's a crime."

"Did Jim have any inkling?"

Olivia rolled her eyes. "I doubt it. Who cares? He loved Douglas so much, he'd probably be happy."

"Mrs. Sean—"

"Olivia, Detective, please."

Morven ignored the plea for informality, struck by an idea. "You are somewhat hard to get background on. Do you mind telling me what your maiden name was?"

It was the first question that had knocked the cool out of Olivia, as she visible clenched. "What? Do I have to answer that? I can call my lawyer."

"You have every right to have an attorney present if you so desire. I'll give you some time to think about it, then we can talk again."

As she left, Olivia still stood holding on to the gate like it was a life raft, staring off into an ocean of space.

Marlowe headed to do his interview solo.

John went back home, as Ainsley would be getting antsy. Not that she couldn't be home alone for a fair amount of hours, but he began feeling a bad dog parent if out *too* many hours. A single dog and a single parent probably always equaled mother-henning. Anyway, he needed some time to think after the morning's scene visit and chat with Marlowe. *I'll never be an action detective*, he thought, jumping past one step on the way to his front door. Too old, knees too creaky. He could hear Ainsley barking.

Soon, they were in the backyard under perfectly blue fall skies playing a rousing game of fetch-tug, Ainsley so excited that she started barking happily at him when he once didn't throw it fast enough. Her high-pitched yapping bounced between their backyard and the surrounding neighbors like a hummingbird of sound. Within a few seconds, he heard other dogs returning the barking, as if a dog telegraph spooled around the neighborhood. Which it did, in a way. For a moment, Ainsley stopped running, listening to the other dogs, before sending up one more bark of her own. Then, back to the game.

They played for an active ten minutes, then on one return trip from the side yard where he had tossed the ball, she dropped it without waiting for him to chase her. Her tongue out panting and sporting a doggy smile so wide it might have brightened a dark room, she stood in front of her outside water dish. The water currently in it slightly dirty, she gave the dish an unsatisfied look. She was as picky about water as a food critic about underdone pasta.

"Quitting time, Ains." Picking up the dish, John tossed the water on the lawn, taking the dish to the tap on the house's back wall. He filled the dish, set it on the wooden deck, then sat on the deck himself. Leaning his head back, he felt the morning sun, offset by a coolish breeze wafting in as if pulled on a string. What a day. What a day for a crime. If this morning's disappearance was an actual crime and not a criminal skipping town. It felt off to him, that scene, though he wasn't sure specifically why. The blood in the driveway seemed too obvious, too pat, as if set up. Was it even Chester's blood?

And what was he missing about Douglas's murder? Ainsley flopped down beside him, dripping water onto his leg. He absent-mindedly scratched her behind an ear. He was missing something about the Douglas scene, or forgetting something. He knew that. Even the finest detectives, even Sherlock, missed a crucial point early in the story. Or if not missed (he didn't want Sherlock's ghost haunting him for considering the master detective could miss something at a scene), a fact not yet clicked into place like that last piece in a puzzle.

It wouldn't hurt to have more facts. Getting more of a dedicated inside view into the police process, he realized how much those facts could be dependent on others—forensics, pathology, officers whose names were farther down in the credits. So many TV detectives, police and amateur, armchair and badged, were-lone wolf types on the outside, but most realized they needed help at some point. Even if solely a person to bounce ideas back and forth with, as well as those outside fact un-earthers working down scene or off scene. Maybe they garnered merely a moment of screen time, maybe a full second billing, but the extended team was important.

Take his newest favorite British TV mysteries. In *Ludwig*, hilarious genius David Mitchell plays a puzzle creator who has to imitate his police detective twin brother when the latter vanishes. He's genius at puzzles, but wouldn't make it through the first season without both his brother's fellow officers and his sister-in-law and nephew. And in *Death Valley*, where bouncy, apple-cheeked Gwyneth Keyworth plays DS Janie Mallowan, Mallowan was stuck in a case until she ran into the legendary Timothy Spall, playing retired actor John Chapel. An actor famous for once playing a popular detective on TV, that background giving him insight into character and motivation. "I'm a highly skilled emotional empath he says," providing the ideal balance for her ambitious detective.

"Gwyneth was a long favorite of your mother and I," John said to Ainsley, who ignored him. "We even saw her in *As You Like It* at the Globe. It's moments like this I really miss her. She could often point out the murderer in a show long before me, picking up on some small clue I'd overlooked." He scratched the dog silently, painful loneliness coming over him like a massive wave, soaking his every pore, causing his body to close inward like it was in a vise, before receding slowly. "At least I have you." His voice had become softer, a flutter causing his last word to break. The change from his normal buoyancy caused Ainsley to raise her head, like most dogs, alert to changes in those nearest them. She stretched, stood, and without warning licked him on the nose.

He rubbed her head heartily. "Ainsley, you always know what to do. Dog instinct. I'll bet you and your dog pals could solve any case faster." She went to lick him again, muffling his words. "I'm all right, Ains. Just missing. You know." That feeling, that loneliness, must be permeating those around Douglas, and Chester too. They may not have been *the* victim, but they were victims. What did Professor T say? 'Crime is inherently traumatic, both victim and witness may fall foul of the hypothalamic pituitary adrenal excess.' That last part may have gotten too scientific, but both victim and witnesses did go through trauma. Solving the case wouldn't make that trauma, or loneliness, go away. But it might lessen it.

"Ainsley." He stood. "I think I'm going to have to go again. Just for a bit. I'll leave you with treats." She jumped at the T word, trotting toward the back door, tail swaying as if chasing away flies. He continued talking as they walked. "I should head back to the station and take another look at the interview and scene notes. And"—he opened the door, grinning nearly as wide as Ainsley had been earlier—"they might have my badge ready."

When Marlowe excited his car downtown, he noticed a few stray croissant flakes on his shirt, nearly identical in color to his pants. Brushing them off with a regret they hadn't made it to his mouth, he realized he should probably do the same to his mustache. A good idea, as it harbored a number of croissant crumbs too. *Don't want to be messy as a muskrat*, he thought, adjusting his suspenders so they were back in parallel positioning, having wandered off sloping stomach sides.

He'd corralled an interview with Chelsea Hinkley right after he called. Lucky break, as her office was in a building two blocks up from the hotel where Douglas had been discovered, which situated it on his route back to the station. Traffic surprisingly mellow on the north to south route, he'd arrived with five minutes to spare. Leaning on the car door, he took a gander at the building in front of him. Four stories, red brick, carrying an older-City charm unmatched by some of the towering steel and iron siblings surrounding it. Part of the building housed the original Douglas Small restaurant, Small's, accessible by a glass door in the southern-most corner. Through a series of stretching glass windows, he could see the backs of bottles and glassware, the restaurant bar running inside in front of the windows. Right after the last restaurant window, a small glass door led into the first Small Bakery location. It catered to take-out orders only, without even a set of stools. First famous for a decadently lush coconut cream pie, one slice of which could add inches to your waistline. Or so the story went.

A pink curtain draped behind the bakery windows, no interior light visible. The restaurant, too, he noticed, gave off no light from within. Both had what appeared from his distance to be typing paper sized notes with black writing on them taped to the doors. He walked closer to check out the bakery sign. It said in block lettering: "Closed due to unforeseen circumstances. Please check back another day. Our apologies." Douglas Small's death was probably well-known already, as the City's news folks weren't known for their reticence when reporting about famous figures. So perhaps there weren't too many disappointed want-to-be customers wandering up.

He walked up to a wooden door just past the bakery. Small Enterprises in exaggeratedly genteel silver lettering took up the middle, with a set of square windows above. He tried the door, which was locked, then noticed a bell and intercom. Ringing the bell, a woman's voice soon followed. "I'm sorry, we are closed, today."

"Detective Marlowe, City Police. I have an appointment."

He didn't receive a reply, but heard a buzz, and trying the door again, found it open. It led straight into a set of dark, creaky wooden stairs, at the top of which a hall stretched out like a wooden tunnel—wood-paneled walls, wood ceiling, wooden doors dotting the sides. The first door was open, and he heard typing within. Stepping through into a square office with walls he'd call puce, a young woman with a cockatoo crest of blonde hair featuring neon-green slashes in it sat behind a wooden desk.

She typed furiously in front of a monitor, long nails clicking keys. Outside of two chairs against one wall and a bookcase filled with Douglas Small books, the desk was the only furniture. Two massive framed pictures of Douglas, one with him holding a whisk, one with a knife resembling that found in his back, adorned the walls. A door stood shut in the corner.

The woman looked up, chewing gum furiously as if in a contest. "You must be the police. Sorry about the lock up downstairs. We're all a jumble, as you might believe."

"No problem. Are you—"

She cut him off. "Nope, I am not. She is through there. And expecting you." A cell phone on the desk starting vibrating. She picked it up with one hand, while thumbing as if hitchhiking toward the door with the other. "Go on in," she said, followed rapidly by, "Hello, Small Enterprises," into the phone.

He left her to it, stepping through the door into a smaller office. Its walls were completely bare outside of a massive dry erase calendar on one, filled with notes in various colors of highlighter, words like little neon signs. While the desk in the front room had been plain, the type you'd find in any 1950s office, the one in this room was ornate—heavily stained oak the color of midnight, carved leaves adorning the sides, a carved lion's head majestic on the middle panel.

The desk wouldn't have been out of place in a 19th century French noble's dressing room, which made the laptop and screen on top of it stand out garishly. There were modern file holders on each end, and a massive ceramic crock near the computer. The crock had Sookie's Dog Biscuits printed on it, but it would have been impossible for any treats to have fit amongst the jammed array of pens and highlighters. A plain-white coffee mug next to a matching plate with half a bagel on it, a full half inch of cream cheese smeared over the top, sat next to the keyboard.

Chelsea Hinkley stood behind the desk, reaching out a hand. As tall as Marlowe and built like an ex-rugby player, she wore well-worn jeans and a cable knit sweater the color of bay leaves. Long, flaxen hair cascaded onto square shoulders. An ample mouth seemingly caught in a permanent wane smile sat below green eyes and aquiline nose.

"Detective Marlowe, I presume." Her voice sounded slightly stretched, as if she'd spent many hours talking.

"Yes, ma'am. Mrs. Hinkely?"

Her hand was soft, but gripped his tightly before letting go.

"Miss, actually."

"My mistake. Thank you for seeing me. I'm sure it's an emotional time."

"It is. Busy, too. Please, sit." She motioned to the single wooden chair in front of the desk. "Not the most comfortable chair, apologies."

Sitting, he agreed internally with her sentiment. The chair was small, and bumpy in a way that no wooden chair he'd ever had the pleasure to sit on could have matched, as if it was made from an unsanded very gnarled tree. He found it impossible to find a spot to settle in to. It seemed designed to promote fidgeting. He couldn't help himself saying as he tried to find an easy spot, "It isn't at that. Are you trying to shy away visitors?"

Her smiled widened. "In a way. It gets busy."

"I'll try not to take up much of your time."

"No, take as long as you need. Stand if you need to. I won't feel intimated." He was sure she wouldn't, already gathering the idea that nothing intimidated Chelsea.

"I'll try and stay saddled. First, how long have you been working with Douglas Small, and what exactly is your role? Assistant, I know, but clarity might help."

She took a sip of coffee. "Thirteen years to the month. I started to be his personal assistant when he was expanding rapidly and having trouble keeping track of his exploding calendar. This was about six months after the first Small Bakery opened. You know, making and helping him keep appointments, keeping abreast of his email and correspondence, general PA factotum stuff. But my role expanded, and I began helping more with the restaurants, staffing and taking care of employee issues, running the majority of his communication, sitting in on meetings around the buildings. General manager, really."

"Pretty big ranch to wrangle."

Her eyes twinkled as she caught his. "It is. Sounds like you used to be a cowboy."

It was hard not be more casual with her. """Only in dreams, Miss Hinckley. Is it a difficult role?"

"Difficult." She took a bite of her bagel, thinking while chewing. "In many ways. Lots to do, for one, but I enjoy that. Firing people, or having to have hard conversations with employees or partners, I don't enjoy. But it's part of it."

"Working with Douglas?"

"Can be difficult. We get along—got along, I'll have to learn to say—but he was a teenager emotionally at times. Genius in the kitchen, charismatic in interviews, savvier businessman than you might think. I had to keep him on the straight and narrow, firmly, at times."

"What do you mean, straight and narrow?"

"He could overstretch his ideas. Try to much, believe he was infallible. That kind of thing."

Marlowe shifted in the chair for the twentieth time, still not finding a serene spot. "I realize you might not be able to say, but how is Small Enterprises doing financially?"

"The accountants are next door. Well, not today." She sighed. "Hard to fathom. You can check with them for specifics, but I'd say fine. We'd made some missteps, but the core restaurants are full."

"How did Douglas get along with the staff?"

"That's an intricate question. For many, he was a celebrity figure more than anything. Each restaurant now has its own chef and floor manager. Bakeries too." Chelsea paused as if searching her mind for a precise description. "He'd float around like a politician when visiting, shaking hands, kissing babies. Certain times, he'd be more hands on, openings, events. Unless he took a special interest in them, he didn't have extensive time with employees, if that makes sense."

Marlowe nodded, raising his right leg off the floor, as it had fallen asleep. "Any issues with specific employees you recall?"

"You mean HR problems." She didn't seem surprised by the question.

"Were there problems that HR came into?"

"Like I said, Douglas could be a bit of a teenager. I don't want to downplay anyone's experience, and know the restaurant world can be a harrowing place. Also, you could talk to HR. Or the company's legal counsel, I suppose." The twinkle in her eye caught his again and held it. "They might tell you that he was never convicted of anything. I did have to have some serious talks with him. He could be a… rake might be the best word. Since he became divorced. Like many famous people."

"Only since becoming divorced?"

"You might have to ask the ex on that, Detective." She took another bite of bagel, finishing it off and chewing with relish. He tended to think anyone who reveled in eating that much couldn't be a bad person. A supposition that had gotten him in trouble in the past.

Marlowe bowed slightly, as if a lawyer facing a judge who just made a ruling. "Will do. You corralled Douglas's email, correct? And phone messages?"

"And phone in general." Noticing his confused look, she explained. "Years ago, Douglas had a slight issue with a phone and pictures on it. You can guess. Teenage boy, as I said. Especially with women. Unless you had a solely business relationship with him, he I felt saw women as objects, indistinct. That phone incident almost turned into a PR problem, but it was smoothed out before blowing up. Since, he never liked to even carry a phone. He had one, but I was in charge of it, as well as email and post. Kept things businesslike on them. He wasn't a technophobe, per se, but didn't want to deal."

"I understand. Not a big techie myself."

"Since meeting you, Detective, I believe it."

"Recently, any threats, things of that nature on his phone or email?"

"Nothing out of the norm. Someone of Douglas's stature is going to get electronic stalkers, mostly passive." She paused again, this time taking a sip of coffee.

Marlowe let the silence descend. It was more comfortable than the chair, and he felt she had more on the topic. In a minute, she spoke up.

"There were some messages via the online channels that veered into death threat territory. I don't manage those, but Bea, who does, you met her outside, she mentioned them. Things like, 'you deserve to die you thief' and 'you'll get yours creep,' that kind of thing. Douglas never glanced at social stuff, unless it was an article praising him. Should I have alerted the police?"

"Not necessarily. The online world's a cantankerous place. But if you could round the most violent messages up and send them, that would be helpful now."

"We can. Anything to help."

"Do you have much to do with the classes?"

She laughed lowly. "I have something to do with everything Small related. But not directly. Why?"

"Was curious if anyone in the recent cake class had reached out through the rivers."

"I think you mean channels."

Marlowe held his hands up as if to say, what can you do?

"I'm not sure on that. Wait, Sarah Sykes had reached out wanting a meeting with Douglas recently. He told me to decline, that he could see her at the class. And the guy he knew as a kid was there. Jim Sean. He emailed a lot, messages as if between close pals. But Douglas never emailed back. Do you think one of the class attendees is responsible? I don't know much of the specifics of Douglas's. . ." She faded.

"Sorry, Miss Hinckley. This is tough to discuss. Only a bit more."

"You can call me Chelsea, Detective." The smile crept back.

"Chelsea." He didn't usually interview with first names, but liked the sound of hers. "We are following all lines of inquiry, and we're nearly done here. Speaking of the class, did you work with Martin Allen?"

"Martin was at the class?" She was either genuinely surprised, or an awfully polished actor. "Didn't realize. I did interact with Martin. And loved his margaritas. Most make them poorly. When he left, the scene he created about the book recipes, not a fun day. The point he made, recipes as IP, is hard to deal with legally. He was definitely a few levels beyond angry. Douglas was going to call the police, but I happened to be at Smalls and talked him out of it, and Martin into leaving. Surprised he'd want to see Douglas."

"The office Douglas used at the classroom, you know it?"

"Sure. Is that where . . ." She trailed off once more, her solidness cracking for a moment.

"Sorry, tough thing to talk about. My question—keys for that office. Douglas have the only one?"

She straightened. "Yes, he made a point of it. His retreat he called it. A sanctum sanctorum where he could think uninterrupted. We had that space many years before the classes started, before he decided what to do with it. He always insisted on having the only key, then left his keyring lying everywhere. Typical Douglas."

Marlowe had taken a notebook from his back pocket early in the interview, and found balancing it while at the same time balancing on what he called to himself The World's Most Uncomfortable Chair™, nearly impossible. His writing covered the page like chicken scratches. "Speaking of the past, do you keep employment records going back all the way?"

"All the way to when Small's opened originally? I wish. Things were very haphazard." There was a "before me" implied, but she didn't add it. "When I started installing more organization, we definitely had hard copies on everyone. Before then, less organized. Then a fire took the hard copies out, so I moved to digital. Would you like to review them? Or have remote access? I might be able to work that out."

Remote access sound like a horse on a very long lead to him. "That'd be awful handy, that access."

"Have someone call, we can figure it out." She leaned her arm over the monitor.

"Sorry, a couple more then I'm out of your hair. What will happen now as far as the restaurants and enterprise?"

"It'll keep going, if that's what you're wondering. Douglas was the figurehead, but there are other investors I'll have to meet with. There's no specific person who can fill his chef's jacket, but Small's as a whole is too big to fail. Even without him. Some restructuring, moving people into different roles. Maybe some of his competitors will try to pick up parts. Early days."

"Who is the biggest competitor?"

"There is no one quite of his stature. Or wasn't. Joel Towell is next perhaps."

"Ah. Met him."

"His charms escape me."

Conspiratorially, Marlowe said, "I can see that. Of everyone we've lit on—employees, competitors, class attendees—anyone stand out to you as wishing Douglas harm?" He leaned to the very edge of the chair, attempting comfort once more. And failing.

"Douglas could be a diva. Like royalty, above the commoners. Part of my job was bringing him back to earth. That attitude leads to resentment. But killing him? Nobody I can think of at a glance. I'll dredge back through recent emails, double check social channels. If I find anything, I'll reach out."

Marlowe stood, his body nearly cheering at him in happiness at leaving that chair. He audibly exhaled.

She also stood, reaching out her hand again. "Sorry again about the chair."

He shook it, surprised at how firm a shake she held. "I survived." He put his notebook back in a pocket, removing a card, which he handed her. "Here's my number. Please call if you think of anything. And if you could send along those messages, very helpful."

She took it, reading, eyes twinkling like stars in the night. "Not sure how I missed it earlier. Marlowe. Like Bogie in *The Big Sleep*. Quite a name for a detective to live up to."

Pulling the door to the outside office partially open, he turned. "Those are harsh words to throw at a man, especially when he's walking out of your office."

As he left, her rich laugh reverberated in the room.

10

John's badge wasn't ready when he made it to the station. Officer Coleman, luckily commandeering the front desk once more, did score him a temporary pass after a few minutes of badinage between the two. He wouldn't let John wander the halls unescorted, however, so John waited in the lobby for an escort. He couldn't chat with Office Coleman, as a short man in a canary-yellow shirt with "If Wishes Were Horses" printed in black scrolling letters on it had wandered in, his beard stretching to the tops of the letters. He'd stopped in to report his car stolen. John couldn't help eavesdropping and heard a tale of bar-hopping with friends through the streets of Settler's Square the night before, leaving the car to take a taxi home after the man realized he'd had a few too many martinis. You couldn't fault that choice, but perhaps the fact that he couldn't remember where he'd parked in the first place wasn't as commendable. John stood and started heading their direction, sure he could help the man pin down the correct street through order and method.

Pausing, he thought, *'It's the hedgehog all over again,'* a quote he remembered from a recent series of the show *Shetland*, about a character who wanted to help any creature in trouble. Maybe Officer Coleman could take care of it without his interference after all. He started to sit back down, when the door at the rear of the room opened.

Weber walked through it with a slightly surprised look. She shook it off, replacing it with a more businesslike demeanor. "Mr. Arthur. I took a call at Detective Marlowe's desk that you were here. None of the detectives are in currently."

"Office Weber." He beamed. There was something about the young officer that seemed familiar. "Thank you for coming down. I was hoping to review some case notes. Maybe you can help."

She considered for a moment. With none of the detectives around, should a civilian be allowed to browse notes? It felt somewhat like letting a dog off leash into a neighbor's yard. On the flip side, Detective Marlowe appeared to put some faith into John's assisting. She decided to take the plunge.

"Surely, Mr. Arthur. They should be back soon. I can take you up." She caught Officer Coleman's eye and gave him a thumbs-up. His mustache moved as he smiled before going back to taking the car-less man virtually through various streets he might have parked on the night before.

Soon, the two were up in the big detective room. John pulled a third chair over to Marlowe's desk, next to Weber on the wall side.

"I hope I'm not interrupting you. What are you currently working on?" John's curiosity for police tasks behind the main stage was unbridled.

"A bunch of things." She relaxed after they sat down. He had such a childlike interest in everything, from elevator posters warning them to be alert for trailing civilians to a notice near the room's front reminding officers to report overtime. "Backgrounds, contacting forensics, and when you arrived, trying to track down bus drivers. Lots happening, Mr. Arthur."

"Please, John. Bus drivers. To see if Chester Himes took himself as opposed to being taken."

He certainly paid more attention than a child. "That's it exactly. But it's Chester Rowan. Outside of the name, very astute."

"Arthur, he sees much." John's Belgian accent caused her eyes to contract, as if she had a headache. A look he caught. "Apologies, Officer. My Poirot accent is poor. And Rowan, I knew that. Chester Himes is one of the greatest mystery writers of all time, crafting the Harlem detective novels in the '40s and "50s. Now, is there any way I can review interview notes, or would that get in your way?"

She flipped open her laptop. He was a curious man, but certainly a friendly one too. Like an eccentric relative. "Nope, not in my way. You can use my log-in. I can get you in to review the notes on *this* case. No surfing around. I'm going to be on a few calls." After a few clicks, she passed it over.

"Thank you, Officer Weber. I'll stay on target, as Marlowe tends to request. And keep it quiet so I don't bother your calls. Just here?" He pointed at the screen.

"Yes, that file folder."

"'Couple of years ago, the governor suspected Mayor Hicks of a dodgy property deal, so he's kept this file on him. Complaints mainly. Wants me to search for anything interesting.'" His English accent was somewhere between drunken Cockney and *Faulty Towers*. Noticing her confused look and sight shift back in her chair, he explained himself. "Sorry, took a turn into Midsomer." Her confusion not retreating, he went on. "*Midsomer Murders*." She shook her head slowly. "No? Classic British TV show, been on since 1998. You don't know it?"

"I wasn't even born in 1998, Mr. Arthur. John. And have only been to the UK once."

"*Mea culpa*, apologies. I watch a fair amount of British TV and have this habit of dropping quotes in on rare occasions."

She smiled, "Rare isn't what I heard."

"Marlowe. Who knows what he's said. I've kept you off task long enough. I will dive in, you go back to bus drivers. No more quotes."

"For now." She picked up the phone, wondering if she'd need to start watching British television.

Marlowe, Morven, and Nelson miraculously arrived back at the station nearly at the same time. Morven parked moments before the other two, but saw their cars entering the parking lot as she headed for the elevator, so waited. They walked into the detective room, where they saw John and Weber.

"John Arthur, here to greet us. Very surprising." Marlowe's drawl touched the sarcastic like dipping a toe in cold water.

"Officer Weber must have let him in," Moven surmised. "I can't believe Officer Coleman would let him wander the halls solo."

Nelson, a half step ahead of them, paused. "It's a good thing, right? Team's all here."

"Suppose you're right at that, Nelson."

"He *is* our civilian contractor," Morven said, pivoting around a chair.

"Glad he's earning his keep. As long as he's not taking Officer Weber off the path."

As they made it to the desk, she hung up the phone. "Detectives. You're back." Her excited tone didn't give away if it was the call or their arrival she was glad about.

"We are," Morven said, slipping out of her suit jacket. Nelson did the same as she continued. "You and Mr. Arthur are here, hard at it."

John stood up as they sat down, giving the scene a carousel moment. "Hello, detectives. Officer Weber brought me up." He glanced at Marlowe. "Hopefully not overstepping. Wanted to review case notes. And we're crowding your desk."

Marlowe shooed him. "Not too crowded. Uncover anything important?"

"Everything is important. On some level. Sadly, that level is subconscious so far. But my brain is hard at work. Much like all of yours. I'm super impressed with the note-taking. Especially the interviews. Bravo." John clapped.

Nelson soaked up the praise. "Thank you, Mr. Arthur. Note-taking skills are an essential part of police work. Did you know we spend 30% to 60% of our days writing? It's a wide range, I'll admit, because of the unpredictable nature of the job."

Marlowe raised a hand before John could reply. Best to keep this cattle drive from straying. "Fascinating for John, Nelson. Matters more prominent beckon. Including recent interviews."

"You met Chelsea Hinckley?" Morven asked.

"Yep. We should round up, all sides."

"Agreed. Officer Weber might have news from this morning as well."

She nodded enthusiastically. Marlowe caught her eye. "Can't hardly wait to hear more. However." He paused, looking around the group. "Am I the only one that skipped lunch?" Noticing four hungry looks, he went on. "Guessing not. A canteen posse is needed. Chow and joe. John?" He saw John had raised his hand.

"Can I accompany whomever goes? I've always wanted to visit a real police cafeteria."

"It's a thrilling spot. Nelson, you take orders."

The young detective sprung out of his seat, grabbing his notepad. "You see what I mean about writing," he said, pen in hand.

A quiet interrupted by chewing, crunching, and keyboarding descended like cotton over their corner of the room. Marlowe currently typed, having made quick work of a turkey sandwich and a bag of barbecue chips, a few letter keys slick with oil and seasoning. A full coffee mug sat on the desk beside him, two empty coffee cups stacked next to it. Morven forked a salad as she typed, a bottle of Guillaume sparkling water beside her, while Nelson gnawed the remaining bites off an apple, an empty bag of mixed nuts nestling next to his own bottle of sparkling water. Weber, having commandeered her computer back from John, balanced it on her lap while she worked. A half-eaten bowl of pesto pasta salad speckled darker green with peas sat on the desk near her, next to cups of unconsumed coffee and water. She'd decided to try the coffee again after Marlowe sung its praises; finding it tasted a like mud mixed with vinegar past its sell by date might, she'd given up after one sip. John stood gazing at the board, a plate in his hand containing a few stray French fires, the grilled cheese that once accompanied them long consumed. "The closest thing on the menu to Peter Diamond's bangers and mash," he'd told Nelson, giving him an in-depth lecture as they walked back on the Bath detective created by Peter Lovesey, one of his favorite authors.

Marlowe wiped his fingers on a napkin, pushed his chair back an inch. "Enough clicking. Everyone's fortified. Let's go through pertinent points from the Rowan scene, if it is, and interviews."

For the next forty-five minutes, he kept them reviewing the day's activities, keeping John from breaking the flow too much via a few well-timed palm up gestures. He wanted to get everything on the table before moving to discussion, while conversations were still fresh. It might help to speak them out before getting the notes in, gathering clarity within the informational clouds. Nelson went first, then Morven, then he went last, telling about his talk with Chelsea. Upon finishing, he took a deep breath.

"That is a whole gully's worth. Let's toss a few opinions around. To begin, Chester Rowan."

"Sir?" Weber gently broke in. "Can I?"

"Of course, Office Weber."

"I spent some time liaising with officers on the scene, door knockers. No neighbors recall seeing him early. No news from forensics yet, but I talked to"—she glanced down to her screen—"Johnathan Arris, and he promised some preliminary information today. More immediate, when you arrived, I was on the phone with City Metro. The Route 17 line runs past the Rowan-Sykes house, with a stop two blocks away. I talked to two drivers from this morning, both of whom say no one matching Chester's description boarded their buses. There is a third driver, the earliest, but I haven't reached him yet."

Nelson set the apple core on the desk vertically, where it instantly fell over. "Do we think Chester took himself away? I thought it was a second murder."

"We think"—Morven speared a last lettuce leaf—"options are open."

Marlowe agreed. "True. Solid work, Officer. Opinions on Chester—victim, suspect, or both?"

Morven put her fork down, standing and stretching her arms overhead. "Unsure. We need forensics on the blood. I suppose if pushed, I'd say suspect. No body."

"Could it have been removed?" Nelson asked.

"Surely. By who is the question."

"One of many," Marlowe chimed in. "Let's back up. Douglas Small. Thoughts currently. Morven?"

"With the information we have, hard to tell. Martin, Kevin, Chester all have or had issues with the chef. Olivia, there is something off about her too. Louisa—"

"Not Louisa, right?" Nelson also stood.

"The first back to his office. A motive, in his behavior to her. But she did seem genuinely upset."

"Others have too," Marlowe mused.

Morven nodded. "Fair point. Hard to take every word at face value. Too many suspects."

Weber spoke up. "Douglas Small seemed to do a lot of bad things, yet people liked him."

Mostly to himself, but loud enough the others heard, John said, "'I certainly did. Killed three people; carried out those murders meticulously, clinically, right under my nose. What kind of a man does that?'"

"John," Marlowe said, causing John to jump a half step and drop his last fry on the floor.

"Sorry, team. Went into *Midsomer*. Which I introduced Officer Weber to, by the way."

"Lucky her." Marlowe chuckled. "What's your take so far on Douglas Small?"

"Oh, I know who did it."

"What?" Nelson exclaimed.

"Not specifically. Generally. It's something in the past. It's always something in the past on every show." He looked at Marlowe. "And I know this isn't TV. But that's my guess. Curious that those employment records from way back aren't available."

Nelson jumped in first. "Right. Douglas Small specifically. Here's a theory, taking the past into consideration. Sarah cheated on Chester with Douglas. Then Douglas left Chester's company instead of publishing more books with him, damaging him financially as well as emotionally. Chester kills him after festering for years, then goes on the run."

"How did he get into the room?" Morven walked nearer the board. "And when?"

"Snuck back pretending to go to the bathroom. Drugging him first. Stole a key."

Marlowe stood. "That's a theory. Could go with Kevin also, if taking in the past. Might be he holds Chester responsible as well. Wife would have access to pharmaceuticals."

"You're right, sir, I didn't think of that. I like him in the frame even better. Carries a ton of anger about Douglas and his dad, was out last night, and could have done the same plan. He's definitely our man." He looked around as if daring disagreement.

Morven shook her head. "Not sold 100%. Where is Chester's body then?"

Nelson's triumph sloshed noticeably into disappointment, like water down a drain. "Yeah, maybe. Probably. But they were focused on making cakes."

"Good point," she agreed, and he brightened back up.

Weber spoke tentatively. "What about Martin? He's got beef with the chef, and a combination of anger and muscles to break the door in, if it needed to be. Even though Chelsea didn't think he had a key, he was a Douglas favorite at one time. Maybe he had one she didn't know about."

"Yeah," Nelson agreed loudly. "Martin is a solid choice. I like the idea of him having a key from the past. We need to check his movements for last night."

Marlowe had been mostly silent as they theorized. "That we do. We need to pin down more facts. Push the class attendees. Get the truth."

"'You can tell one lie, or two lies, or three lies or even four lies, but you cannot lie all the time. And so, the truth becomes plain.'" John's Belgian accent was back.

"Plainer than that accent," Marlowe chided. "Point well taken, whoever pointed it first. We need more. More from forensics. More interviewing. More insight, even." A movement on his screen caught his eye. "Here's an email from Chelsea. Could help."

"Chelsea?" Morven's questioning tone had an undercurrent of humor, like a salmon swimming near the water's top.

Marlowe's mustache hid most of his blush. "Miss Hinkley, I mean. Notes on social stuff. Online employment records. Nelson, want to wade through it?" His agreement was written so plainly on his boyish face that Marlowe didn't wait for a reply. "Thanks. My take, feel free to disagree, is that we treat Douglas and Chester separately for a bit. Morven, you lead on Chester. Follow his trail. Nelson and I and John will continue digging in on Douglas and class folks. How does that sound?"

Everyone nodded, Morven speaking up. "Very logical. Small team, two parts. I'll interview this last bus driver in person, keep after forensics, revisit the scene. I'll take Officer Weber, if that works."

"Works. Let's roll."

John turned from the board. "Very police-like, Marlowe. A solid scene-ending line."

"John?"

"Yes, Marlowe?"

"I am police."

Weber and Morven were in the latter's car, heading to interview the third bus driver.

"Why do you want to interview Dain Planter in person?"

"Fair question." Morven smoothly passed a car going ten miles below Highway 98's fifty MPH speed limit. "Two reasons. First, in general, I like interviewing face-to-face. It gives a better chance to read expressions, push without seeming telemarket y. Second, my guess is if Chester did take a bus, it would have been the earliest possible to avoid neighbors. Mr. Planter drove the early route. He is our best chance to make inroads on the question of suspect, victim, or other. And I thought you might like to get out of the office. I guess that's three reasons." Morven pulled off the highway onto a side street.

"That makes sense," Weber said, looking out the window. "The City has so many great trees, especially up north here out of downtown. Check out those two massive Douglas Firs. Hundreds of years old."

Morven pulled the car to a curb, parking. "You into trees, Weber?"

Slightly sheepish, she said, "I have a degree in wildlife biology, and it involved knowing about trees and plants as well as wildlife. Before I decided to join the police."

"That's awesome. We need officers with diverse backgrounds. Helps with perspective. And if our bus driver has tree questions, we're ready. Speaking of." She opened the door, Weber following. They were parked directly across from the City Zoo. The side they were on was mostly small, boxy apartments, with one brick Episcopal church's attempt at neighborhood gothic architecture breaking the routine. Dain Planter's building was a dusty red fourplex, two up, two down.

His apartment was 1B, at the top of a short flight of stairs. On Morven's knocking, a high-pitched yapping could be heard. The door opened a quarter wide to reveal a man probably pushing fifty, thinning salt-and-pepper hair, slightly rectangular face, long rectangular torso perched on short legs. Not the body you'd expect from someone who drove buses for a living. He wore jeans, and a white windbreaker over checked blue and white collared shirt, the type a 1950s sitcom dad might don on a Saturday. A black button with white printing saying "I Roll" adorned his coat.

"Hello, Mr. Planter. I'm Detective Morven and this is Officer Weber. We called earlier."

"Yep, I remember. Wanted to talk to me about a passenger or some such."

"Correct. Could we come in?"

"As long as you enjoy dogs, I'd love for you to come in." There was just a pipette's worth of leering in his words as he gave both a top-to-bottom glance. "He's a small one," Dain continued. "Cambyses, back up." As he backed into the living room directly off the door, a fifteen-pound, black, pointy dog encircled his feet. Somehow, he managed not to trip.

"Have a seat, officers." Dain motioned to a tan leather couch, casually bumpy as midwestern rolling hills. A chair sat opposite, behind which was a fenced-off area, probably the dog's spot when Dain was at work. They sat gingerly on the couch as he took the chair. The room was bare outside of a door-sized TV and robust video game console on a small shelving unit.

"Cambyses. That's quite a name." Morven reached her hand down so the dog could smell it, which it did for a second, before sprinting back to begin chewing on one of Dain's shoes.

"Big name for a leeetle dog," he said, accented badly. "He seems to like it. How can I help you lady officers?"

"You drove the 17 bus this morning, the first run on the schedule."

"I did. I don't always like the super early morning routes, but it fits my schedule, gives me time to come walk the dog after, before I head out to play D&D later. Really, I don't mind that route. It's not too full, and you get an interesting mix of people. It can get dark in winter, but that means less traffic, and people still need the bus no matter what they're up to. Some coming home from courting, a little rouged if you know what I mean, some trying to be early birds at the office, some hungover, some wrapped in spandex for early gym rounds. You look pretty fit, by the way."

Dain was a talker. Morven knew the type. Usually lonely, but could go on. "Today, did you have any passengers board the bus at the 32nd and 58th stop?"

"You know your route 17. I'll keep an eye out for you. No, nobody boarded at that stop today. A nice young lady I'm guessing coming from her boyfriend's boarded at 65th. I won't forget her. A looker, you know?"

"Where does the route proceed after that stop?" Weber asked.

"You need to ride the bus more, it sounds like. I drive straight down 32nd until I hit the locks and the botanical gardens. Been there?" Neither said anything. "Suppose not. Pretty place. Not too crowded. Then I turn onto 54th, which shortly turns into Locks Place, then onto Exchange Street into the neighborhood's central area, and then from there it turns—"

Morven cut in as mildly but firmly as she could. "Did anyone board the bus this morning near the 32nd and 58th stop? The one preceding or directly after?"

"Well, let me consider. A couple people did, yes. Just a handful, mind you. Early birds."

Weber pulled a photo of Chester out of her pocket and reached over to hand it to Dain. "Was one of them this man?"

"He up to no good?" He gave what he probably thought was a conspiratorial smile. Noticing their serious faces, he looked down. "No, I don't think he did. There weren't many boarders, as mentioned. Sometimes they blur together, unless they're in a fluffy hat like this one lady arrived adorned in one day, a boa to, if you believe it. And pants so hot—"

"Could you give another look, to be sure." Morven started to second-guess her idea of coming to interview in person.

"Sure, Detective, for you, anything." He stared more closely. "Actually, maybe. Not so sure."

"Yes?"

"He definitely didn't board near that stop. But at the Exchange Street stop, that's the busiest one, more folks boarded. Gets blurry, but I remember the last boarder because he seemed out of breath, panting to beat the band. Dark cap on, dark jacket, dark jeans. Being friendly like, I asked if he was okay. He glared, and his eyes I remember, sunken and beady while also frantic, if that makes sense. Like a thief who's been in a dungeon too long. It might well be the same guy, but I can't swear to it. That give you what you need?"

"Do you remember where you dropped this passenger?"

"That's a tough roll. Downtown proper gets busy. Let me think." He went quiet, then appeared to be counting off on his hands. "Won't swear to this either, but I believe he got off at 2nd and Johnson, the last stop. It's a crowded area, as there's our stop, Metro, plus the Greyhound bus stop up a block. Those drivers aren't like us, not as safety conscious."

Morven stood, and Weber followed suit. "Thank you for your time, Mr. Planter, this has been helpful."

Dain stretched up, the dog who had been lying down encircling his legs again. "Sure, happy to assist the women in blue. It's near five o'clock, though, so you have to be clocking off soon. Want to stay for a drink? I was about to make a 7 and 7."

They turned down the offer as quickly as possible, and were soon back in the car.

"That's a positive development, right?" Weber asked as Morven started the car.

"Interesting, as Marlowe might say. You up for heading downtown, seeing if we can find any friendly shops with security cameras near that stop?"

Words flew out as if from a catapult. "I am for sure. I mean, yes, Detective."

"Let's roll." Morven laughed, pulling out.

John leaving to go take care of Ainsley and "percolate his thoughts" left Marlowe and Nelson alone in the office corner. It felt too quiet after having the fuller group, cavernous. Both had been busy. Nelson catching up on paperwork and inputting, as well as scrolling the list of social messages and accounts Chelsea sent and taking a break to do push-ups. Marlowe caught up on his own paperwork, sifting like a baker through what information they'd gathered and gotten so far.

He raised his head from the laptop screen. When working on the computer, Marlowe found himself often getting nearer and nearer to it, as if an art critic checking brushstrokes or Sherlock with a magnifying glass. Knowing leaning in wouldn't help make the mystery clearer, his head dipped closer anyway, until he realized it and backed away. Tipping the pens out of the olive-wood bowl on his desk, he raised it toward his face, taking a big breath in. Olive trees, grassy Umbrian hillsides, a smell of red wine that would cause the back of the throat to catch in a beautiful way, his ex-wife's perfume, all swirling impossibly in his brain. *Oh, to be a shepherd in those hills. No murders, no crimes to solve.* The thought appeared out of nowhere, like a refrain of a song he didn't remember hearing.

"Um, excuse me?" A man's voice accompanied by a small squeak broke his reverie.

"Mr. Johnny Arris." Marlowe set the bowl down with a longing look, swiveling to face their visitor. "As I live and breathe."

"Detective Marlowe, Detective Nelson." Johnny nodded greetings. His beard and mustache, tightly trimmed and matching his jet-black hair in color, barely moved. With a thin, handsome face, eyes managing to mingle puppy's sadness and scientist's curiosity, and a wide, friendly mouth, the forensics manager could have been a character actor the audience never forgets. "No Detective Morven?"

"Out at the moment."

A sigh escaped from Johnny unbidden, as if a bird slipping through not quite close enough bars on a cage.

"Can we help?" Nelson kept an encroaching smile in check. Both knew the man had a crush on Morven.

Johnny shook off the melancholy. "Yes. Or maybe I can help you. We are still a ways out from processing the scene, or scenes, completely, but I do have a few initial facts that might help. I can try to answer questions if you want." He made sure to give both of them direct looks as he talked, as if not wanting either to feel excluded.

"Any help appreciated. This near the starting line especially."

"Sure, I get it. You know we aim to please, but science takes time. First, Chester Rowan. I know that blood is top of mind. We will do more extensive tests, but a rapid test showed A positive. Checking with the wife, that was his type. Pretty common."

Nelson rose from his chair excitedly. "That puts the spotlight on abduction I'd say, if not murder."

"Easy does it, Nelson." Marlowe pulled on imaginary reins. "More to tell, Johnny?"

"It's for you to investigate, but nothing else out of the ordinary at that scene yet. We're running fingerprints, etcetera, but no obvious signs."

"Douglas Small scene?"

"That one is more confusing. The classroom setting, fingerprints, food particles. The amount of flour alone everywhere makes it difficult."

"Appreciate the effort, from you and your team."

Nelson jumped over, causing Johnny to flinch. "Agreed. We appreciate it. Especially if you have more information."

"As mentioned, that scene will take time. However, we do know that the substance on the—I guess it's a rafter—that dripped down on the victim was unsalted butter. Basic stuff. Not sure on the brand."

"Cow paste," Marlowe said, "as we thought."

"Never heard that one, Detective Marlowe. But yes. A few more notes, knowing tests are ongoing."

"We'll keep that in mind."

"Please do. The door. Very confusing. The victim appeared to be locked in, both door lock and hook lock, as the latter was broken recently, in my opinion. If that had happened farther back, we'd expect less evidence of it. We did check shoes at the scene and are processing those findings. I was there for that, however, and I would wager nearly all walked in the office at some point after the crime."

"Felt that way."

"Right. Loads of fingerprints to process from the office and classroom, as well as the murder weapon."

"Other objects in the office too?" Nelson asked.

"Naturally, Detective. One note. We did run analysis already on the coffee, I believe Doc told you." He looked from one to the other and got two nods. You couldn't fault his manners. "Great. The coffee was mixed with an amari, by the way, the Italian digestif. Probably fifty-fifty amaro to coffee. Not a hundred percent which brand, but on the bitter side of the amari spectrum is my guess. The smell was obvious. That would have hidden the drug's taste. We are testing the bottles there for fingerprints."

Marlowe grinned. "You like the amari, Johnny?"

"I do. I'm doing a study to be able to tell brands by aroma, but haven't gotten too proficient yet."

"A solid area of study. More from the scene?"

"Nothing substantial. We'll keep working." He gave a short salute to both and turned to leave. Pausing, he said, "tell Detective Morven I said hello."

"Will do," Marlowe hollered to Johnny's retreating form. "Thanks kindly."

Marlowe and Nelson stayed at the office for a while once Johnny left, discussing the case between bouts of push-ups for Nelson, some against the wall, some on the floor, some leaning on the desk. By the third round, his boundless energy began to make Marlowe tired. It had been a long day—another long day—and though he knew that television lead detectives often miraculously went days without sleep, surviving on coffee and the occasional late-night takeout, in his experience the mind worked less well without a break. He called Morven and caught up on the Chester Rowan case, as she and Officer Weber were on the hunt for any sort of trace of the man. Telling her not to push it too far into the evening's hours, he decided to take his own advice.

"Nelson," he said to the back of the man's head, currently moving up and down like a hammer along with the rest of his mid-push-up body. His voice caused Nelson to stop, angling Marlowe's direction without standing. "Feels we hashed it enough for one day. Need recharging."

Nelson popped up like a spring. "Recharge the little gray cells." John Arthur's influence on the young detective perhaps had gone too far.

"All the cells. Quitting time."

"If it's okay with you, Detective, I'm going to stay a little longer. Continue reviewing the Small socials, and the employee records Miss Hinckley sent."

"Dandy. Appreciate the effort. Don't let the moon rise too high on you."

Nelson swiveled down into his chair in front of his laptop. "Check. Have a good night."

"Until tomorrow." Marlowe ambled out of the room, into the elevator, out the station's front door, and into a surprisingly temperate fall night. The clouds remained tucked in their beds off the horizon, and while it was dark, there was an almost summery tang to the air, a smell somehow of fresh-cut grass. Whether memory or real, he wasn't sure, but it drew his legs to walking down the hill toward Settler's Square, away from the station parking lot and his car.

The mood or night or need for a friendly non-case-connected face took him past the long-vacant lot across from the station, empty of all but earth mounds and rubble for years, supposedly the spot for a new apartment building, as if the City needed more. Large fences covered in boards and plastic sheeting blocked it off, there long enough they had become a tattered outdoor art project, layers of graffiti rainbowing.

His route traveled the outskirts of the bustling bar, restaurant, and shop neighborhood, where even on a slow Sunday night people congregated. A group wearing matching Osprey football jerseys, the local team playing on the road that day, stood outside a bar drinking beer from bottles and discussing the earlier game Across the street, a group of drag queens did the same. Two men in matching porkpie hats played chess on a card table set up in a tiny corner park, candle burning on the table. He turned a corner and nearly ran into a tousled-haired teenager in jean jacket enveloped with pins, one hand holding a red leash attached to a rottweiler weighing more than the kid. As Marlowe scooted around them, the dog gave his hand a surreptitious lick. *That's probably giving me good luck*, he thought.

And he was right. When he walked into Gary's, his favorite stool, one near the bar's corner and front door, was free. He tossed his sport coat over the stool, sitting on it. The bar was busy, three-quarters full of people ranging from more football fans in branded gear, to a neon-mohawked couple, to people playing Yahtzee (he could tell by the name yelled as he walked in), to two couples who only had eyes for each other. The Clash's "Jimmy Jazz" came out of speakers mounted high in corners. Gary himself poured beer behind the bar.

After depositing two pints to a table, he approached Marlowe. "Kit." Gary tended to call him after the playwright whose name he shared. "Chockablock here. Nice to see you. What'll it be?"

"Negroni okay?" Marlowe had fallen for the currently wildly popular everywhere drink when visiting Italy in the past.

Gary pulled bottles from shelves. Beginning to pour into a metal mixing tin, he said, "Always. How goes the struggle?"

"You know. Busy as a Dodge City roundup."

"I understand. People here are falling over each other in their haste to get drinks."

"Does seem so. Nice night."

"Tis that." He paused, gave the room a glance. "Did I ever tell you the story of the Negroni?"

Only a hundred times, Marlowe thought. "Might have."

"Better I have, as I see an empty G and T. Cracking tale, however. Next time." He raced around the bar out onto the floor like a bearded greyhound.

Marlowe sipped his drink, gazing over the small sea of humanity the bar represented. *The bitter, herbal, sweet poetry*, he mused, not sure if he meant the drink or the people, but forgetting about the case completely for a few minutes.

11

The next morning, the police members of the team were in their spots early. Marlowe arrived last, but only by a few minutes. He'd stopped to pick up croissants on the way at Sampson's Sips. His Venti coffee, which he called The Big One, nearly half consumed by the time he sat. The detective room as a whole bustled at a level much higher than the last few days. Officers sat at desks clicking computers, stood talking about cases and the weekend, laughs breaking above the general din regularly, movement and noise bouncing in all directions as if it were the first day of school.

Croissants handed out, Marlowe took in the team. "Well," he drawled around a bite. "Who's first?"

Nelson's hand popped up, adding to the school atmosphere. Slight dark circles ranged under his eyes, but his normal energetic nature didn't seem tamped down.

"Nelson, you seem raring. What's up?"

He popped up to stand in front of the board, a piece of paper in hand. "I was trolling Small social accounts and messages sent to them after getting the passwords from Miss Hinckley. There were, as she mentioned, a number of very threatening messages sent to Douglas within the last two months. Everyone in the public eye, so to speak, gets weird social messages and comments. Sadly part of the modern world. These seemed persistently threatening at another level. Things like 'you deserve to die, you thief,' 'you'll get yours creep,' 'choke on your drink, and more. One even said 'don't let the knife slip,' which felt very pointed." He took a breath. "Sorry about the pointed. I think the messages could be important, coming so soon before his death and being so aggressive."

"They could be," Morven said. "Maybe we can track down who sent them, digital forensics it."

"Might take some time." Marlowe knew things didn't always move quickly.

Nelson excitedly held up the paper. "We may not need to. I have an idea who sent them."

"Do tell."

"You see, I grouped the threatening message, noticing they were sent mainly by two accounts, same across social channels. Neither account has any other activity, so seem created for this purpose. One is called *my fathersson* and one *straightnochaser.* The first one sent most of the very threatening ones, the die ones and the knife one. The other sent just a few, and all had obscure drink references in some way threatening the victim. I believe they could be Kevin Holman and Martin Allen, Kevin being so focused on his father and Douglas stealing the restaurant, and Martin being a bartender, it makes sense." Even Nelson had to take a deep breath after the rapid outpouring of words.

"Nelson, that's focused work." Morven took the paper to read as Weber nodded her head enthusiastically in agreement.

Marlowe rapped knuckles on the desk. "You earned that croissant. However." He paused. "We can't be sure. We'll still run it by the computer folks, but should press spurs in on Kevin and Martin. Interviews. Here. Under caution."

"Yes, Detective. Maybe they'll crack under the pressure and admit it all. Or one of them. Unless they were working together."

"Let's not put the cart before the horse, Nelson. But solid work. Speaking of people who didn't like Douglas. Morven and Weber, latest on Chester."

Morven, with a few additions from Weber, told them about their meeting with Dain Planter and how they decided Chester might be more on the run than abducted.

"Chester Rowan taking it on the lam." Nelson's voice had a hint of disappointment. "Are you sure it was him?"

"Not *positive* the person the bus driver saw was him, but we think it was."

"There's more in that gully, I'm guessing."

She laughed. "Guessing correctly. We made a few further stops last night after Mr. Planter. First, we revisited the scene to get a look and try to talk to Mrs. Sykes. Weber?"

She didn't hesitate. "Mrs. Sykes appeared originally reluctant to talk. Oddly so, I felt. We did ask her specifically about the clothes worn by the man Mr. Planter saw. She went to check, and it did seem a hat and jacket matching the description were missing. She still emphatically believed he was taken. We asked if she knew where he might go, and she couldn't come up with any ideas. She asked us about the Douglas Small investigation, but we gave her the lines on inquiry."

"Nice." Nelson approved of all standard police lines.

"One note that hasn't been brought up; Johnny Arris stopped by last night." Marlowe gave them the updates from forensics.

"That adds to the Chester side for sure." Morven sat on the corner of her desk, gazing out the window. "His blood. An attack he escaped from, or trying to throw us off his trail? Could be either, or both. Our night didn't stop at the house. We headed downtown to where, if it was him, he might have been dropped off."

"Dogged. A pull on a tenuous line sometimes reels in the fish. To mix animal metaphors."

Morven smiled. "It's morning, Marlowe. All metaphors are fair game. Anyway, we did some door knocking, open shops and restaurants, to see if anyone saw someone matching the description. Not a ton of luck at first. Then we stopped in Grouty Gyros."

"Did you stop for a snack?" Nelson was hungry, even after he'd finished his croissant at medal-winning speed.

"We did, falafel wraps. You might not expect it from the non-tasty home improvement name, but pretty good food."

"Very tasty falafel," Weber offered.

Morven continued. "But only after the owner, young guy, begged us to. He had CCTV mounted outside the door and happily said we could review it. Big police supporter, or enthralled with Weber, I'm not sure." The younger officer slightly blushed. "It was difficult to see perfectly, but I believe we caught the person from the bus. Same outfit, same size as Chester. Hunched over, hat pulled down. Wouldn't pass in court, but could be him."

"Where was this?" Marlowe wanted to know for the case, but he also liked a good falafel sandwich.

"Between the bus stop and the Greyhound bus station."

Nelson smacked his hands together. "He's on the run. He did it."

"Easy, Nelson. We don't know for sure it was Chester. We need to visit the bus station now that it's open."

"Seems a plan. Keep following that trail?" Marlowe left the question hanging until getting nods from Morven and Weber. "Nelson, get those interviews set."

"And you, Marlowe? Besides more coffee." Morven noticed his cup was empty.

"More brown gargle first. Then I have my own interview. Set for"—he made a motion as if checking a watch—"not many ticks away. Ruth Small. Reached out, as it feels the ex-wife should know more background, as well as a few of our class attendees. Didn't want to push too much right after Douglas's death. She volunteered to come station side. Okay, let's fly at it."

"Before we fly, is Mr. Arthur in today?"

"John might stop a spell later. Ainsley had an appt this a-m." Morven and Nelson, who both knew the dog, looked concerned. "Nothing serious. Annual dog checkup, I'm told. Now, I need to check up my coffee level."

Ainsley's checkup went smoothly. She wasn't overly enthusiastic about visiting the vet, but at the same time, *was* overly enthusiastic about meeting people, which caused vet visits to be a mélange of nervous panting, wild tail wagging, and hand licking of any vet tecs or vets who came in the room. A list that today included her regular vet, the tall and sturdy Doctor Mortimer, who always made John think of John Mortimer, the British barrister and writer who created TV character Horace Rumpole, eventually turned into a TV series *Rumpole of the Bailey*. He didn't bring it up to the doc, instead keeping the appointment doggy-focused. John didn't drop the TV talk into *every* conversation, even when the opportunity presented itself so perfectly.

They made it out in record time and with a record number of treats being consumed by Ainsley. The day was pretty as the previous. Two fall days with no rain and blue skies so deep they'd make Monet instantly set up an easel in the middle of the street. Walking back to their car, stopping every few feet for Ainsley to smell a streetlight, hydrant, or the sidewalk, John realized he was opposite of Sourdough Home Sales, Lucille Crow's real estate office. He saw lights on inside behind the big glass windows.

I shouldn't, he thought, stopping his walk. Which caused Ainsley to also stop, sit, and gaze up at him with a plea for more treats in her eyes. Marlowe would be upset if he interviewed one of the class attendees solo, would give him that frowning mustache he'd caught pointed his direction a few times. He wasn't actually a police officer. But he was, he decided as he angled Ainsley toward the nearest crosswalk, a consultant. One who maybe might want to sell their home one day. It was awfully big for just the two of them.

He was lying to himself, of course. He would, he knew at heart, never move from the house he'd lived in with his wife, as well as the past dogs they'd owned there—Sookie, Rory, and Pina, a trio of jolly rottweilers.

It might provide enough of an excuse, however, to derail Marlowe for a moment. He was so close to her office. In front of the door, as a matter of fact, a door he pushed opened, holding it for a moment so Ainsley could slip through without getting bumped. The minute they entered, two voices called out.

Lucille said, "No dogs in—"

While at the same time, Madison said, "She is so cute." Ignoring Lucille, she bent down to begin scratching Ainsley while saying, "Is it okay if I pet her? It's okay, right?"

"It's great. She's very standoffish, as you can tell." Ainsley's paws were now on Madison's shoulders, and she was licking the woman's face. Madison sat on the floor to make it easier for the dog, her legs in blue-green-and-red striped pants on either side of Ainsley, arms in a black long-sleeved T-shirt petting, hair pulled up in an orange ribbon bouncing to the pets like a massive mushroom in wild wind.

"She's adorbs. What's her name?"

"Ainsley. I can pull her back."

"No way. Ainsley, you're so cute."

"She is cute. For a dog." Lucille had walked up without John noticing, looming over him in her single-button black blazer, black pants, and white T-shirt.

"John Arthur." He tried to reach out a hand, but it was the one still holding the leash and pulled back. "Sorry, she's excitable."

Madison exclaimed. "Are you kidding? She's amazing. Luc, you need a shop dog."

"I need a lot of things. That might not be one of them." Her tone was slightly fierce, but her face watching the other woman and Ainsley told a different, friendlier story. "I'm Lucille Crow, and that dog-petter is Madison Bernard. You don't have an appointment, which is fine. How can I help you? Looking for a home with a yard?"

"I was actually," he started, then stopped himself. He felt bad about lying. "Actually, no new home for us today. I was hoping to ask you a question or two about the other night."

She bristled. "What are you, a reporter?"

The phrase *consulting detective* settled on his mind like a deerstalker hat, but he ignored it. "Civilian police consultant. Contractor. Helping the police."

"That was awkward." She smiled. Madison kept petting Ainsley, sprawled onto the white tile floor.

"Sorry. I was honestly passing and thought I'd stop in. Hopefully not a problem."

"Not too much. Civilian police contractor on a juicy murder case. You'll probably be dining out on that for years."

"I'll get Ainsley some treats from it, if nothing else." Ainsley was blissfully being petted and didn't notice the T word. "Thanks for talking to me. I know you've talked to the detectives already. I wondered if anything else about that evening, or the previous, had occurred to you."

"Not that—"

"One thing." Madison looked up while petting. "Remember, Luc? That big fella, Jim. We remembered he was out of the room longer than a pee break."

"Maybe he wasn't peeing."

"Eww, Luc. It was strange."

"A little strange."

"That's good to know." John broke their back-and-forth. "Did everyone spend time in Chef Small's office at some point?"

They both considered, before Lucille spoke. "He did little, more personal consultations for most."

Madison chimed in. "Not us. We were supposed to be that night."

"How did you like the space? For baking, I mean."

"For baking. As opposed to murdering a famous chef."

"Oh, Luc, you know what he means. I thought it was dreamy. So much equipment. Those oven mitts with flowers on them you kept tucked in a pocket. Pretty stuff."

"I doubt he cares about my fashion sense. It was a nice space. Top-shelf equipment. Wonderful appliances. Wish I had those fridge-freezers. You could make an icicle the size of my arm in there."

"Why would you want that?" Madison asked, causing Ainsley to jump up, then lie back down.

"Extra-cold drinks."

"Murder weapon that melts," John said, then regretted it as they both gave him an odd look. "Sorry, I watch a lot of television mysteries. And read them."

"Figured that one out myself. Maybe I should detect instead of selling houses. Which I should be doing."

"A moment more?"

"You can stay all day, as long as Ainsley does too." Madison gave the dog a dreamy look. "Can I give her a treat?"

"Wait, you have dog treats?" Lucille said in mock exasperation.

"I wish."

"I have some." John reached into his pocket, pulled out a wallet with the Marvel character Doctor Strange on it. Setting the wallet on the nearby desk, he reached deeper into his short's pocket and pulled out a few small cheddar biscuits, which he handed to Madison. As they talked, she dolled them out to Ainsley.

He went on. "You were in back when the door was broken down. Was anyone alone in the office around that time?"

"Alone?" they said in tandem, before Lucille went on. "I see. Time for the..." She made a stabbing motion. "I don't remember. Chester was back there, the big guy, before he went running out. The other older guy, Kevin. We were all running around a little like headless chickens. I suppose one of those chickens might have been there. Only for a moment."

"Murder most fowl," Madison said mock solemnly. Noticing both staring, she said. "Chickens. Fowl, with a W. Sorry, bad joke. Learned bad jokes from my dad, and they pop out."

"Did he teach you to be a smart-ass too?" Lucille tilted her head back, braying a laugh, large shoulders rippling.

"I thought you meant the Agatha Christie movie. Foul with a U. Margaret Rutherford as Marple." They stared blankly. "No? One more question then. I should get Ainsley home. Who was the best baker?"

Again, they spoke simultaneously.

"Luc."

"Louisa."

Madison continued first. "Luc here is fantastic. I didn't think Louisa was an option."

"She's amazing. Especially taking into consideration she had to deal with Douglas's abuse." Lucille gritted her teeth.

John let that lie for a second before following up. "Besides you and Chef Sweeney, any others who stood out?"

"I'm not that good a baker, Mr. Arthur, don't listen to her. She just wants me to buy her a cupcake later. Sarah wasn't bad, I suppose. Flynn needs seasoning, but has the skills. The glamourous one—I can't remember her name—was better than you'd imagine with those nails. Is this helpful?"

"'A person who likes baking is either sincere or a very serious criminal indeed.'"

They both laughed, before Lucille said, "What was that, a British accent?"

John ducked his head. "Sorry. *Father Brown*. British TV show. How did you two meet, by the way."

"Slipping in another question. Very detective-y. We've know each other for years."

"Luc, you're so modest. She saved me. My hero." Madison beamed at the older woman, who rolled her eyes. "Really, Mr. Ainsley owner, I was in a bad way. Bad boyfriend way, after a bad father way, if that makes sense. Wandered if here one day when avoiding the former, who was on a rampage. Luc helped me out of the situation, got me working for myself. She's a hero. Like you're a detective."

A phone on one of the desks rang, and Lucille went to grab it. "Takes all kinds. I'm the has-to-work kind."

"We'll leave you to it. Thank you." John gave Ainsley's leash a gentle tug, and she languidly stretched from nose to tail tip before moving to the door.

"Bring Ainsley back anytime, anytime," Madison singsonged as they left.

Marlowe was in one of the station interview rooms with Ruth Small. They sat in gray metal chairs at a gray table, surrounded by four walls appearing washed gray with moldy green notes under fluorescents.

Ruth took it in. "This room is the definition of drab." Her long princess coat, which she left buttoned the whole time, was the color of a ripe Roma tomato, contrasting the surrounding.

Marlowe's just-under-burnt toast-colored sports coat draped his chair back, red suspenders with gold stars sharp against white shirt. "Sorry for the surroundings. But thank you for stopping by." He'd called her earlier, and without prompting, she suggested talking at the station.

"Happy to. Had shopping to do, and lunching with Rebecca."

"Captain Innocent."

She smiled. "That's the one. What can I help you with, Detective Marlowe?"

"A few questions. First, do you know anything about the contents of Douglas's will?" He knew he'd probably need a court order to get a view, but felt asking her might give some insight.

"Unless he's changed it, and he was horribly absent-minded about matters like that, I believe most of his assets come to me. Plus a bequest to the local culinary school for a scholarship in his name. That's what it was, at least. You should talk to Douglas's lawyer, Harry McCabe."

"Will do. Thank you. Wondering if I could run some names by you.

Attendees at the class Douglas was teaching. See if any stand out."

"You think it was someone at class who did it? Must have been. I've been trying not dwell on it."

"It's a difficult situation."

"It is, but I want to help. Do you have a list I could look at?" He handed her a list, and she bent slightly, bringing it nearer her face, brushing a strand of hair out from in front of her eyes. She took a minute, a minute hum vibrating from pursed lips every few seconds, before she spoke again. "Strangely, I know a few on here. Should I . . ."

"Start with those you know best." He had a notebook and pen out.

"Not sure I know any on here closely. Longest would be Kevin and his wife, Claire. Surprised they'd take the class. His father was Douglas's original investor, or partner-investor, in the first restaurant. Kevin was around some. Then Douglas bought his father out before becoming a bigger name, expanding the empire. He, the father, spiraled down, and Kevin thought it was Douglas's fault. Just business, but he made some scenes, even getting you all called in once. Douglas refused to press charges, wanting to sweep it under the rug for PR reasons. You believe he's involved?"

"Getting background, ma'am."

"Ruth is fine. Martin I remember too. My involvement in the restaurants was lessening during his time with Douglas. If memory serves, he left angry. Douglas wasn't always easy to deal with for staff. Another surprise on the list. Martin, I do remember, had a tendency himself to be hard for coworkers to deal with." She leaned in conspiratorially. "Temper."

"Any other names stand out?"

She hmm'd, then said, "Not really. I mean, Sarah and Chester I know, or knew. She had an affair with Douglas. Gave him the shiniest review ever, which got him national attention. Did Chester know? Seemed nearly common knowledge. One of the reasons for our divorce. Plus his… issues, let's say, with staff in the bakery and restaurant." She gave the list another look. "Oh, this name I vaguely recognize. Jim Sean. Did he know Douglas as kids? I think so. Douglas used to hide in the back when he'd come to the restaurant, make fun of him. Olivia Sean must be his wife."

"It is." He kept it short, to not stop her flow.

"Don't know that I met her, but the name, Olivia, sounds familiar somehow." She paused. "Nope, not sure why. Lucille and Madison, familiar too? Not standing out enough to define. Sorry."

"Not at all, this is very helpful."

"I'll keep mulling, reach out if I remember more. Anything else? I need to hit the salon before lunch."

Her hair already appeared to him as if she'd stopped before coming in to the station. He stood, moving to the door. "Nope. Will reach out if so."

They traveled the industrial hall leading from interview rooms to lobby. As they entered the lobby, Marlowe trailing as he held the door, he heard a familiar voice.

"Chels," Ruth exclaimed, trotting over to Chelsea Hinckley, who was talking to an officer behind the glass.

Chelsea hugged her as she spoked. "Ruth, you aren't…"

"Helping the detective with his inquires, as I've learned to say." A giggle burst like bubbles in Champagne.

"That's why I'm here. Hello, Detective Marlowe."

For reasons he was having a hard time identifying, he blushed. "Howdy, ma'am. Miss Hinckley."

"Detective, I remember we decided on Chelsea."

Ruth gave both a grin. "I see you know each other. And I need to scoot, so will leave you to it. Coffee soon."

"Yes please," Chelsea said as Ruth swept toward the lobby doors. "Detective Marlowe, I'm unexpected."

"A bit. Nice surprise."

"I was going over our last conversation and wanted to follow up."

"Surely. We'd be tickled for the help." He instantly regretted tickled as a word choice. "Can you follow me."

"I'd be tickled to."

Soon they were in the same room he'd just excited. She had on jeans, a black sweater with a white star in the middle, and a puffy seafoam vest she'd unbuttoned on sitting.

"Beautiful place you have here." She laughed, her voice lighting up the plain room like bright sunshine.

"Interior tones by Caravaggio."

"Cowboy references and art. You do have hidden depths, Detective."

He tried not to blush. Failed. "What can I help you with, Miss—Chelsea?"

"I've been thinking about our talk, and wondered if I could take a look at the class list. I wanted to make sure I didn't know any more of them. I want to aid in getting who did this, if I can."

"Sure." He handed over the paper with names on it. She took it. "I do recognize some of these as mentioned: Sarah, Chester, Martin, Flynn. Jim Sean even, from emails. I've heard of Kevin Holman too. You know that background." She saw Marlowe nod, went back to gazing at the list. For a moment, neither spoke, and unlike many past times he'd spent in the interview room, this silence was comfortable. Finally, she said, "This might be a long shot, but is it okay to use phones in here? I want to try and track down a picture. Unless you have them?"

"Sadly not at hand. Mobile away."

She pulled a smart phone out of her pocket, typing rapidly as a teenager on it. "Could be."

"Discover a cow hidden in the brush."

She laughed, and Marlowe couldn't help smiling along. More seriously, she went on. "It's hard, her appearance is very different from what I remember. Thinner, more glamorous. Olivia Sean, if I'm not wrong, is Olivia Fair. Worked at Small's long ago, but only for a day or two if memory serves. The phone issue I mentioned Douglas had? That was her. He was pretty awful to her. She left the restaurant, almost went to court, but then didn't."

"Interesting." He took back the paper.

"Helpful with your inquires?" He didn't immediately reply, and she said, "I'm guessing you can't say too much."

"Could be. How are you feeling? Rough times, I know."

"Too busy to be sad most moments."

"Understandable. Sorry to break into a busy day, but glad you stopped by."

"Me too." She stood, buttoning her vest. "If more comes to mind, I'll stop by again. Or call."

"I'd be—"

"Tickled." Her laugh rang out once more.

When Marlowe returned to the detectives' room, he discovered Nelson reclining in his chair like a tiger that had just eaten after a hungry few days on the hunt.

"Nelson," he exclaimed, causing Nelson to instantly sit up student-straight. "You look like the coyote that caught the cat."

Turning as Marlowe walked by, he replied. "Detective, I might have. It took a number of calls and some time, but I finally have both Martin and Kevin coming in for interviews this afternoon. Felt we could each take one with Morven out."

"Well wrangled, Nelson. Ideal timing. Need to try and set up one more." He told Nelson about his conversations, including the Olivia revelations.

"Olivia Sean. Or Fair. That's a motive right there." Nelson couldn't stop a smirk at his rhyming.

As if someone were reading his thoughts, Marlowe's phone rang as he reached to call Olivia. He picked it up, Nelson able to overhear half the conversation. "This is Marlowe. Hello, John. You did what? Yeah, okay. Yes, you can come down. But we are busy. Interviews. No, not an interview montage. Actual interviews. See you then."

"John Arthur?" Nelson asked.

"The very one. Stopping by later."

"Detective, what's an interview montage?"

Marlowe ignored him, picking up the phone to try and reach Olivia Sean.

12

John made it to the station before any of the interviews started. First, he made an abbreviated stop home, long enough to let Ainsley out, throw the ball five times, convince her to go to the bathroom, apologize to her for leaving again, cut up a handful of treats and scatter them on the ground to entertain her. "The game," he said to his doggy Watson before leaving, "is afoot". Then he was off again.

On his way downtown, fall skies took a U-turn, turning rapidly a bloated lead color that promised rain. A promise delivered on before he made it halfway, drops scattering across his windshield like action painting. Nothing hard yet, but even drops had a way of clearing downtown streets.

As he drove, people who not long before had been grabbing coffees and then lingering before heading back to offices sped up to reach roof-covered spaces. Vacationing couples holding hands, dawdling beneath pretty skies as they whispered pretty words, uncoupled, sprinting for restaurants, bars, hotels. Dog walkers letting every sniff stop take as long as it takes—which for most dogs can be quite long—all of a sudden developed a need to cajole canines past even the smelliest spots. The rain hadn't increased in volume when he reached a parking spot near the station, but the idea of it, the City's wet reputation, moved the masses indoors.

Once within the station, his wish was finally granted. The genii in this case Office Coleman, who had John's police contractor badge ready. Blue, as he'd expected, with his name and City Police in black on the bottom and a picture of him he'd sent in on it. Contractor printed on it, too, though with precise placing of his thumb when holding it out in front of him, it might be read as just John Arthur, City Police. He was trying out various manners of displaying it when Marlowe arrived in the lobby.

"John." His tone didn't attain the usual friendliness.

John placed the lanyard the badge hung from around his neck. "Marlowe. I know, no interviewing suspects. In my defense, Ainsley did have her appointment next to, or near to, Sourdough Sales. And I have been mulling over downsizing into a smaller place."

"Downsizing? Where would the books go?"

"Fair point." John noticed a tiny smile creep into Marlowe's sterner look, like a break in the clouds. "I hadn't planned on stopping, believe me. 'I've got my honor as a gentleman at stake don't forget.'"

"No time for accents. Interviews happening soon."

They stood quietly, as if waiting for the other to speak. John, meaning for his words to be to himself, softly broke the silence. "Just go twenty-three under hand deal."

Marlowe heard the confusing sentence. "What in tarnation, John?"

John smiled. "Sorry, was thinking about the *Chelsea Detective*. Show staring the thoughtful Adrian Scarborough playing Detective Inspector Max Arnold in the Chelsea district of London. Lives on a tastefully tattered houseboat among the millionaires. Down-to-earth, but a muser too. Funny, as before that show I tended to think of him as a BST lock when he'd show as a guest star. You remember BST."

"Your theory on the biggest guest star being the killer. How could I forget."

"Touché. Anyway, on one case he uses that phrase as a mnemonic to remember a license. *I* was trying to remember something, thought saying it might help."

"Did it?"

"Not yet. 'You ever get the feeling your brain is trying to tell you something?' That's another *Chelsea Detective* quote that feels apt."

"Little brain cells tired."

"Marlowe with the near Poiroting. Who'd have guessed."

"Hang out with John Arthur enough, and you have to cut him off from his television talk, because interviews are about to happen."

"Interview montage time. Another TV favorite."

"Hard to montage when they aren't happening all at once, if my montage definition memory serves," Marlowe said.

"There are half montages and staggered montages." Noticing Marlowe's eyebrows beginning to raise, he quickly went on. "Where you'll have one interview that trails into a montage, or where they don't happen simultaneously, but are edited that way." The eyebrows fully up, John pivoted. "We can go over that later. Can I sit in on the interviews?"

"Not sure the lawyers would approve."

"Lawyers? Very serious. Is there a control room with video feeds? There's one whole British show, which has now crossed borders into other regional copies, called *Criminal* that takes place just in the interview room and the control room behind the two-way mirror. Guessing you have a room like that"

"We do," Marlowe admitted.

"And?"

"Yes, you can sit there. Quiet."

"As the proverbial mouse."

"Let's give it a look. Only a handful of minutes before the first. Olivia Sean."

Marlowe opened the door, and as they walked down the dreary hallway, John couldn't help saying in a stage whisper, "The montage begins."

John ensconced in a room with a wall of video screens showing the interview rooms, bubbly as a glass of newly opened sparkling wine, Marlowe and Nelson waited in the lobby.

"Detective Marlowe, if need be, I could solo this interview. I have my I-POA. I'm ready."

"You are, Nelson. I get lonely, however." Internally, he wasn't sure that Olivia's charms wouldn't overwhelm Nelson.

At that moment, she walked into the room, wearing designer jeans that gripped her legs tightly, a cream-colored cashmere sweater, and black Chelsea boots. She was accompanied by a very thin, very tall woman with a round face accented by a silver bob, wearing a suit a shade darker in color with creases that seemed to slice the air.

They approached the detectives, neither extending hands. The tall woman spoke first. "Detective Marlowe. Did we really have to come down here?"

"Miss Church. I didn't know you were Mrs. Sean's lawyer." He'd had interactions with Lauren Church before and knew she was a formidable lawyer.

Lauren raised her hands in a gesture that implied his phrase was obvious. "Can we move this along."

"Surely. This way. As you remember."

She sighed in answer, but shepherded Olivia behind the detectives. Soon, all four sat in Interview Room 6 at a metal table, walls the color of dehydrated grass surrounding them. Before Marlowe or Nelson could speak, Lauren rapped the table as if bringing a court to order.

"Why are we here?"

"A few questions. Need any tea, coffee, or water before we start?" Marlowe felt courtesy might disarm. Nelson looked a little like a bunny caught in the stare of a large cat. Olivia's nearly alien beauty combined with Lauren's teacherly ferociousness had thrown him.

"You're stalling, Detective," Lauren said. "We're fine." Olivia stared at the table.

"Holler if you change your mind. Mrs. Sean, when you talked to our colleague Detective Morven, you admitted to having an affair with Douglas Small."

Lauren interrupted. "Affair? Mild flirtation. Which is legal. And which, as you said, Olivia admitted to."

"True. Did your husband know, Mrs. Sean?"

"Olivia answering a question about her husband's knowledge would be hearsay," Olivia's lawyer said condescendingly.

Olivia put her hand on Lauren's arm. "It's all right. I don't believe he did, Detective, but you would have to ask him."

Lauren smirked, cocking her head.

"We can," Nelson muttered, but even with a low level of vocalizing, hearing his own voice seemed to snap him back into focus. He sat a little straighter.

Lauren shot him a patronizing glare, but Marlowe spoke first. "Mrs. Sean, is it correct that before your marriage, your full name was Olivia Anne Fair?"

"What could that possibly have to do with? No comment," Lauren said.

"I'm sure Olivia is more than capable of saying 'no comment' all by herself. If she wants to." His words hung in the air like balloons for a moment of silence before Olivia punctured it.

"No," she began, then paused. "Yes, that's my name. Or was."

"Why not tell Detective Morven earlier?" Nelson asked, looking at his notes.

Lauren was about to speak, when Olivia again put her hand on the lawyer's arm. "It's fine, Laur. I didn't tell her because it didn't seem relevant."

"Is that true?" Nelson's words increased in pace as he continued. "Or is that you didn't want us to know you used to work for Douglas Small and had a contentious history with him?"

Olivia gulped as if gasping for air, and Lauren gave Nelson a look that carried a thick layer of contempt in it, like jam on toast.

"Water, Mrs. Sean?" Marlowe gently asked.

She lowered her head a moment, before raising it while wiping her eyes, which caused thin lines of blue eye shadow to trace over her cheeks. Lauren whipped a white-as-paper handkerchief out of a pocket and handed it to her. Olivia spoke while wiping her cheeks.

"I'm fine. Contentious isn't the right word. I hated Douglas Small."

"Olivia, maybe—"

"No, I want to say it. It feels good. I hated him."

"Why?"

She paused, hands gripping into fists. "I used to visit Small's, years ago. And really wanted to work there, as it seemed up-and-coming. Exciting. He was a chef getting famous, and I, like others, fell for him. Fell under his spell. He flirted incessantly when I'd come in to sit at the bar. When I said I wanted to work there, he promised a job, the moon, and more. He was married at the time, so I tried to resist. I hadn't had many boyfriends then." She ran her fingers through her hair, the gesture done as if to remind herself of her own attractiveness.

"I didn't look the same. Heavier by twenty-five pounds, for one. Different hair. Just different. Douglas never saw an attractive customer or waitress he didn't want to bed, however. It was like he saw us as disposable for his needs. Not as specific faces, people. The great chef. My first night, after a party of five I was waiting on left late, it was just us two in the restaurant. He convinced me to have a few drinks, talked about how great a job I did, how I was sure to do more great things as his empire—he actually said empire—expanded. If only . . ."

"Olivia, are you sure you want to tell this story?" Lauren's voice was tender.

"Yes. Douglas took advantage of me. I was nearly passed out. Too much to drink, which he gave me, then gave me some more." Olivia's coolness had long been dropped, like a jacket out of season. "And then he took pictures of me on his phone. Not the kind of pictures you'd want shown, or to even see yourself. Lucky, I guess, since he didn't have a compassionate bone, he didn't show them to everyone else at work. But he started taunting me with them on my second day. Showing them to me when someone else was steps away. I tried to fight back, but he had all the power."

"I wish I'd been your lawyer then." Lauren could have been a mamma lion.

Marlowe and Nelson kept quiet, knowing sometimes it was best to let a suspect have their leash, take the conversation whichever direction they wanted.

"Me too. But you weren't. I couldn't take it. Thought about taking him to court, but couldn't take the embarrassment. I quit the restaurant. Spiraled, to be honest. Had a few bad days, then weeks, then months, and wasn't sure how I'd end up, where I'd end up. Then had a moment where I realized I'd let him win. Sounds weird, I know, but I woke up one day and decided he wasn't going to win. Changed my life, and my appearance. Met Jim. Who, misplaced love of Douglas aside, isn't a horrible guy."

"You decided not to press charges."

"I knew no one would believe me. He's a legendary chef, a pillar of the community, rich, famous. I wasn't. Who would believe me over him? I should have, though. I'm sure his predatory behavior didn't end with me."

"Why take the class?" Marlowe was surprised she'd ever want to see Douglas again.

"I realized when meeting him with Jim at restaurants that Douglas didn't have any idea who I was. My appearance had dramatically changed, but I'm not sure he noticed female faces as distinct people. I wanted to get him to fall for me, then make him suffer like I did."

"And so you killed him." Nelson jumped like he was heading off the high dive.

"What?" both women said, Lauren following it rapidly with, "Detective whoeveryouare, that is outlandish. With no facts."

Marlowe tried to calm the waters. "Maybe that was a leap at this stage. We appreciate that story wasn't easy to tell, Mrs. Sean. The night of Douglas Small's murder, can you walk us through it from your perspective."

"This has gone on far enough." Lauren partially stood.

"We'll just have to bring you back down," Marlowe replied.

Olivia pulled Lauren softly to sitting. "Let's get it over with. We were working on our cakes. Douglas was flirting with me. My plan was to record him or something. He tried to kiss me in the dishwashing area. Slime. But mostly, class was same as always."

"Demonstration, then baking."

"Exactly." She spoke as if wanting to get it out fast so they could be done. "He loved having everyone watching him before he'd go back to his room like some famous actor post curtain call. Jim would moon by his door, knowing not to interrupt. This time, after he'd been back longer than usual, it was a jumbled couple of moments. That little assistant of his going back to check on him, then returning, freaking out, shouting that he didn't answer her knocking. Not sure why she was so worried at that point. I think she went back again with those two women bakers, then came back with one of them, more shouting about the door being locked, him not answering. Then some of the men trailing back after a few minutes of it, before a group went. They broke down the door from what I could hear. Jimmy returned out-of-it after he saw Douglas and ran down the stairs."

"Very helpful." Marlowe considered. "Did you go back to the office?"

"I did go back. I wanted to see exactly what happened. I wasn't sad, but I didn't kill him."

"Detectives, Mrs. Sean has been more than helpful. We're done here." This time when she stood, Olivia didn't stop her.

Kevin's and Martin's interviews were only available to be scheduled at the same time. Marlowe hadn't met the former and originally decided he would interview him and Nelson the latter. Then they switched, Nelson making a plea for Kevin as he'd already met him once and figured he "could pry the truth from him." Marlowe wasn't sure on the pry, but liked the detective's zeal, like a horse unable to sit still before a race starts.

He was doubly happy with the decision when Martin walked into the lobby with lawyer Shane Buchanan. A lawyer who usually only represented the rich and powerful, Shane tended to want to interrupt an interviewer into submission, throwing around legal terms as if he were a circus juggler and they were bowling pins. Marlowe had dealt with him before. Nelson had not, which could make for an interview that mirrored that circus.

Both detectives were waiting when the duo arrived, Kevin having not yet shown. Martin wore his typical scowl, along with a black T-shirt and black jeans, hair combed back ferociously enough it must have hurt. The lawyer had a pinstriped royal-blue suit on that must have cost about what Marlowe made in a month, but which for all the dollars propping it up, hung awkwardly on the man, like he'd borrowed it from a person two inches taller. Shane strode across the lobby upon sighting them, Martin trailing in his wake.

"Detective Marlowe." Shane reached out a hand, which Marlowe shook. The man's palm was as dry as the shake was short. "Not sure why we're here."

"Didn't realize you'd be here." Marlowe ignored his question.

"I'm Joel's lawyer, and he asked me to step in, make sure Martin's rights aren't trampled."

A sharply worded reply about elephants and lawyers floated near the front of Marlowe's mind, but he ignored it. "Please follow me." Without waiting to allow Shane to protest, he walked to the door leading to the interview rooms, holding it open. Realizing the futility and awkwardness of not following, Shane went through the door, Martin in tow.

Marlowe opened the door to Interview Room 5 a moment after the other two had passed it, making them retrace a few steps to enter. After settling down in chairs, none removing coats, Shane jumped in.

"Is this necessary?" He waved his arms like a pitchman to an invisible audience. "The interrogation room. The depressing walls. The two-way mirror. My client has done nothing."

Marlowe knew better than to rise to the lawyer's banter, but the words slipped out. "You sure on that, counselor?"

"I'm here, correct?" The question obviously rhetorical. "I don't take cases I don't think I can win."

"There isn't a case to win today. We would just like to ask Mr. Allen a few follow-up questions."

"Mr. Allen has been very kind in offering to come down. Please, let's keep it short, shall we?" Shane either didn't realize they'd had to track Martin down as if a pack of fox hounds to get him to the station, or was ignoring the fact. Marlowe would have put money on the latter.

"Before I begin, would either of you like some water, tea, or coffee?"

"Detective." Shane's tone was as if he thought he'd caught Marlowe out. "Can we stop with the good cop, bad cop routine. Let's wrap this up."

Good cop, bad cop? The temptation to pretend another officer was sitting next to him was strong, but Marlowe overcame it. "Take that as a no then. Martin, thank you for coming down." Martin's jaw clenched tightly enough that Marlowe worried he'd crack a tooth. "We just have a few follow-up questions."

"Are you charging my client with a crime, Detective?"

Nelson remained in the lobby after Marlowe, Martin, and Shane left. He stood away from the front desk, smoothing wrinkles off his wrinkleless suit coat absent-mindedly with one hand, papers gripped in the other. Seeing Marlowe's jaw go firm under his mustache when the lawyer arrived, a far cry from the older detective's normal laid-back cowboy round the campfire personality (as Nelson thought of it), made him almost wish he was in that interview with them. To see if Marlowe decelerated back to mellow or kept up the intenseness. He both looked up to his boss and felt he had to look out for him; his good nature felt easy for some to take advantage of. But maybe he was wrong and there was a layer to Marlowe he hadn't seen.

"Get your head back into the game," he whispered to himself. An elderly woman sitting three seats away, waiting to talk to the front desk officer about her neighbor who kept moving her trash cans, gave him a curious look. Catching her eye, he switched to a toothy smile that turned curiosity to a blush that, for a moment, made her appear twenty years younger.

He was beginning to believe Kevin Holman might be standing him up, when the man walked through the door, alone. The man seemed even more drooping than before, skin folds visible under chin lines, hair missing the brush, eyes red even from a distance, sunken behind circles the color of two a.m. He wore scruffy jeans, mustard-yellow polo, and a brown sports jacket creased like an old map folded for years in the back of a drawer. The fingers of one hand were still bandaged.

Nelson made a rapid approach, causing Kevin to stop short. "Mr. Holman, thanks for coming."

"Wasn't sure I had a choice." Kevin ignored Nelson's proffered hand.

"We do appreciate you visiting the station. Could you please follow me." Nelson moved toward the door, Kevin in his wake like a floundering ship behind a shiny tugboat. Soon, they were ensconced across from each other at a table in Interview Room 4, Nelson sitting straight as a T-square, Kevin slouched, seemingly oblivious to the room's drab walls, low lightening, and overall institutionally depressing appearance.

"Would you like any coffee, tea, or water?" Nelson found a kernel of compassion starting to grow inside him for the other man. He was so defeated. There was no doubt Nelson liked to win, but he couldn't help feeling sorry for those on the other side.

Kevin shook his head. "Should I have gotten a lawyer?"

"No charges. We asked Martin to come in and help us with our inquiries."

"Then we can leave immediately." Shane leaned forward, as if he was going to spring out of his chair.

"You could. We'd still want to ask the questions. Leaving might look mighty suspicious."

Shane settled back.

Martin finally spoke, words coursing through teeth just partially unclenched. "Ask your questions. I didn't do anything."

"You worked for Douglas Small for a few years in the past, correct?"

"You know this, Detective," Shane said before Martin could reply, though the latter did nod.

"During that time, he had the office at the classroom space."

"Yes." Martin held the word a moment, as if considering its taste, before speaking more. "It wasn't a classroom space at the time. More storage. Even the great Douglas Small could make mistakes, and at the time, everyone felt renting that space was one of them. The classroom idea came later. Probably thought of by someone else, as Douglas was prone to stealing ideas." The last words smeared with sneering.

"Did you visit the office back then?"

"I suppose so. Sometimes the space was used for bar storage. And for testing recipes, as the sink and stuff were there."

"You and Douglas both there during those visits?"

Martin shifted in his chair, the tightness of his jaw receding. "Often. We got along well back then. I didn't know the real him, yet, and we'd make drinks together, talk about the bar program, where I wanted to take it, how to align it with the food program. I liked him. Back then. We were out in the main space mostly, but spent time in his office noting down recipes, discussing cocktail ideas while testing cocktails. Didn't realize at the time he was going to take the recipes I came up with."

Marlowe kept his voice measured. "Ever visit the office solo?"

"Sure, bunch of times."

"Did you have your own key?"

Before Martin could reply, Shane cracked into the conversation like a muddler cracking ice. "Objection! This line of questioning is irrelevant and immaterial."

"Not a courtroom, counselor."

"Martin, you don't have to answer."

Martin sighed. "I know. I can though. I didn't have a key, Detective."

"How'd you get in?"

"You are certainly within your rights to ask for a lawyer," Nelson answered Kevin, "though you haven't been charged with anything."

"Couldn't afford one. Maybe couldn't have ever afforded one."

No sure how to respond, Nelson briskly moved on to a standard opening. "We just need to ask you a few more questions about the incidents of the past few days."

Kevin had been staring at the tabletop, but now met Nelson's eye. "Incidents? More than one?"

"There has been another incident, yes. You may have heard. The disappearance of Chester Rowan."

"Oh, him. I thought you wanted to talk about Douglas."

"I do, so let's start with him. You had a long-standing grudge against Mr. Small, correct?"

A ripple traveled Kevin's body, as if a spider had crawled on his back. After, he seemed more together somehow, less lost child and more aggrieved teenager. "You call it a grudge, when he stole my life from me? I call it more than a grudge, wouldn't you?"

Not sure exactly what the man meant, Nelson moved on. "Yet you still signed up for the class."

"That was Claire's doing. Good intentions, bad idea. She deserved more fun than she'd had. We told you about this already, Detective."

"Just clarifying. With your, feelings, in regard to Douglas, did you find it difficult to be around him?"

"Feelings. How are your feelings in regard to those who've stolen from you? It was hard, but I did it. For Claire. Thought I could finally get him to give me what's mine, what he took from my father."

"Do you feel he acted alone, or were others involved?"

Kevin stood up, pacing the length of the table. "He didn't do it alone. Those other two at the class, Sarah and Chester, they helped. Pushing him as this god of cooking, not giving credit to my father's contributions and then being part of the swindle in a way. Yes, I think they were involved too."

"Mr. Holman, could you please sit down."

"What?" Kevin seemed shocked to find himself standing, as if he were a bird suddenly in flight without remembering taking off. He held the back of the chair in white-knuckled moment, then sat back down. "Sorry. Got hot."

"At the class, you confronted Douglas."

"Did, a little. Claire kept me civil. Just wanted him to… you know."

Nelson had planned a gambit in his I-POA to catch Kevin off-guard, get him to admit the online threats came from him. Then, when he was wobbly, get him to admit to the murder. He may feel sorry for the man in a way, but that wouldn't stop him from going for the big score.

"Did you use the same threatening language that you sent him on social media?"

Martin sighed at Marlowe's question. "I borrowed Douglas's key to get in the office."

"With his knowledge?"

Somehow, when talking about the past, the anger had seeped out of Martin. He seemed more empty than aggressive, like a balloon once full of air, now limp. "Mostly. At the time, we were close. I thought. Being creative, designing drinks and a bar that would rank among the top."

"Why would you visit the office by yourself?"

"Detective." Shane ran fingers through her well-coiffed silvering hair, for a moment looking nearly cinematic—perfectly balanced features, chin a coaxing curve, aquiline nose, clear skin, few worry lines. Then his small eyes went a squint smaller, pushing him from leading man to supporting role to villainous. "That's years in the past. My client isn't a tape recorder."

Martin spoke softly. "It's okay. Easy enough. Most visits by myself I would go work on cocktails to show Douglas later. Wanted to impress him."

"Most visits."

"Near the end, I went to look for proof he'd stolen my recipes, but didn't find any."

"That stealing must have festered over the years."

"Argumentative!" Shane pounded the table. Both ignored him.

"It did." Martin's jaw tightened again.

"Which led to you threatening Douglas on social media." The statement led to a confusion of voices from the other side of the table, Martin and Shane talking over each other rapidly.

"What, how—"

"Martin has nothing to—"

"It was—"

"Hearsay, Detective!"

Marlowe held his hand up high above the table, the gesture causing both to stop and stare at his hand as if they were dogs and he was holding treats. "Hold steady. Let's agree you did send some messages."

"What?" Kevin's one-word answer to Nelson's social media question didn't scream confusion as much as you-found-me-out. It was like he'd been playing hide and seek and never dreamed he'd be found.

Nelson read off one of the sheets in front of him. "You deserve to die, you thief. You'll get yours, creep. You should be killed for what you did. Don't let the knife slip."

Kevin didn't respond, mouth open.

"You sent these messages, Mr. Holman. Very—" Nelson nearly said *pointed*, but caught himself. "Direct. Very threatening. All sent before the class."

Kevin stuttered as if a car with a bad starter, the charge not cleanly reaching engine. "I, I, didn't. Didn't."

"You did send these."

"I did," he gasped out. "But they were words. Just words."

"Which you then acted out at the class when you killed Douglas Small."

If possible, Kevin deflated more. "No. How could I have?"

"You managed to get a key to Douglas Small's office from your real estate career." The idea had just popped into Nelson's mind. Real estate agents had lots of keys, he thought. "Once in, you stabbed Douglas, cutting your hand in the process. This, after you had drugged his coffee with drugs you got from your pharmacist wife."

Shoulders slumped, Martin replied to Marlowe's question about the messages. "Not threats really. I still want—wanted—him to admit blame for what he did. But he didn't. And now never will."

"Did you make a copy of the office key back when you used to visit?"

"Detective, that is supposition of the most heinous sort," Shane said, exasperated.

"Question, not statement. Martin?"

Before Shane could interrupt again, Martin said, "No."

"You sure you didn't make an extra key, holding on to it in hopes you could gain entry to the office during the class?"

"No."

"Look for some evidence of Douglas taking those recipes? Have it out with him in private."

"You're badgering the witness, Detective."

"Not a witness on the stand. At the moment."

"I believe we've been cooperative enough. This fishing expedition is over. Next time you want to talk to my client, have a warrant."

"I suppose that would be the next step." Shane had a way of getting up Marlowe's nose like a thistle up a horse's.

As the two men went back and forth, Martin's eyes locked onto a corner of the floor. Shane grabbed his arm, shaking him. "Come on, Martin. We're done here. This is turning into a sideshow." He dragged the other man up.

Marlowe slowly made his way to the door, where the other two waited. "Okey-dokey. Let me walk you gentleman out." He opened the door, and as they walked out into the hall, the interview room next door also opened.

Nelson's use of the word "wife" caused a change in Kevin. He went from shaky and soft to harder, as if the thought of Claire being dragged in as an accomplice drove the self-pity from him. "No," he said simply. "That didn't happen. Claire would never have drugs lying around. And real estate agents don't have random keys. It's been years since I was one, anyway. And I cut my hand when punching the desk after one of Douglas's snide remarks."

This time, it was Nelson slightly deflating. He'd expected the man to admit guilt when pushed. Instead, the opposite had happened. For a moment, he remembered a cartoon where it appeared the bunny would be caught by the coyote, but instead it was the coyote over the cliffside. He gave himself a small pinch, looked down at his notes.

"You wanted to harm him, as the messages indicate."

"I admit I sent the messages, and that I was angry at Douglas Small. Have been for years. Am still, even with him dead. I wanted him to feel some fear, like I fear. Bills. Life. Being a bad husband. Those message were my way of doing that. But I didn't go farther."

"Don't let the knife slip."

"He was a chef, Detective. It's fairly obvious."

Nelson decided to switch tactics. "You said you also hold Chester Rowan accountable. And you've admitted you were out, with no witnesses, the night he disappeared. You wanted vengeance, and so killed him too."

Kevin's more serious manner wasn't mislaid by Nelson's accusation. "I was rambling earlier. Wouldn't I have needed a car to get to their house and do whatever you're suggesting? Claire would have noticed. I went for a walk. End of."

"You've carried around this anger for a long time. You finally acted on it. To both men."

"Detective, how could I have killed Douglas? Someone would have noticed. And I barely knew Chester. I think you're off in the weeds. I'm not saying more without a lawyer." Standing up, he seemed taller than when he'd walked in.

Nelson hated admitting it, but Kevin was probably right. "We may have more questions. And you can bring a lawyer next time, as mentioned." He opened the door, and walking out, nearly ran into Marlowe and his group in the hallway.

13

Morven and Weber were at the City's Guild Train Station. A large Beaux Arts brick building, with marble statuary high above the main entrance—a woman with unfurling robes riding a horse-driven chariot, waves cresting on either side. Dramatically impressive, but a spot hundreds walked by every day without looking at. Morven felt it hidden, in a way, by its very uniqueness and history, having been in the City for over a hundred years, many of those derelict before a local billionaire restored it, winning a national renovation prize in the process.

Walking in, she felt a touch of awe. The entrance hallway wasn't too remarkable—wooden walls, a few marble columns, a rack of tourist brochures, snack and water machines—but when you went through into the main waiting and ticketing hall, it was like walking into a grand ballroom from some Victorian palace. Barrel-vaulted ceilings of gilded arched ribs, longitudinal beams, flowery crown moldings towering high above wooden benches, with faux-stone decorative painting adorning walls, simulating cut blocks of natural stone. There was a mural depicting a forest scene, lofty evergreens in front of a snow-capped mountain.

Weber paused as they entered. "Wow."

"Never been here before?" Morven smiled as she asked. The room had the same effect on her even though she'd been many times. Often not to take a train, just sipping a coffee, soaking in the atmosphere.

"No. It's like, if you moved the benches, they could have a ball here. Steel-caged crinolines and Champagne."

"They have used it as film and TV location."

Weber beamed. "I can believe it."

"Sadly, we've no time for dancing." She walked to the ticket windows along the southern wall. They felt tiny in the room. Weber trailed a step behind, still staring at the ceiling. Only one window currently had an occupant behind it, an older woman with curly, blueish hair wearing a blue smock that matched the sky in the mural, the train company logo stitched in red on right pocket. She was knitting what looked to be a rainbow-colored scarf.

Setting down needles and yarn at their approach, her voice would have reminded anyone of a kindly aunt. "Yes, dears? Tickets?"

Morven held up her badge. She wore a tailored, long-sleeved, pewter-shaded suit with button cuffs over a white shirt. Weber was in full uniform. But police officers took trains, too, so the question made sense. "We are hoping to ask a few questions, if that's all right."

"I've always been happy to support the local police. My name is Frances Bee." Her eyes twinkled kindly.

"Thank you, Mrs. Bee."

"That's miss, dearie. Always an aunt, never a mother."

"Miss Bee it is. We're trying to check if a particular man took a train yesterday morning. Do you happen to have CCTV we could view."

"Sorry, any CCTV cameras you see are only props. Budget cuts have left us more 1950s than modern." Noticing the looks on their faces, she quickly continued. "However, I worked yesterday morning. Not a lot of trains leaving then. The Coastal 70. Intercontinental 120. Northern States closer to noon."

"That's good to know. Were you the only one working?"

Giving them a knowing look, the older lady replied, "Budget cuts. Which is to say, yes."

Weber pulled Chester Rowan's picture out of a pocket. "Would you mind taking a peek at this picture. Did this man get a ticket yesterday?" She passed the picture through the window.

Frances stared at the picture. "Let me see, dear. My eyes aren't what they were twenty years ago. Then, I could have told crow from raven at hundred feet."

"He may have been wearing a hat pulled down low," Morven prompted.

Frances held the picture at arm's length. "There's something in this weak jaw." She considered, then said happily, "Yes. I do believe this man came through. Got a ticket at the last moment for the Coastal. Not very friendly. Furtive, my nephew Andy would say. Is that helpful?"

"Very. Thank you, Miss Bee." Morven, for a moment, wished she could stay chatting with the friendly older woman all day. Having a cup of tea, sitting within the majestic waiting room. She sensed the woman was the type who brought cookies. But work beckoned. "Could we get a schedule of the stops that route makes."

Frances reached under her counter, grabbing a folded route map. "Of course. Glad to be able to assist such delightful officers."

"Thank you," Weber said brightly, Morven echoing the sentiment a second behind.

As they turned, Frances spoke again. "Excuse me, dears. Before you leave, would either of you like a cookie? I brought chocolate chip today."

Morven pulled her Kia into a parking space directly in front of the Sykes-Rowan mock-Tudor house. They'd called Sarah, discovering she was still at home, taking days off from her job as restaurant critic and columnist for the City's biggest—and now only, after its main competitor had misread the advance of the internet—daily newspaper. Rain dappled the windshield lightly with fat drops that portended a serious incoming storm. With the City's weather as unpredictable as a wild boar, as Marlowe had once said, they'd both grabbed dark-blue police slickers, donned after exciting the car.

Walking up to the house, Weber asked Morven a question. "Do we think Chester Rowan committed the murder, is currently on the run, and we are tracking him down?"

Morven considered a moment. "At this stage, best not to think anything 100%. Collect facts, follow them as we uncover them. He is a person of interest, whom we would like to speak to. Tracking sounds a bit like we should have bloodhounds bounding through a forest."

Weber laughed. "But we are trying to find this person of interest, so why not follow the bus?"

"Fair question," Morven replied. She was glad Weber was taking such an interest. "We could have followed the bus, stopping at each place it stopped, asking folks working at the individual stations if they'd seen him. It wouldn't have been a bad strategy. I felt, however, that if we questioned Mrs. Sykes, maybe we could narrow it down, see if we could cut the time needed to find him."

"I get it. That makes sense."

"To jump back to your other point. Keeping our avenues of thought open, Chester could be responsible for Douglas Small's death. There are some points around means and opportunity to decipher. The how, as Mr. Arthur said. But Chester could be running because he's afraid for some reason we aren't aware of. Hopefully, we can get more facts and Mrs. Sykes can point us in the right direction."

Then they were trotting up steps to a front door that opened before they had a chance to knock. Sarah perched slightly behind the door opening. She didn't appear completely frazzled, but was more disheveled then normal, a few hairs escaped from tight bun, a smudge of the right lens of her low-on-the-nose glasses, a dusting of flour unwiped on black yoga pants, one button unbuttoned on her black shirt.

"The police have returned, like an over-spiced meal." Her greeting wouldn't have been used as an example definition in Webster's. "You haven't found my husband yet?"

Morven's measured tones didn't rise to Sarah's aggression. "Mrs. Sykes, I'm Detective Morven, this is Officer Weber. Could we come in?"

Sarah's haughty manner slipped. "Wait. Is this bad news?"

"We just have a few more questions at this time."

Sarah backed up. "You need to give yourself more time in the proofing drawer. Tough to get a taste for what you're trying to accomplish."

They perched on the same couch Nelson had sat on earlier. Morven decided to dive right in. "We currently have reason to believe your husband left the City voluntarily."

Sarah's look was hard, even coming over her old-fashioned glasses. "What do you mean? He's been kidnapped, or worse. Someone is targeting revered food figures. It's taking the Yelp culture to another level."

Weber's eyes widened as Sarah's voice went up in pitch, but Morven kept on in the same calm tone. "We believe he wasn't kidnapped, as mentioned, and are hoping you can help us narrow down where he might have gone. If you're up for a few questions."

Sarah gave her head a shake. Breathed out. "Why would he have left? Are you forgetting the blood in the driveway?"

"Can you think of somewhere he might have headed?" Morven asked, ignoring her question. "The sooner we find him, the better."

"He did seem stressed. But I don't think he would have gone anywhere. It's not like we have a hidden boat. Or some airplane behind a tree."

Weber spoke up. "He hasn't been in contact with you?"

"Of course not." Sarah's words held a hint of scorn, but Weber's words did seem to bring the writer back in focus. "I would have admitted that as an ingredient to this conversation."

"Are there particular places you two like to visit?" Morven knew that suspects, witnesses, and criminals on the run tended to head to places they know, or knew, by instinct.

Sarah harumphed. "Paris. I suppose you'll call the Prefecture of Police, get a free trip out of it, have a Gâteau St-Honoré."

Morven kept pushing, never rising to Sarah's jabs. "Anywhere closer to the City?"

"Because of my job, we've traveled the region looking for bright young chefs. We don't sit on the couch eating store-bought doughnuts. This is a waste of time."

"I appreciate this can be frustrating, but we *are* trying to find Chester, and you can help." She let that lie for a moment, holding eye contact with Sarah until the latter looked down. Then she continued. "Specifically, is there anywhere between the City and the coast?"

Sarah looked back up, replying a little softer. "I can't— Wait, we have spent a few weeks on the west coast proper. There is a little bakery in Westdock that makes delicious cranberry fritters. There are cranberry bogs that way. Some good new farm-to-table places popping up. It's a regional cuisine story."

"Did you stay in Westdock?"

"Three times, yes. Once at Pearland. Wanted to try a winery near. Not enough depth of flavor in their Chardonnay."

"This is helpful, Mrs. Sykes. Thank you. Can we have the addresses of those places?"

"Sure, I'll get them." She picked up her phone, began clicking. Soon, she read off two different addresses, which Weber wrote down in her notebook, Morven watching Sarah closely.

"You think he's at one of these places? I feel I'd know if he booked one, they'd send an email. I've tried to call him."

"But he didn't pick up?" Weber asked.

"Nope. And now his phone seems disconnected completely. Can you find him?"

Morven stood, with Weber following suit. "Thank you very much the help, Mrs. Sykes. We will keep you informed. If you think of anything else, or hear from Mr. Rowan, please contact me. Here's my direct line."

Sarah had stayed sitting as they rose, so Morven bent and handed over a card before moving to the door.

Sarah stared at the card as if it contained the answer to a riddle. "Sure. Shut the door, please."

Pulling the door closed behind her, Webersaid, "A please. I can't believe it."

"She's in shock but won't admit it. I'm in shock at this rain." The earlier drops had grown up into a downpour. "Let's run for it, but watch those steps."

John sat in the video room adjacent to the interview rooms. Marlowe and Nelson and their various suspects had just exited. About to do the same, he paused in front of screens focused on the empty rooms—chairs, tables, drab walls, low lighting, ceiling corners in shadows any spider would approve of.

How many had occupied those rooms? Suspects, witnesses, lawyers, officers, bereaved loved ones. Angry and sad and suspicious and sulky and surreptitious people. A long road populated by all genders, races, even ages, funneling through either to help the police in their inquires or to be the eventually incarcerated. Hardened criminals, bankers, IT consultants, gardeners, baristas, real estate agents, accountants, pharmacists. Tall, short, fat thin, luxurious locks and spackled beards, brown, blue, hazel, green eyes staring back at walls that had heard it all. The tearful confessions after aching hours of back-and-forth, the arrogant lies like flies refusing to be still. Facts unearthed like bones thought long hidden, words carrying so much weight it was surprising the rooms themselves weren't drawn down through the floors into the earth like the dead.

The ghostly memories of those words, those people, for a moment to him felt real, tangible, as if he could stretch his arms miraculously through the screen's glass, following by touch their wiring, escaping within the walls, into the rooms. *I must be even more tired than expected,* he thought, knowing he'd tossed and turned for hours before drifting off the evening before. Ainsley had even huffed in her sleep at him from her dog bed as he flipped from one side to another. *Last night was like Gwyneth Keyworth said in Death Valley*, he thought, the quote arising unbidden. *'It's like when you can't sleep and the theme to Eastenders is running through your head.'*

"But for me," he spoke softly, rising from the chair, grabbing his notebook, "it wasn't *Eastenders*. It was the theme to *The Great British Baking Show*, and then various intro theatrics, piling onto to each other. All this"—he motioned to the screens—"because of a baking class." There was something niggling at him, and he paused. A thought, like a whisp of well-whipped cream on the tip of the tongue, hovered. "There's something . . ." He snapped his head back in the direction of the door, grabbed the handle, and headed out.

Once he left, the room didn't go silent. A hum of electronics remained, the true soundtrack to the modern world, the lights of the computers and audio equipment glowing, flickering on and off as if eyes in a woods at night even if there was no one to see them. Except for the ghosts, which weren't only in the interview rooms. Here, they were made of the memories of the people who'd watched. The police officers, sergeants, detectives, captains. Those not doing the interviews, but an important part of the process, leaving an earthy smell of hard-earned sweat tinged by the acidity of stale coffee, pen marks on wooden tables like hieroglyphics. As the door shut, the room might have appeared lonely if rooms had feelings. But it wasn't. It knew there'd be more occupants soon.

Walking—nearly skipping—down the hall, John soon reached the door to the lobby. It felt like those last musing moments alone covered hours, but he was only a step behind Marlow's and Nelson's groups. Swinging open the door, he had to put a hand on the latter's back to keep from running into them like an elderly bowling ball into pins.

"Detective Nelson." John's voice was surprisingly loud, cresting over the lobby's mumbling sound collage. "Sorry about the bump."

Nelson, Kevin, Marlowe, Martin, and Shane turned at the same time, their unexpected unison of movements like the precursor to a flash mob dance. The unison only lasted a moment, replaced by the more mundane individuality of limbs taking different paths, voices rising to different notes at the same time.

"Mr. Arthur," Nelson said.

"John, what in the…" Marlow said.

"Your honor," Shane said, making as much sense as normal.

"Get off me," Martin said, shaking off an invisible hand.

Kevin said nothing, staring at the door shutting behind John as if an enemy he'd rather forget.

A strong, lone female voice cut through the male chorus like a lightning bolt illuminating a cloudy sky, its touch of humorous ironic detachment such a different strain of speech that the others were silenced. "Decided to reconvene the class at the station? Or an attempt to bring the phrase 'herding cats' to life."

Lucille, who had been talking to the officer at the front desk when they'd excited the door, now walked over to the group as the hubbub of John's bumping Nelson commenced. She wore a suit the color of deepest ocean over a green shirt, her heft and size somehow shading the others.

Before the din of many voices out of tune could commence, Marlowe spoke. "Miss Crowe. A surprise."

She raised an eyebrow. "For me, them, or you?" Everyone but her seemed oddly embarrassed. "Doesn't matter. Your civilian sidekick here"—she thumbed in John's direction, wagging a wallet—"stopped by the office earlier and forgot his wallet. I thought I'd bring it down. Didn't know such a crowd would be here to greet me. It's enough to make a girl blush. If I was a blusher."

For some reason, Nelson started blushing, trying to balance out the rush of blood by reverting to formalities. "We are following multiple lines of inquiry, and these people are helping us with our inquiries."

"I'm sure you are, Detective." Lucille smiled in a way that made Nelson feel like an awkward teenager.

Shane had been silent long enough, by his reckoning. "Is this some kind of ploy, officers? First, this random man runs into us, possibly eavesdropping on confidential conversation, and now this woman does the same. Because I really must object."

Lucille chuckled. "Now I'm a ploy. Who says chauvinism is dead."

"You're misconstruing my words and—"

Before Shane could continue, Marlowe cracked open his sentence, raising his hands and pressing against air as if he were pushing sounds to the ground. "Mr. Buchanan, that'll do. This is Miss Crowe, who was at the class. She's already said why she's here. Thank you, Miss Crowe. If you don't mind." He motioned at John, who stepped up and reached out to take his wallet from Lucille. "One thing solved. This, Mr. Buchanan, is John Arthur, a civilian contractor with the police, who has a habit of walking into crowds."

John reached out and took Shane's hand from his side, shaking it as he gave the man's shiny suit a once-over. "You must be a lawyer."

Shane's confusion over the shaking was writ large on his face. "Must I?" He seemed to be asking the question of himself.

Marlowe gently started herding Shane, Lucille, Martin and Kevin in the direction of the door. The latter two hadn't spoken in the back-and-forth, just glaring at everyone and the floor respectively. "I believe we are done. Thank you for coming down."

He hadn't noticed John right behind him until the older man spoke up. The way he spoke was as if he was talking to himself, but his tone rather loud. "You know what I need to do is return to the scene. Tomorrow morning. There's a clue at the edge of my thoughts. That should bring it into focus."

Everyone in the group looked back at him expect Marlowe, who kept moving them forward and out the door, as if crowd control at a concert no one wanted to leave.

Back at desks, Marlowe and Nelson sat. John came up in their wake, surprisingly silent during the elevator ride. He perched in front of the board, eyes moving from it to the small notebook he held, not rapidly but routinely, as if checking off a series of boxes on both.

Taking a deep breath, nose ensconced in the olive-wood bowl, Marlowe ended the quiet. "John, what was that about?"

John didn't turn. "What was what?"

"That last spur into our little unexpected convoy downstairs."

"Just thinking out loud." He turned, smiling. "That lawyer is perfect."

Nelson had been beginning to type in his interview notes, but looked up. "Perfect is not how I'd describe him."

"Perfect as a humorous, intentional or otherwise, reoccurring small part in a show. As a lawyer."

"I get it," Nelson said, not getting it.

"Did you find watching the interviews useful?" Marlowe knew John well enough to see the gears churning in his mind.

"I did. Thank you both. Interesting, as a certain senior detective might say."

"He might at that."

"Do you really plan on visiting the SOC again?" Nelson pronounced SOC as if it was the word sock.

"The sock?" John's bemusement was kindly.

"S-O-C I mean. Scene of crime."

"Should have known. Yes, I do."

"Do you have a theory?"

John slipped into an accent, slightly Belgian, slightly waffling. "Arthur, he always has theories. None completely baked yet." He pulled his phone out of his pocket, clicking it to check the time.

Marlowe watched him curiously. "Maybe we should bounce those theories around before you head off to the—" The phone on his desk rang, cutting him off. "Morven, glad you checked in. Really?" Urgency flowed through his voice like water through a sluice. "Yes, we can."

Nelson's eyes were glued to the other detective. Neither noticed John Arthur as he left. Ainsley had been alone long enough.

The rain maintained its steady movement from skies to earth when John got home. But dog walking must commence no matter the weather. Somewhat like the postal service, he decided, which was an intriguing confluence of ideas considering how many dogs like to bark at postal delivery people. When he got home, he didn't even take off his wet coat. He instead put a subdued pink one on Ainsley, on top of her harness and leash. A process made more difficult by the fact she was so excited to see him that she kept jumping on and off the couch like an ad for springs that never lost their bounce. Eventually, she was suited up, and he had poop bags in one pocket, treats in another.

Then they were walking in the rain, his blue cap pulled tight. Ainsley didn't like rain, but didn't hate it either. It fell into the nuisance category, somewhere between squirrel and bunny, nowhere near hated cats. She still stopped to sniff bushes, grass, sidewalk, every few minutes. Unlike when it was dry, the stopping itself interrupted by occasional full-body shakes that started at tail's tip and ended with nose, sending drops flying off her body like people fleeing a sinking ship. In this case, though, she was repopulated by more water in minutes, causing more shakes.

John would have tried to speed the process, but knew Ainsley would win that battle of wills. He didn't want to deny her the joy of the walk, which even in the rain provided a change of scenery and the chance to catch up on neighborhood dog gossip, delivered by smells and scratches along the way. What stories must the streets give up to dogs that we can't ever grasp. She had a few choice humans she watched for, slowing in front of particular houses in case they were working in yard, exiting cars, dismounting from bikes. If one happened to be around, her tail would begin helicoptering and she'd pull their direction, knowing a pet and head scratch were on offer.

"Nobody out today," he said to her, causing a pause in her trotting as she cocked a head his direction, wondering if his vocalizing equaled a treat. When it didn't, she started up, passing a thick hedge between houses, then pulling hard on the leash. A woman at the house they were in front was hauling a ladder to a corner of her house. Hearing Ainsley, she set it down, crouching doggy height.

The woman was exceedingly thin, but muscular too somehow, long black hair pulled partially into a ponytail half plastered to her head by the rain. She wore yellow rain pants and a red hoodie cut off elbow length. John felt bad he never remembered her name. She was one of the on-the-walk humans Ainsley liked best, as the woman wasn't above crouching to the perfect petting height.

"Ainsley," she greeted the dog, her voice scratchy as a rose bush branch. "What are you doing out in the rain?"

"Dog walks are weather proof." John laughed. She laughed, too, but didn't look at him, busy petting Ainsley and fending off the dog's attempts to lick her face. "What are *you* doing out in it? Not yard work?"

She was a habitual yard worker. "No, not even me. A wasp nest up in the eaves. Rain stirred them up or something. Got sick of it."

Ainsley's tail kept wagging as the woman moved back to the sidewalk, dog instinct telling her petting was over. John stayed in place, his eyes for a moment glazing. "'Wasps have noses,'" he said, his English accent barely audible in the rain.

"What was that?"

"Oh, sorry. Thought of something. Be careful on that ladder."

She nodded, and he and Ainsley started off down the sidewalk. After a few steps, she sat, and he fished a treat out of his pocket. "This is a very productive walk, Ains. The wasps reminded me of a *Chelsea* quote, and at the same time clicked a few facts back into place. Often, just the idea of a good TV detective is enough to push me along. I think—" She pulled on the leash. Enough of this standing, there was walking to be done.

Marlowe's evening after he'd finally clocked off had been uneventful. He'd raked over the case with Nelson before leaving the office, catching him up on Morven and Weber's activities and plans, bouncing ideas around before leaving. He felt progress was slow, trickling forward like a river that needs a good rain. A funny analogy, as rain pounded on the roof of his apartment. That rain had kept him from stopping at Gary's on the way home, as had a niggling feeling in the back of his brain that he was missing something. He couldn't define it, couldn't put words or place or person to the feeling, but knew it would worm its way out eventually.

So, he let it go. Ordered a mushroom-onion-extra-mozzarella pie from Poole's Paradise Pizza. Put his feet on the coffee table while he ate it and read, very slowly, Dickens's classic *Bleak House*. John had convinced him he had to, saying Marlowe was like "a kinder, moderner Mr. Bucket." While he didn't like it as much as the last Dickens he'd read, *Dombey and Son*, finding the beginning slow going like trudging through mud, he'd doggedly stuck to it. Fields that delivered delicious crops weren't always easily ploughed, as his grandfather used to tell him. Here, he was right.

Munching a fourth slice, he found himself drawn into Dickens's world. The case, for a few moments, put aside for Victorian, foggy London streets and courts and pubs and country drawing rooms. Every so often, that ghost of a thought came back, then left without unveiling itself. He'd read the phrase "duty is duty, and friendship is friendship," four times before realizing he should probably hit the proverbial hay. Tomorrow would shed new light on the case, light he'd be better suited to step into if he got some sleep.

Waking up the next morning, that phrase popped back into his mind like a daisy opening in sunshine. "Duty is duty, and friendship is friendship." Sometimes, that's how he felt about John Arthur. Maybe his friendship with the man had led Marlowe to give him too much rope, not sticking to his duty as an officer of the City police. That scene at the station, where John had mentioned— Wait. John had talked about going back to the original scene and looking for clues in front of multiple suspects, suspects who knew others who might be suspects. Marlowe's mind raced. Suspects who could be murderers. And who might murder again. John said he was returning to the scene this morning.

Before many more minutes passed, Marlowe was in his car heading to Tolltown, to Hotel Herre, to Small's Cooking Classroom. He parked the AMC Matador in a loading zone and grabbed a wrinkled sports coat the color of dry tumbleweeds off the back seat, shuffling in to it as he walked. The sky above was heavy with low clouds, as if, as John had once said probably quoting someone, a great gray tarp had been pulled from one corner of it to another. Streets were dry, rain having let off around midnight. Walking past the front desk, he flashed his badge, taking the first step on the stairs at a bound.

Reaching the landing, he noticed a red stain surrounded by red splatters. Blood, with more drops heading in the direction of the classroom.

14

Westdock was a welcoming small town on the state's coast. Tourism brochures would call it charming or cozy, but neither word quite captured its combination of fishing business, both historically and as a going concern, and vacation spot. Coming to easy grips with that balance became difficult for locals, many of whom still went out on boats to catch salmon, cod, rockfish, and tuna. For them, the town wasn't a playground but work, hard work. But long stretches of untarnished sandy beaches, a current creating waves big enough to surf on, water temperatures mild enough to wade in, and quaint restaurants and shops that had sprung up to cater to the influx of summertime tourists kept the months from May to September crowded.

The other months were more deserted. Occasional tourists would wander in, stopping at the Mermaid Fish Market, The Old Oar Pub, the Maritime Museum, and more watery spots. Only the bravest then ventured into the water, as temps dropped rapidly once the seasons shifted. Because of the tourist trade, many Westport dwellings stayed empty for months at a time. From newer condos painted stark white promising easy beach access, to Cape Code style houses decorated with shells and local artists' paintings, to cheaper spots closer to shack than house (though touted as the latter online), solid summer bookings faded to offseason echoes. During that time, seagulls perched on top of empty buildings, wondering why dropped bits of fried fish, ice cream cones, and salt and vinegar chips they'd gotten used to had disappeared.

Early mornings on fall days like these tended to be quiet, the weather as cloudy as within the City most hours. When a sunbreak appeared out over the ocean, it didn't lack for dramatics, expansive view streaked with momentary color, waves wild as if ridden by a fleet of invading Atlanteans. Morven stood looking at a view exactly like that for a moment, thinking that if she were a painter this would be the landscape she'd want to paint. Moving, wild, mother nature at her energetic finest. *But*, she though, *I'm a cop, with no time to stand around looking at seascapes.*

She turned to look behind her, where Weber and a group of five local police officers, all in uniform, trailed. Morven and Weber had spent most of the night on Chester Rowan's trail, checking in at bus stops along the route, ending up here. They'd alerted the local police they might need assistance, and were welcomed in the same friendly manner most Westdock locals welcomed tourists. Even the saltiest fisherman tended to the outwardly amiable side toward visitors. Something about living near the ocean instilled a calm, even-keeled nature, she and Weber had decided.

They'd made it to the town during the dark hours, deciding to wait on their next step until morning. Catching up on the town map with the white-haired Westport Police Chief, a perfectly named John Salmons, they'd spent an hour planning the next move, then a few hours crashing on cots. Not the most restful night, but the station's coffee was leaps and bounds better than at the City Station, carrying a hint of chicory, and the chief had brought them the town's famous cranberry fritters for breakfast. The doughnuts lived up to reputation, with tart cranberry balancing out doughy sweetness.

Now they and their crew of local officers were at the corner of King and Copper streets. Giving a keep-calm-and-quiet gesture, Morven pointed to a house three doors down the latter street. It was a well-kept, one-story Cape Cod painted a blue that matched the top of a still ocean, trim a blue closer to the ocean depths, and white accents like the froth on waves. Surrounding homes mirrored it in style and coloring, as if the stretch of street were a planned development, only deviating in names, which each house had on a plaque out front. Cutter's Cottage, Deep Reef Retreat, Captain's Hideaway.

The one she pointed to, Fisherman's Folly, was the single house where a light was visible. Only a weak glow, like a candle or hooded lantern, but visible in the darkness. None of the other houses looked inhabited, the whole street whispering of absence. At the end of the stretch of sidewalk connecting front door to street, Morven huddled up the rest. She pointed at one officer, a twentysomething man named Ronald Rye who had a hint of brown sideburns trailing out of his hat.

"Go around back," she whispered. "In case there's an exit. We'll give you two minutes. Keep it quiet."

He nodded, before moving off around the house's north side, ducking under window height.

"Let's move up to the front door. I'll knock, but in case no one answers, Officer Laughland, you have the ram ready." A six-foot-three man who would have made a good Hercules for a local production—curly black hair, biceps straining uniform stitching—lifted the metal door-bashing tool in his hand up and smiled. She smiled back. "Stand behind me, and Weber, you behind him."

Weber nodded, eyes gleaming. She knew she should be tired, but the adrenaline of the last few days hadn't worn off. What a lucky break she'd had. Not only a part of the detective team for this case, but getting to be a part of a chase across counties for a criminal on the run. She'd be tired later, she knew. For now, that tired could be shelved like a book you knew you'd have to finish reading at some point.

Leading them to the front door, Morven stopped, made sure all were in place. Then she delivered a hard series of three knocks, the sound of knuckles on wood breaking open the muted morning like a bell announcing invading forces. The instant her hand hit, the light inside the house vanished. Not a sound came from within. She knocked once more, loudly.

"Police! Open the door or we will be forced to knock it in."

Still nothing from inside. She moved out the way. Officer Laughland filled the space where her body had been, everyone else giving him plenty of room. Like pushing a hearty child on a swing, he pulled the metal ram back and then wooshed it forward, blasting the door backward with that single blow, wrenching locks from wood like a blow from an axe into a log, splintering any quiet the morning might have held on to. Finishing door destruction, he rapidly slid out of the way, allowing Morven to enter first.

"Police." She said it loudly, the word traveling through the unlit room. "Put your hands up.." She scanned the entryway consisting of a short hall leading into a shadowy room. Reaching out to the paneling, she found a light switch. Flicking it on illuminated the hall and room. She'd missed a sign hanging on one section of hall, white words on three faux driftwood slates connected by rope: "Welcome/Home/Sailor."

"Police. We are entering the room." Moving into the living room cautiously, her gun in one hand, there was a smell of sweat and fear and, strangely, cheddar cheese and burnt toast evident. The room presented a white couch and chair, wooden floors, and a wooden table in front of a TV mounted on matching wood stand. The chair held bundled blankets, the table home to a half-eaten piece of toast that looked as if it had been cooked over the extinguished candle in front of it. A bottle of red wine, empty except for a last pour, was near the chair.

"Mr. Rowan, we know you're here." Her voice was loud as the waves against the pier on a windy day. "Officers surround the house. Please come out, save us and yourself any more trouble."

Rounding the corner into the living room, it opened-planned into a small kitchen, which must lead to the back door, though it wasn't readily visible. Coming from that direction, Chester Rowan slowly took a few staggered steps into the light. Haggard as an old dog after a long walk, his stubbled face and shoulders appeared to drag as he moved, jeans dappled with mud, shirt with stains that could have been anything, a collage of rushed meals had one after another. He had a knife in his right hand. His eyes seemed to be having a hard time focusing.

"Put the knife down." Morven's urgency traveled through each word. "Get on the floor. Arms spread."

Confusion spread like a rash over his face. "Knife?" he mumbled, looking at his hand as if it must have belonged to anyone but him. "Oh, knife." He dropped it, moved sluggishly to his knees, then lay down. A sigh escaped him once he reached the floor.

Morven, Weber and the rest of the officers moved in.

Marlowe paused at the door to the classroom. The blood drips had continued the whole way. He didn't as a rule like to use a gun, desiring to rely on words and intuition while letting other officers more suited wield the physical threats. The strategy had worked, but at the moment he was wavering. His hand went to his shoulder holster, then into a pocket to grab his phone. Not wanting to alert anyone possibly inside, he texted Nelson to meet him at the classroom ASAP. With backup. He knew the young detective would operate with all possible speed.

He also knew he couldn't wait. Cautiously, as if approaching a wild horse, he eased the door open and walked into the classroom, where he saw John Arthur sitting at the tall table closest to the door. Not the one where Douglas Small held court, so to speak, but one of the two nearest it. On a stool, John stared absently in the direction of the hallway leading to the office where the body had been found. He didn't seem to be focusing on anything, holding a whisk in one hand, absently twirling it as if aerating a batter made from air above his head.

Marlowe didn't see anyone else in the room. It had been partially straightened since the forensic teams finished with it. Some clutter was still in evidence, but much of the strewn flour, half-made cakes, and chaos caused by the crime and the proceedings that always follow were no longer in evidence. A stray foot-and-a-half of police tape clung to one wall like a memory. He eased in, cautious, unsure if John was the only inhabitant. The man didn't appear wounded. He was, Marlowe heard as he neared, whistling a barely audible tune, notes tracing directions Marlowe didn't recognize.

Marlowe's low-pitched voice broke the tune off. "John. Everything good?"

John swiveled on his stool. He looked the detective over as if his appearance was expected. "Marlowe. All good. Just reviewing the multiplication tables for the number seven, like Montalbano. I wasn't sure who would arrive first."

"You're not injured."

John's mock-French indignation would have embarrassed any native Parisian. "Moi? Not at all." He considered a moment, giving the whisk a final whirl before setting it down. "Healthy enough. For my age, that is."

Marlowe motioned backward. "The blood, not yours?"

Understanding spread over John's face. "Ah. That is not mine, no. Sorry to worry. That's actually our friend Drogo's. My fault, I must admit." Noticing a moment of consternation cross Marlowe like a shadow, he laughed. "Not that I caused it by assault. Don't get the cuffs out yet. Arthur, he has not crossed into criminality. An accident. He was sleeping here, on a couch out on the landing. Girlfriend, or cousin, trouble. When I came up, I startled him. He fell off the couch, nose straight to the floor. Ran to the stairs, then back to the classroom, then I moved him into the dishwashing area, where we got some towels to stop the bleeding. Once it was under control, I sent him off to the clinic up the street. Might be broken. Not sure. He did manage to call out, 'Oh man, not my nose, it's my best feature.' Five times, I believe. Quite a character, Drogo. Memorable supporting cast."

John's storytelling was less fast paced than usual. Less focused as well. Almost as if the man was carrying on two conversations, one with Marlowe, one in his head.

"Got it. But is all well with you? You seem—"

John broke in. "Sorry, lots going on in—"

Marlowe returned the favor. "Your mind."

"Indeed. See, it's a 'bit awkward really. I think I may have just solved the murder.'"

Marlowe tried to keep the excitement out of his voice but failed. "Wait. Are you telling me you know who murdered Douglas Small?"

"'I do, and I think I'm about to get a confession.'" He said it with the hint of an English accent, which Marlowe was so used to it barely registered.

"From me? I don't see anyone else."

"No, not from you, Detective. I slipped into a *Ludwig* quote there. Did I tell you about *Ludwig* yet? Newer British mystery show, fantastic. Features triple-threat, comedian-actor-author David Mitchell playing twins who—"

Marlowe's upraised palm caused John to stop mid-sentence, before restarting.

"The palm stop. I'll never tire of it. Such a classic police gesture."

"John." Marlowe pulled the name into two syllables, managing to put a hard accent on both.

"Right, rambling. Save the *Ludwig* for later."

"Seems a smart idea."

"Anyway, I believe we will have another attendee to our little *mise en scene* arriving in minutes. I wonder if we should move. You might scare them off."

John stood up, walked over to the wall next to the door into the classroom. Marlowe followed, making it impossible to see either if glancing in through the door.

"Perhaps we should whisper too." John followed his own advice, theatrically.

While Marlowe found himself wishing for a second that John was an officer he could instruct to drop the stage manners, he knew the man had to follow his own fiction-driven trains of logic. And knew from past history that if John said he knew who the murderer was, he probably did.

So he played along, whispering. "Can you tell me who we're waiting for?"

From one angle, it was a ludicrous scene. A heavyset senior police detective sporting a mustache that might have won awards, and an elderly, retired writer in a blue baseball cap, brown shorts, and aqua knee-high socks with tan capybaras swimming on them. Both crouched against a wall, whispering. John couldn't help chuckling softly, even knowing the gravity of the situation.

"I could, but shall we go through some suspects first?"

"As long as my knees don't give out."

"Aging, it ain't for sissies. Right, first, as John Chapel might say, we need to focus on the character of the various suspects."

Marlowe couldn't stop himself asking, "John Chapel?"

"Legendary British actor Timothy Spall plays him in a show called *Death Valley*. Funny enough, the character John Chapel is also an actor, who used to play— You know, maybe we'll save that for later."

"Amazing restraint," Marlowe dryly replied.

"Thank you for noticing. Onward. Let's start with perhaps the most obvious. Kevin Holman. Revenge, simmering for years. Not a bad motive. The past is always influencing the deeds of the present, as nearly every British mystery show has taught us. But his character, from what I've seen and read in the reports, seems far too wishy-washy to carry out such a decisive and planned murder. Because it was, curiously, both spur of the moment and yet full of thought, the process of the crime. His wife, perhaps. And she as a pharmacist would have access to drugs. But she seems decisive in a healing manner, if that makes sense."

"Somewhat. Continue." Marlowe wasn't completely aligned with John's logic at each step, now or in the past, but knew the man usually found his way. Like a dog, he supposed, on the scent of a rabbit.

John beckoned with his hand as if coaxing someone off stage. "Martin Allen. His character is certainly an angry one. Violent, even. But is it the violence of a murderer, or of a potential bully? Someone who wants to appear a hard man more than actually is. I believe so. He hated Douglas, and knew this space better than anyone. Maybe he could have had a key from the past, but I don't see Douglas giving those out easily. Too controlling. Martin is an easy answer, but it's never the easiest answer. And anyway, I don't see a bartender as a killer."

"Does that make sense?"

"Probably not." John laughed in a whisper. "But Martin doesn't fit. Too much bluster, and this was a crime of precision. Dislike of Douglas could lead to confrontation, but murder? Don't see it. Something deeper is involved." He paused, listening for a moment, before continuing.

"No one yet, but they'll be here. Time for a few more. Olivia and Jim Sean. Him we can put aside. His love of Douglas was genuine, if misguided. But her history with him, and her character, which seems calculating in a way, smart. And damaged by Douglas's shameful behavior toward her, like many others. Perhaps?" He shook his head slowly. "But no. She wanted to embarrass Douglas as he had her, make him feel small. Killing him would have meant she couldn't see him suffer, wouldn't be able to watch him go through what she did. Him being gone takes that away."

"Smart point." Marlowe nodded.

"She did provide a final clue." John's voice had a note of sadness in it. "Good memory, I suppose."

"What clue is—"

"Shhhh," John cut him off.

"What in tarnation?"

"Thought I heard something. HVAC I suppose."

Cocking his head in the door's direction, Marlowe asked, "You really believe someone is gonna show?"

"Eventually. But until then, two more. Chester and Sarah."

"Chester—"

"Has been tracked down by Morven."

"Very astute. Yes."

"His character was too wobbly, though he has the past indiscretions and grievances. Enough to make him angry, furious, obsessed with Douglas, with making him pay Enough to make Chester lose his grip, if that makes sense. But I don't believe he's a killer. Make Douglas look silly by putting butter in the rafters to drop on him mid-class? That's Chester's poor idea of style. But in his mind, harboring thoughts of revenge, he felt connected to the actual crime."

Marlowe was genuinely surprised. "You think—"

"Shhh," John whispered. "This time I did hear a noise."

Marlowe hadn't heard a peep, but could believe John's hearing was sharp. The man certainly had keen senses in general. Maybe living alone since his wife died had raised his senses higher, like an arm getting stronger when the other is lost. Maybe spending so much time with Ainsley, borrowing on her advanced dog senses. Before he could continue the train of thought, the door pushed open.

Lucille Crow walked in.

She wore jeans, a rain jacket the color of rain clouds, and carried a silver tray with plastic wrap covering the items on the tray. Her presence and size seemed to fill the room like an empty balloon suddenly inflated. As her stare rove around, John walked up to her, Marlowe right behind him.

Noticing both, she spoke heartily. "Mr. Arthur, you brought company. How thoughtful."

"And you brought?" He gestured to the tray.

Setting the tray down on the same table she'd sat at during the class, the same John had been at, she carefully removed the wrap to reveal what appeared to be five perfect tarts. Ignoring Marlowe's hand on his arm, John walked up to her to gaze at the pastries.

"Tart au citron." His voice was breathless in admiration. "Perfect crust it appears. My favorite."

She smiled. "The wrap did a number on the merengue kisses, but thank you. I guessed you as a citron lover. Something citrusy in the eyes. You, Detective . . ."

"Marlowe," he said, walking close enough to grab her if need be.

"Right, Marlowe. Like—"

"Just like."

"That's a cross to bear for a police officer. Sadly, didn't know what you'd want. My guess…" She looked him up and down. "Croissants. Too much work. Apologies."

"None needed."

John brought his gaze up from the tempting tarts. "Mrs. Crowe, thank you for coming down. I guess I should try a tart." He reached for one, but Marlowe stopped him.

"John, not sure about that."

Lucille laughed loud as a trumpeting elephant. "You don't think I'd poison tarts, do you, Detective? My pastry skills may shock people, but they don't tend to put them in the hospital…or the morgue."

"Just figured talk first, treats later." Marlowe wasn't sure if John was right in his reasoning as far as Lucille being the murderer, but he wanted to be safe. Though he had to admit to himself, he liked the woman and hoped John was wrong.

"Okay, talk."

John beat Marlowe to speaking. "Mrs. Crowe—"

"Lucille is dandy."

"Lucille. Not exactly sure how to begin. I'm taking it for granted you came down here because you heard me say in the station I was returning, and you figured I'd a lead on the case, or solved it."

She nodded. "I try to treat people as if they're smart until I find out they're an idiot."

"Good logic. Sadly, they so often are. You aren't. You *are* a murderer, but not an idiot."

Marlowe tensed, but Lucille just sighed, air flowing out of her body slowly. "How's that?" she said, but it came out more a question of logic than a desire for him to repeat the statement.

"I don't believe I'd need to tell you the how, but if you'll forgive my digressions, I'll go through exactly what I have figured out, see if it matches." He looked at both, but as neither spoke up, he continued. "First, I always thought this was a crime both planned and unplanned."

His hint of a French accent made Lucille's eyebrows purse, but John didn't notice. He started to pace slightly in front of the table. "A crime undertaken with precision and daring. A crime that could be done by a fantastic baker, for example."

"The how?" Marlowe nudged him.

"No digressing. I hate to say, but it's a mundane solution."

"Mundane solution?"

"A popular British television trope. Happens all the time. Crime seems impossible, turns out to be a simple idea." Lucille's and Marlowe's blank gazes caught his eye. "Maybe not the time. Here, it's fairly straightforward. You opened the door, which was never locked, killed Douglas, locking the door on the way out."

"I believe Louisa tried the door first." Lucille said.

"Louisa would never barge in on Douglas. He had used her, abused her the way he used others, and she was under his thrall. Interrupting the great Douglas Small's break by walking in uncalled for? Never. She knocked, got no answer, came and got you and Madison, and you pretended to try the door in front of them while holding it tightly shut. Seen it happen in multiple British shows, *Father Brown* for one, not to call your originality into question. I believe even if they went to help you try to open it, you're easily strong enough to have kept it shut."

"If that's a compliment, not sure I'll accept."

"It was a bold move. One you had to make, as your first idea didn't work. Which was to make a key. Douglas always left his key ring around. You swiped it while he was demonstrating and all were gathered round, made an impression in clay, then returned it."

"And I did this bit of legerdemain how?" Lucille seemed slightly amused by John's performance.

"A baker of your skills certainly didn't need to watch Douglas demonstrating. You don't seem easily flustered. I found some clay in your drawer where you'd hidden it. Probably left over from the pottery class you took."

"I am impressed."

John bowed low as Marlowe said, "If Miss Crowe made a key, why not use it?"

"My surmise is that thinking it through she—I mean you, Lucille—realized it would be trackable. You'd have to take the mold to a key maker, that kind of thing. So, the key making was discarded like a bread that didn't rise. My guess is you made the key second night, then realized it wasn't going to work. So you resorted to drugging Douglas in his doctored coffee the third night."

Lucille didn't agree, just watched him.

"Then it was more waiting, for Louisa to knock on the door and have a mini breakdown. I wondered at first if you locked him in somehow on a feigned trip to the bathroom. Now, I believe you trusted in Louisa not checking the door. A bold move. From there, it was just going to help, and then when Louisa and Madison left, operating at extreme speed. Opened the door, stabbed Douglas, and then locked it before anyone else came back, pulling out the hook lock so it appeared he'd locked himself in. You wore an oven mitt to handle the knife and to pull out the hook, but really, everyone's fingerprints were in that office. Audacious, still, because you had to have perfect timing. Audaciously perfect timing. Just what an accomplished baker would have."

"Why would you think I was so accomplished? I was taking a class."

"When asked, everyone around the class said you were the best baker. And look at these tart shells. Immaculate. Anyway, you once *were* a baker. For Douglas."

Lucille's smile was rueful. "You *are* clever."

John blushed. "It was Marlowe's team that did the work. I solely read the reports, watched a few interviews. And wasn't completely sure I was right until recently. But it's your story. Would you like to take over?"

"Why not. For the first time in my life, I put my body on the line to stand up for my beliefs and do the right thing. If you caught me, so be it. I was the original baker in the first Small Bakery. Went by Lucy then.

Crow without an e. It was early in the Small empire." She ladled scorn on the last words. "Barely kept employment records. I hoped you wouldn't discover it. I came up with the original bakery recipes. All I wanted to do was bake, bake and please Douglas Small. It's sadly an old story. He took advantage of me. Abused me, straight out. Then ditched me and it got hushed up like so many of his crimes. I didn't bake again for a long, long time. Went to therapy. Had to be medicated for many years."

"Some of which you used to drug Douglas?" John slipped in, half-questioningly.

"Yep. Appropriate I felt. And you were spot-on in the timing. Realized what I wanted to do first night. Brought clay to make a key impression the second night. But when working on the Swiss roll, Douglas went on and on about cracks in the cake, which I heard in my head as cracks in the case. Made think through the key idea. Then I saw Drogo try the door to the office later that night. I was heading to the bathroom. He just opened it, and Douglas, who treated the poor kid as subhuman, yelled to leave him alone. Douglas didn't want to be bothered, but didn't bother to lock the door."

"He didn't recognize you?" Marlowe asked, finally joining the narrative.

"Lots of changes to me, Detective. Lot of time in care, loads of medication, as mentioned, and my body changed. I've gained probably fifty pounds, changed my hair, changed to contacts, worked out with weights. Time passed. My appearance now is nothing like the little baker I once was. And Douglas didn't see those he abused as individuals, I think. He didn't look at women's faces much, if you know what I mean. Even when I worked with him every day, I was more prop than person."

"So it was revenge," Marlowe said.

She didn't reply for a moment, then looked at John. "It's your show. What do you think, oh armchair detective?"

John blushed once more. "More like dog-walking detective. It wasn't revenge, not really. Revenge might have been getting a case against him. It was to protect Louisa. You saw how he treated her, just as he treated you. Saw where it was going, more violence against a woman baker by Douglas. Saw yourself in her, maybe. You're very protective—much like you brought Madison into your life to protect her. You weren't going to let him destroy another young life."

She bought hands together in a quiet clap. "You mixed that like a genoise. Exact amount of air."

"I take that as quite a complement from you."

"Now what? You know, no offense, but I believe I could easily outrun you two."

"But probably not me," Nelson said, briskly walking in the door.

"Detective Nelson," she exclaimed. "I missed you."

"I didn't want to interrupt Mr. Arthur." You could tell by his beaming face that he'd been practicing the line, or one like it, and couldn't believe he'd actually got to say it.

"Detective," Marlowe said. "Glad you could make it. Miss Crowe, I suppose we should continue this at the station."

"I suppose we should. But first, these tarts. They aren't poisoned. I can take a bite out of each if you want."

John picked one up as she talked and took a bite. "Delicious. Absolutely perfect. Better even than those I've had in Paris."

"Well, that's a relief, I can tell you." She gave the room a final look, then crooked her elbow out as if waiting for an escort to take her into a formal dining room. "Detective Nelson, would you be so kind as to accompany me?"

"Yes, ma'am. I mean, could you please come with me and the officers outside, Miss Crowe. I will read you your rights on the way."

"Ohh, that's something to look forward to." She laughed as they left the room.

Marlowe stood, taking it in for a minute. "John, you might have filled me in sooner."

John chewed slowly, savoring. "I wasn't sure myself until she showed up. Not 100%. But she fit. When Olivia said she only saw Madison come back into the room during the initial chaos, I knew."

"Makes sense. Still seems chancy to eat that tart. What if she was planning to kill me?"

"She might have, but not via baked goods. Too devoted to the art. Though maybe they are poisoned." He pantomimed holding his throat as if choking and started to bend over, a display of acting that would have made a third-year drama student blush.

"John?" Marlowe drawled.

"Yes, Detective?" John straightened up, taking the last bite of his tart.

"Stick to watching, not acting."

15

Marlowe eventually ate one of the tarts. They were exceptionally delicious. The sweetness of the meringue against the kick of sharper, but not too sharp, lemon citrus, the play between tang and sugar, and the flakey lightness of the crust, as if bread made heavenly air. *It was*, he had thought for a moment within the pastry euphoria, *hard to believe the tart was made by a murderer.*

But even if at times he wished he didn't, he knew murderers came in all shapes and sizes. Emotions or circumstance or momentary madness, whatever you wanted to believe, could drive the most mainstream, the friendliest, the talented to murder. As much as the public might want to believe in criminals being a class unto themself, it just wasn't always the case. As his grandfather would say, even the calmest horse can buck you into broken bones with the wrong gust of wind. How the horse acted after that was hard to predict. Maybe back to being calm. Maybe buck more. Maybe they'd never be the same horse again.

Continuing to hold interviews with Lucille at the station, her court-appointed lawyer in tow, she'd taken the path of being calm, being the same person she'd seemed before. Slightly ironic at times, wryly humorous, dropping the occasional baking reference (once, she called Douglas a bitter caramel, overcooked and teeth-cracking). Never trying to dance around the fact she'd murdered him—at the beginning of the process, that was.

Until realizing that if she plead guilty, she wouldn't get a trial. Then she changed her tune from sweet to a savory note, talking less and less, finally not talking. Only saying she wanted to be able to speak to a jury in open court. It ended with one of Marlowe's strangest interview sessions. Lucille asked to speak to him alone, off the record. A strange request, but one he'd decided to accommodate, as she'd been mostly cooperative. When alone, she spoke first.

"Did you ever try those lemon tarts?" she asked with a smile.

"I did. Delicious. But you don't need me to tell you that."

"Do you think I'll be able to bake in prison?"

For a second, he wondered if she was being facetious. There was a twinkle in her eyes, and she seemed to be holding back a grin. "Not sure. Depends. You changed the plea, so why sure about prison?"

"Between us? I don't plan on denying it when all's said and done. But." She took a deep breath. "I want to be able to tell my story in court. To out Douglas in front of the public for what he was, what he did, what was papered over because of his celebrity. Could be it'll help others in the same situation."

"Could be," he mused. "And could be they'll let you bake. Once they know your skills."

She laughed loudly, noise filling the room like the scent of freshly baked bread.

It had been three days since they'd arrested Lucille. Marlowe headed down the hill from the station to Settler's Square at a trot. The late afternoon sky's fading blue clearness and crisp sun a waning but welcome change from the past few days' on-and-off-and-on rain. Promising a round on him at Gary's, he'd sent Morven, Nelson, and Weber that direction, with word that John and Ainsley were meeting them. Then he'd had a few things to do at the office, which took a tad longer than expected. He hoped they'd gotten a round in without him.

Walking in, the first thing he heard was John finishing a sentence in an English accent. ". . .I was detecting." The second was a high-pitched bark coming from under the table the four were sitting at, an extra, empty chair at one corner. The T. Rex song "Bang a Gong" played softly. Gary stood behind the bar polishing taps, bemusedly watching John. He caught Marlowe's eye as he entered the room with a nod, then turned to grab a flute glass.

"Marlowe." They spoke in chorus, seeing him at once. Ainsley left her spot under the table and stretched her tan-and-black brindled body to what seemed an extra three feet to sniff and lick his hand as he walked up.

"Sorry, Ains, no croissants."

John scratched between her ears. "She's fine. Gary's been giving her treats."

"And here, Kit," said the bartender, walking up, "is a glass for you. You deserve a treat too."

Weber whispered an aside to Morven. "Kit?"

"Tell you later," she replied. Then, louder, "Glad you could make it, Marlowe. We're into the prosecco. Nelson, do the honors."

"On it." He grabbed the bottle on the table, filling Marlowe's glass.

Marlowe gazed intently at the straw-colored effervescent liquid in the glass, and everyone went silent. He spoke with mock seriousness. "To you. Solving a tricky case. Or cases, in a way. Though only one charged."

"How did it end up with Chester by the way?" John asked.

Marlowe tilted his glass Morven's direction. "This one's yours."

She took a sip before replying. "It was odd. Sad. At first when we found him, he didn't say anything, had a tough time concentrating. Then he said he was guilty. Back at the Westdock station, he talked more, but in a rambling manner. Hard to decipher, but we made sense of it eventually. He really only placed the butter in the rafters and turned up the heater. A prank in a way, to embarrass Douglas. But he'd carried so much anger toward the victim for so long, about the books, and even more about the affair with his wife, that he wished on some level that he could do more, something violent. Even if he wasn't a violent person normally. The idea kept churning in his mind, damaging his mental health. I believe this mental state convinced him that his butter trick was somehow responsible for Douglas' death, too. I've checked in, and it appears he's getting the help he needed."

John shook his head. "Publishers. Very tightly wound. It vaguely reminds me of a show."

Marlowe cut in. "Glad he's getting help. And sorry I'm late. Tying up a few things."

Morven stretched her arms. "No worries. We told Gary it was on your tab."

"I didn't know I had a tab."

Gary's goatee bobbed. "You do now, so no scarpering without paying. These lot are at it. Rapidly." He laughed, walking off.

John gave Marlowe a noticeable once-over, causing the detective to stare back. "Well, John, what is it? Ketchup stain?"

"Detecting."

"And?" Marlowe could match anyone for taciturnity.

The others wore matching curious looks.

"'Allow me to elucidate,' as John Chapel might say. You're getting ready to go on a date." John's smidge of smugness couldn't be contained.

"What?" Nelson asked loudly, a sentiment echoed by the other two.

"How do you figure?" Marlowe's face matched a statue.

"Your sports coat is recently brushed. You're wearing a pressed red button-down, and I've only ever seen you in white. That tie is ironed and immaculately tied. Even the shoes, freshly polished. Though Ainsley may have licked one. Sorry about that."

Marlowe stared at him. The man could be uncanny. Then he smiled, but didn't say anything.

John smiled back. "I'll bet another round I know who."

"You're on," Morven chimed in.

"Chelsea Hinkley."

Marlowe sighed. Uncanny. "A gentleman never tells." Sometimes John's insightfulness was too much.

"'I don't mean to blow my own trumpet,'" John replied, bringing the English accent back, "'but I'm a very fast reader.' Even of clothes. And reports. I thought I sensed something when reading your interview notes. A dark horse, you are. Leading to another bottle I believe." He caught Gary's eye, and the bartender walked their way. "Not for you, Marlowe. Don't want you to be tipsy for your date. Speaking of gentlemen and tipsy, do you know the Trollope quote . . ."

Marlowe sighed as John's accent returned, and got out his credit card.

AUTHOR'S NOTE

The names, characters, and situations represented in this novel were all invented, and have no relation to any real people, places, or pastries. Except those names and characters from cited television shows, movies, and books. And Ainsley the dog, who is definitely based on a real dog, one that is begging for a treat as I type.

I'd like to once again give a huge thank you to Ainsley for her invaluable assistance in writing this third book featuring Arthur and Marlowe. Also, giant thanks to my wife Natalie, for her reading the books – unlike the first two, which were birthday presents, this was given to her as an anniversary present. Also, even more thanks to Jon and Nik, for all their help and assistance in making this book, and to Elizabeth White, the most amazing mystery book editor on this or any other planet (and one who makes swell title suggestions). Thank you, also, for reading it. My guess is you've read the first and second The American Who Watched British Mysteries books already, but if not, I hope you enjoy them, too.

www.ingramcontent.com/pod-product-compliance
Lightning Source LLC
LaVergne TN
LVHW100525110826
845146LV00002B/780

* 9 7 9 8 9 9 2 6 4 1 5 4 7 *